Praise for Anna Snoekstra's
Only Daughter

"Snoekstra's excellent debut stands out in the crowded psychological suspense field with smart, subtle red herrings and plenty of dark and violent secrets. Recommend to genre aficionados and readers who enjoyed Lisa Lutz's *The Passenger*."
—*Library Journal* (starred review)

"Unreliable narrator thrillers are practically a subgenre of their own, and there are two unreliable narrators here as well as a wickedly twisted and fast-paced plot that leaves numerous questions unanswered.... Readers who enjoy a creepy thriller that will keep them guessing will be unable to put this down."
—*Booklist* (starred review)

"*Only Daughter* by Anna Snoekstra is a dark meditation on the secrets we keep about our families and about ourselves. Twisty, slippery, and full of surprises, this web of lies will ensnare you and keep you riveted until you've turned the final page."
—Lisa Unger, *New York Times* bestselling author of *Ink and Bone*

"In Anna Snoekstra's dark and edgy debut, a young woman slips easily into the life of a girl missing eleven years, only to discover the grisly truth behind the disappearance. Will she be the next victim? Truly distinctive and tautly told, *Only Daughter* welcomes a thrilling new voice in crime fiction."
—Mary Kubica, *New York Times* bestselling author of *The Good Girl*

Also by Anna Snoekstra

Only Daughter

Little Secrets

ANNA SNOEKSTRA

mira

mira

Recycling programs
for this product may
not exist in your area.

ISBN-13: 978-0-7783-3109-4

Little Secrets

For questions and comments about the quality of this book, please contact us at
CustomerService@Harlequin.com.

BookClubbish.com

MIRABooks.com

Printed in U.S.A.

For my sister.

Prologue

By the time the first wisps of smoke rose into the night, the arsonist had made their escape. The streets were empty. A dull orange glow emanated from the courthouse, not yet bright enough to challenge the moon or the neon beer signs of the tavern across the road.

The smoke thickened quickly. Angry, dense clouds were rising in rolls, and yet when a car drove past, its only response was to speed up.

Soon, orange flames grew from the roof, replacing the smoke. The fire was so dazzling now that a contracted pupil could no longer distinguish between the dark gray and the black of the sky. People emerged in time to witness the windows exploding, one after another in a series of dry pops. The fire extended its arms out of each window, waving crazily at the gathering crowd.

Sirens began, but no one could hear them. The sound of the fire overtook everything, its low, light roar like the warning sound made at the back of a cat's throat. Two girls appeared from the tavern, late to the party. One ran toward the flames, asking if anyone was inside, if anyone had seen anything. The other stood still, shoulders fixed, her hand over her mouth.

When the firemen pulled up, the bright street looked like daytime. The crowd had stepped back, the ones who had been closest damp with sweat. Everyone's eyes were wet. Perhaps from the ashes in the air, or perhaps because by now the news had circulated.

Yes, there was someone inside.

PART 1

'Tis a lesson you should heed:
Try, try, try again.
If at first you don't succeed,
Try, try, try again.

—Proverb

1

Laura hurried to keep up with Scott and Sophie, her school-bag thumping against her back.

"Wait for me!" she yelled, but they never did.

She had hesitated at the memorial outside the burned-out courthouse. A big picture of Ben was surrounded by lots of flowers and toys. The flowers were all brown and dried up, but there was a little plush cat that would have fit perfectly in the palm of her hand. Ben didn't need it; he was dead. But when she'd gone to take it, she'd looked up at the photo of him. His accusing brown eyes looked straight into hers. So she'd left the toy there, and the twins hadn't waited and she'd had to run as fast as she could to make sure they didn't leave her behind.

The sun bounced off the twins' blond hair, making Laura squint. They were sword fighting with sticks now. Galloping and fencing up the street, screaming "En garde!" at regular intervals. They wore the same white-and-green school uniform as Laura, except her shirt was no longer quite white. It was a pale alabaster from being washed a few hundred times at least. It had belonged to Sophie once, and to their older sister, Rose, before her, as had her shorts.

Despite her every possession being a hand-me-down, Laura was unique. She knew that she was the cutest child in her kindergarten class. Her fringe was cut blunt, accentuating her large dark-lashed eyes. Her nose was a button, her mouth a little pink tulip. She lived for coos and pats on the head.

"Hurry up, Laura!" Scott yelled.

"My legs aren't as big as yours!" she yelled back, her little black school shoes clip-clopping on the pavement as she hurried.

Then she saw it.

A bee.

She slid to a halt. It was the shape of a jelly bean, with mean-looking yellow and black stripes. The bee buzzed in front of her, blocking her path as it hovered near a bush of pungent purple flowers. Laura was overwhelmed by the urge to see what it felt like. Squishy, she was fairly sure. She wanted to pinch it between her thumb and forefinger to see if it would pop. Laura had never been stung by a bee but Casey at school had once and he had cried in front of everyone. It must hurt a lot.

Very slowly, she inched around it, walking like a crab on the very edge of the pavement until there were a good two meters between the bee and her.

When she turned, the street was empty. Sophie and Scott had turned one of the corners, out of Laura's sight. If she really thought about it, she would probably know which one, but she couldn't think. The suburban street seemed to be growing bigger and bigger and Laura felt like she was shrinking smaller and smaller. A sob rose slowly and heavily in her throat. She wanted to cry out for her mum.

"En garde!"

Laura heard it loud and clear from her left. She ran, as fast as she could toward the sound.

Sophie and Scott changed into T-shirts then continued their sword fight in the backyard. Laura wasn't invited. They didn't like to play "baby games," even though Laura told them that now she was at school she was officially not a baby. She sat up at the kitchen bench, listening to the screams and laughter from outside and staring down at the three plates of crackers that Rose had left for their afternoon tea.

Laura could hear Scott yell so loud it came through the glass. "You're dead!"

She watched as Sophie feigned a dramatic and violent death. It was a stupid game; she wouldn't have wanted to play anyway. While they were distracted, Laura quickly reached over, took two crackers from each of their plates and stuffed them in her mouth.

She chewed happily, swinging her legs and kicking the bench. The house filled with the banging sound. She knew she was being naughty. If her mum was at home she'd be in big trouble. But she kept kicking, trying to leave some little brown scuffs to blame on either Sophie or Scott. She hadn't decided yet.

Rose's bedroom door opened and Laura stopped kicking. Her older sister stamped down the corridor. Some days Rose would want to braid Laura's hair, or put makeup on her and tell her how pretty she was. *Just like a little doll*, she would say. Laura hoped it was one of those days but the angry stomps of Rose's feet told her it wasn't.

"How was school?" Rose pulled open the fridge door and put her head inside, as if she was trying to absorb all the cold.

"It was good. Nina said she could climb the big tree but she couldn't and she fell out and broke her bum."

Rose stuck her head out and looked at Laura, a can of Coke in her hand. Her lips were tugging up as if she was going to laugh.

"Really?"

"Yep!" Laura began to giggle, and then Rose laughed too. Laura liked it when she made Rose laugh. Rose was the prettiest girl Laura knew, even when she frowned, which was most of the time. When she laughed she looked like a princess.

"Poor kid," Rose said. She stopped laughing and rested the Coke against her forehead.

Laura didn't say anything. Nina hadn't really fallen out of the tree. Actually, she had made it the whole way to the top and then bragged about it all afternoon.

"What was that banging noise before?"

"Dunno. Can we braid my hair, Posey?"

"You know I don't like it when you call me that."

"Sowwy," she said. Sometimes when she pretended to still be a baby, Rose would like her more, but this time Rose didn't even look at her. Instead, Rose cracked open the can and took a swig. Laura looked at the pictures on Rose's arm. They went all the way from her elbow to her shoulder and looked like pen, but were there forever. Laura thought they were beautiful. Rose looked up at the clock and groaned.

"I'm going to be late. Fuck." Rose slammed the can on the bench, and little specks of brown liquid came out.

Laura gasped. She didn't know what that word meant exactly, but she knew it was one of the worst ones.

"I'm telling!"

Rose didn't even care; she just walked right out of the kitchen and back to her room to get ready. She was definitely not going to braid Laura's hair.

Laura jumped down from her stool. "I'm running away. You can't stop me!"

She ran to the front door and opened it and slammed it shut. Then she very quietly tiptoed away, so Rose would think she had left.

Laura decided to hide under her bed. She wriggled down on the floor and pulled the box of her winter clothes in front of her. If she stayed there for long enough, someone would notice she was gone. They would look for her but they wouldn't find her. Hiding was the one good thing about being small.

After a while, she started to get bored. It smelled funny under there, like the sports socks she wore all week long for her PE classes. She pulled herself back out. She was sick of this game now. As she sat cross-legged in the middle of her room, deciding whether it was the stuffed turtle's or the fluffy dog's turn to be played with, she noticed a shadow pass her window. Someone was coming to the front door of the house. Maybe her mum was home early!

She scampered to the entrance hall and opened the door but there was no one there at all. A wave of disappointment washed over her. Then she looked down. Someone had left her a present! She knelt down to look at it, wondering if it was a gift from Ben's ghost. To say thank you for not taking his little cat.

2

The denim shorts and tank Rose wore to work were crumpled in the corner of her bedroom. They were in need of a wash but she hadn't bothered today. Tugging the wrinkled clothes on, she could smell the sweat and beer caught in the fabric. By the end of her shift she'd reek.

Rose slipped her phone into her back pocket. Her fingers itched with its absence. All day, she had refreshed her email again and again and again. It was difficult to be patient.

She took her shoes out from under the bed. They were new, after the soles of her old ones had split from the canvas. They had been held together by threads and then she'd tripped on a beer keg and they'd ripped open like a mouth, her foot left exposed in the middle like a tongue. These new ones were cheap white sandshoes that already looked dirty. They had rubbed her heels raw last night. She winced a little as she pulled them on. Hopefully soon the material would soften, or her feet would harden.

Rose pulled her hair into a ponytail as she walked down the hall, her wrists flicking expertly. At first she didn't notice Laura, who was sitting on the floor, her back to Rose. It wasn't like her to be quiet. The only time she ever was was when she was hiding under her bed.

She knew she'd be late, but still Rose stopped. Laura looked so tiny when she was quiet. Her shoulders were narrow as she hunched forward over her crossed legs. Moving closer, Rose realized she was talking very, very softly in a strange high-pitched voice.

"No, I want chocolate, please. Thank you. Yum, yum, yum."

"What are you doing?"

Laura looked up at her. "None of your beeswax!"

Rose squatted down next to Laura to see what was in her hands. It was an old-fashioned doll, with a porcelain face and hands and a cloth body. It was nothing like any of Laura's other toys. Weirdly, she noticed that it looked just like Laura, big brown eyes, brown hair in a bob, cut sharply at its jaw.

"Why'd you cut its hair? You've ruined it," she said.

"I didn't."

"Yes, you did."

"Did not!"

"You did. You cut its hair so it would look like yours."

"I didn't! The person who gave it to me did it. They left it outside the front door. It's a present for me."

Rose touched the soft skin under Laura's chin so that she would look up.

"Are you fibbing? I won't be mad."

Laura held the doll in front of her and put on the high-pitched voice again. "Posey's just jealous. You're all mine!"

A strange feeling crept inside Rose then, a sense of something not being right. She considered taking the doll away, but Laura looked so content playing with her tiny twin. She was being stupid, she decided; of course someone didn't leave it for Laura. She must have borrowed it from another girl at school.

Leaving Laura to play, Rose left the house. She pulled the flywire screen door shut behind her and poked her finger through the broken netting to snip the lock closed. The thing was pointless. She remembered when she and her mother had installed it, years ago now, for security. These days it wouldn't have a hope of keeping intruders out; it would barely even protect them against blowflies.

The door was just like everything else in her life, in this town. After the car factory shut down, Colmstock had quickly lost its sense of purpose. Once, it had been pleasant. The largest town in the area and right off the Melton Highway, it was considered a nice place to stop off for a night on your way to the city. Small enough to have a strong community, but big enough that you could walk down the street without knowing every person you passed.

These days everything in Colmstock was broken and ugly. People weren't so friendly anymore. Too many residents had swapped a social drink or two for a meth habit. Crime rates were up, employment was down and yet the population stayed the same. It was as though everyone felt a sense of loyalty to the place. Well, Rose certainly didn't. She was getting out of here. Even the idea of it made her smile. The idea that this wouldn't be where she lived anymore, that she could have a whole different life. Realizing that her pace was slowing, she forced herself to stop dreaming. Her new life would start soon, but right now she was late for work.

Rose headed for Union Street, waving a hand over her face to keep away the flies. Even though the sun was up, she didn't feel safe walking alone. There was a much quicker route, but it meant going past the fossickers. She wouldn't do that no matter what time of day it was, so she had to circle around the long way. Slipping her phone out of her pocket, she refreshed her email again. Nothing. Her heart sank. They'd said they would get back to her today. She couldn't bear to wait any longer. She had never been so ready for anything.

Since she was a kid, she'd always wanted to be a journalist. There had been a lot of setbacks, the local paper *The Colmstock Echo* closing being the worst one. Then she'd got an email saying she had been long-listed for a cadetship at the *Sage Review*, a national paper. A week later she was told she had been short-listed. Still, she hadn't let herself get too excited. It was just too good, too amazing to happen to her. Then just eight days ago she was down to the final two. It was just her and one other hopeful person out there refreshing their emails today.

Her friend Mia was certain she would get it. Rose had laughed and made some joke about whether she'd seen it in her crystal ball, but really, she had believed her. In her gut, Rose knew she was going to get the cadetship, for the simple fact that no one could want it as much as she did. It just wasn't possible.

She hurried past the lake, which was surrounded by dry knee-high grass, home to snakes and mosquitoes. It reeked of stagnant water. Next to it, the bare frame of a swing set stood, taken over by an insistent flowering weed. Someone had cut down the swings a few years back, leaving the skeleton of the frame. She wondered if the swings had been rehung in the backyard of one of the nearby houses or if they had been destroyed just for the entertainment of a few kids.

Rose turned away and picked up her pace, the rubber soles of her new shoes slapping against the sticky bitumen, trying not to remember how, once upon a time, when the water was still blue, she'd gone for picnics by that lake with her mother. Her mother, who had sat mute next to her new husband Rob James when he'd told Rose it was time for her to move out. It was okay, since the cadetship was in the city and board was part of the deal, but still, it had hurt.

She crossed over toward Union Street, careful to hop over the cane toad that was squished into the road. Here, people would swerve onto the wrong side in order to squash one. They'd stay there, flat as pancakes, covered in ants, until they turned stiff and hard like dry leather in the baking sun.

The main street of Colmstock was three blocks long. There was only one set of traffic lights and, farther up, a pedestrian crossing in front of the squat redbrick church. Not far from where she stood was a pub. She could see the dog racing on screens through one of its grimy windows, which were often splattered with blood from bar fights by the time it closed. There was the Chinese takeaway joint with its loud red lit-up sign, nestled between the Indian restaurant and the antiques store, which had both closed years ago.

Farther down was the primary school and the Colmstock council building. From where Rose stood, waiting for the lights to change so she could cross the street, she could almost see the burned-out courthouse. It stood between the library, which had escaped the blaze, and the grocery store, which hadn't. In front of the steps to the courthouse was the memorial to the kid who had died there, Ben Riley. The picture of him was fading, bleached by the constant sun. The building was cordoned off with plastic tape. Barricades should have been put up, but it hadn't happened yet.

Rose stared at the charred remains. Now that all the files inside the courthouse were ashes and the computers were melted blocks of plastic and wire, did that mean the scheduled trials wouldn't go ahead? Did it mean that people who would have been criminals no longer were? Would the law be put on hold until they rebuilt the place? Even from here, she could smell it. The burned wood, bricks and plastic frying in the sun. It had been three weeks and the smell hadn't gone away. Maybe that was just how Colmstock would smell from now on.

Her pocket buzzed. Forcing herself to keep her hand steady, she took out her phone. She half expected it to be some dumb text message from Mia or a spam email. But it wasn't. She opened the *Sage Review*'s email, her mouth already tugging at the corners, ready to grin, ready to hold in a scream of excitement.

Dear Ms. Blakey,
Thank you for applying for the *Sage Review* Cadet Program. Unfortunately

Rose didn't read the rest. She couldn't.

Her mouth hadn't caught up yet. She was still smiling a strange hollow smile as she crossed the road to Eamon's Tavern Hotel.

3

Like many of the businesses on Union Street, Eamon's Tavern Hotel had once been one of the grander houses of Colmstock. It was larger than the others and more imposing with its wide stoop and double windows. However, any opulence the place had once possessed was long gone. It had been due a fresh coat of paint about twenty years ago. Now the facade of the building was crumbling and dirty. In the windows were neon beer signs: Foster's. VB. XXXX Gold.

Inside Bruce Springsteen played on repeat. The smell was musky: stale air and beer. The lighting was always dim, probably an attempt to hide the deterioration. Still, no darkness could hide the fact that everything was just a little bit sticky. It was the kind of place that had a few motel rooms around the back but no one would ever want to sleep there if they weren't drunk off their arse.

The bar was half-full of tradies and cops downing their paychecks, sitting heavily on dark wooden chairs. The place was popular with the law. The police station next door served the smaller towns in the region as well as Colmstock, though the boys didn't like to drink more than a stone's throw from the station. Seeing the things they saw some days, even walking the ten paces to Eamon's felt like too far for a beer. The other pub down the road was where you went if you wanted it to be clear that you didn't like the company of cops. Still, anyone who still drank in public rather than staying home with a baggie of crystal and a glass pipe was considered an asset, no matter where they chose to do it.

Underneath a faded black-and-white portrait of the Eamon family, the original occupants of the house, was the L-shaped bar where Rose chatted with Mia. They had worked at the tavern together for years and had spent hundreds of hours doing exactly what they were doing now: leaning against the bar, drinking Coke and talking shit.

Laura wasn't the only one who thought Rose looked like a princess. Senior Sergeant Frank Ghirardello, for one, was watching her from the corner of his eye as he drank his beer. Even with the tattoo up her tricep, she looked as pure and perfect as a movie star. That first sip of cold amber poured by Rose herself was the closest thing to bliss he knew. Frank had been keen on Rose from her very first shift at the tavern. She had served him a beer with foam six inches deep. The way she had looked at him, he was sure in that instant, she was The One. So he had taken the beer, tipped her and tried to drink the thing even though he had received a face full of froth with every sip. Frank had never been big on alcohol, but in the last few years he had developed a small drinking problem just to be close to Rose.

Around him, his squad discussed their theories on the most recent case, which had already replaced Ben Riley in their minds. Not for Frank. Some arsehole pyro had been causing a stir all year. It had been small blazes at first, a bush or a letter box smoking and smoldering. They'd liked to believe it was bored teenagers, although that had never been very likely.

The high school had shut down this year because of low enrollment, the class sizes less than a quarter of what they used to be. Most of the teenagers either worked at the poultry farm or had adopted the pipe full-time. The ones on meth were still committing crimes, assault and robbery mostly, but none of them seemed to have the patience to light a fire just for the joy of watching it burn.

Then, last month, it had escalated very suddenly. The psycho had been too trigger-happy with his lighter and burned down half a block of Union Street. Ben had only been thirteen, and he was what they called "special." "Brain damaged" was the real term. The boy acted more like a little kid than a teenager, but he was the darling of Colmstock. A smile for everyone. His parents owned the grocery store and sometimes he would play in the storage shed behind the courthouse next door. He had made it into a little cubbyhole. Poor kid had no idea the smoke meant run.

At first he'd been sure it was Mr. Riley, his dad. The guy had made a mint from the insurance and Frank suspected that he wouldn't have been opposed to lighting up his own son if it came to that kind of cash. But he had an airtight alibi. Frank had checked it and no way it was bogus.

Around him, the other men were joking now. Enough was enough. It was no time to be laughing. He cut into the conversation.

"Any headway?" He was looking at Steve Cunningham, who was the council chair. He knew what the answer was going to be, but he asked Steve every time he saw him anyway. He needed them to demolish the wreckage of the courthouse; it'd been almost a month. The rest of the group stopped talking and looked at Steve.

"Not yet," Steve said, and even in the dim light Frank could see his shiny bald patch reddening. "We're still trying to bring together the funds. It'll happen."

"Right," he replied.

"I'll get the next round," Steve said, standing. "Frank?"

"I'll pass, mate." He knew it wasn't Steve's fault, but he liked to have someone to blame. That black mess felt personal to him. It was a sign, blaring his failure to the whole town.

Frank had seen a lot of bad things. Of course he had. But seeing Mrs. Riley, telling her the fire was already too bad, that he couldn't go inside, that he couldn't save her son. The expression on her face as she was forced to stand back and let her child burn. He'd never forget it.

He ignored his friends again and watched as Rose finished pouring Steve's round and went back to flicking through the newspaper. She was talking quietly to Mia Rezek, whose father, Elias, had been a cop himself before he'd had a stroke about five years back. The two of them were acting as if they were hanging around at home rather than on the clock. Rose smoothed a hand over her hair. The movement was so simple, so casual, yet it made his throat constrict. God, he wanted her. It was almost unbearable.

He leaned back in his chair. The tavern was just quiet enough for him to hear what she was saying.

"'With Saturn lingering in Aquarius, nothing is off-limits,'" Rose read. "'Something unexpected will surprise you today.'" She snorted back a laugh. "Look out, single gals."

"It doesn't say that," he heard Mia say. Then their voices quieted.

Raising his head, Frank saw they were looking over at his table. He quickly downed the dregs of his drink and made his way toward them.

"Ladies, what are you staring at us for? See something you like?"

He flexed his biceps at Rose, but she wasn't even looking at him. She was already pouring his beer. Mia had noticed it though, and she smiled. He noticed the pity in her eyes and hated it.

"Don't waste your breath, Frankie," she said, leaning her elbows on the bar. "Rose is getting out of here."

"I still have a few weeks, don't I?" he asked. He was hoping she, or Mia, might give him news on the program Rose was hoping to get into. They'd talked about it like it was already guaranteed, but he didn't think it was. Or at least, that was what he hoped. His life would be so empty without her.

Looking at Rose, he saw her hand shake ever so slightly, spilling a droplet of ale onto her wrist. She rubbed it onto the seat of her shorts and handed him the beer.

"Something like that," she said. He was about to question her further, probe her like he would a perp in his interview room, but Mia interrupted.

"Let's see, then." She picked up his empty glass from the bar and peered into the foam inside it intently.

"Anything about my love life in there?" he said, looking at Rose again. Her smile back at him was thin. He should stop; he knew it. He should ask her out for real, not keep making these lame, obvious jokes. He was past thirty now and he was acting like a horny teenager. It was embarrassing.

"Well," said Mia, spinning the glass around, "I'm seeing a lot of positivity here. It's telling me that nothing is off-limits. That something unexpected is coming. Something that will surprise you."

They looked at each other, not knowing that he was in on the joke. It didn't matter; he took the opportunity.

"Is it an invitation for a double date? I think I could convince Bazza."

Frank's partner, Bazza, a newly-minted sergeant, was a

good-looking guy. He was tall, he had muscles and he used to
be one of their best footy players a few years after Frank had.
Frank loved him like a brother, but even he knew the guy was
more Labrador than man. His eyes lit up with pure delight
every time Frank mentioned lunch, he eyed strangers with
suspicion and he was as loyal as he was thick. Frank was fairly
sure if he told the man to sit he would do it, without a thought.

They turned to look at him, just as Bazza burped and then
chuckled to himself.

"We'll let you know," Rose said, and Frank smiled as if he
was only kidding, turning before the hurt could show on his
face. He had to grow some balls and ask the girl out properly.
Otherwise she'd leave town and that would be that.

Behind him he heard Mia say, "You know, I think Baz is
kind of hot."

His shoulders tensed, hoping like hell that Rose wouldn't
agree.

Thankfully, he heard, "He's a moron."

"Yeah, exactly."

They laughed quietly, and he sat back at his table, thank-
ful it wasn't him they were laughing at, and took a sip of his
beer. He could picture it: Mia with Bazza and him with Rose,
barbecues on the days off; Bazza at the BBQ; Mia tossing a
salad; Rose bringing him a beer and sitting on his knee as he
drank it.

4

Rose heaved the keg onto its side. It was heavy, pulling on the sockets of her arms and tightening the ligaments in her neck. She let it fall the last few centimeters, for no other reason than to enjoy the violent thud as it hit the cement floor. The windowless storage room at the rear of the tavern smelled like damp. Squeezed into the small space were the beer kegs, a large freezer full of frozen meat and fries, and a few boxes full of dusty beer glasses.

Bending over, butt high in the air, she pushed the keg around the tight corner into the back corridor with little baby steps. She looked ridiculous. If Frank could see her now maybe he would stop looking at her like she was hot shit. Or maybe he'd get off on it. The thought of that made her straighten up. She hated having men's eyes on her. It made her feel as though she didn't own her own body. As if by staring her up and down they were possessing her flesh. If it weren't so damn humid she'd wear long pants and turtlenecks and never, ever shave her legs.

She was starting to get blisters. Every step she took her heels grated down against the rough fabric of her shoes, slicing through another layer of skin. She was starting to wince as she gently kicked the keg down the corridor. She passed the stain on the carpet from where Mark Jones had puked up his beer and the crack in the wall that seemed to be getting slightly bigger every day. She tried to remind herself that sometimes she didn't totally hate this job. Quiet nights goofing around with Mia could be fun. But right now she wanted to pull her hair out. Every night, for years and years, the same bloody thing, one shift identical to another. The only difference was the aging of the patrons.

The numbness she'd felt earlier had worn off now. Her stomach was crumpling inward with shame and disappointment at the email from the *Sage Review*. She hadn't told Mia yet; she couldn't. If she did, then it would be real. Mia would ask her what she was going to do, where she was going to live, and she didn't have the answers. Instead, she kept her body moving and tried to breathe. Rose had written about everything she could think of. She'd written about the financial crisis and its effects on her town; she'd written about the search for the arsonist who had killed poor Ben Riley and burned down the courthouse. She'd written film reviews, celebrity gossip and, worst of all, attempted an awkward video series on YouTube.

Regardless of the topic, the rejections were always the same. "Thank you for submitting..." they would begin, and already she knew the rest. Everyone always said the only person who stood in your way to success was yourself. She knew that; she really did. Rose just needed one good story, something truly unique. If she just had a great story, they couldn't say no.

This cadetship had been made for her; she'd fit the requirements exactly. It had been so perfect, so exactly right.

The corner of the keg whacked against the wall, causing a framed picture to fall to the floor.

"Fuck." She hadn't been paying enough attention. She couldn't cope with this. There was now a large crack in the glass across the photograph of the Eamon family: the husband with his war medals, the wife with her strained smile, the little curly-haired girl with her curly-haired doll and the boy with his frilly shirt. Rose hung it back on the wall.

The feeling in her stomach was turning to pain, and she was struggling to swallow it away. It was like acid reflux, spilling out from her gut in a poisonous torrent and into her throat.

She put her head into the kitchen. "All right if I take my break now?"

"Sure," the manager, Jean, said, not turning around as she chopped a mound of pale tomatoes.

Sometimes she took her break up at the bar, attempting to eat something Jean had made and continuing to chat with Mia and whoever else was sitting there. But if she was going to get through today she needed to have a few minutes to herself. She grabbed the first-aid kit off the shelf and went back into the corridor. She pushed open one of the motel room doors and sat on the end of the bed. Carefully she slid one of her shoes off and examined her heel. The skin was bright red. A blister was forming, a soft white pillow puffing up to protect her damaged skin. Carefully, she traced her finger over it, shuddering as she touched the delicate new skin.

Unclipping the first-aid kit, she rummaged through the out-of-date antiseptic and the bandages still in their wrapping until she found the box of Band-Aids in the bottom. She pulled one out and stuck it on her skin, stretched it over her blister and then fastened the other side down. The process of putting on the Band-Aid reminded her of being a little kid. Of being looked after, of knowing there was someone there to make everything okay. Her throat constricted and she couldn't hold it in. Holding a hand over her face to muffle the sound, she began to cry. Horrible, aching sobs rose from inside her.

Clenching her eyes closed, she tried to force herself to stop, but she couldn't. She was so tired, too tired. Her eyes turned hot, tears overfilling them and burning down her cheeks. Crying was easier than not crying.

She stood, looking up to pull the door closed so there would be no chance they would hear her at the bar. Through her watery vision she saw someone. A man, standing in the hallway, staring at her. She tried to reset her face, wiping her cheeks with her hands.

"I'm sorry," he said and, weirdly, he looked like he might cry too. She stood, her hand still on the doorknob, staring at him, not knowing what to say, so aware of her crumpled forehead, of a tear inching down one of her wet cheeks. His eyes flicked away from hers and her face prickled with humiliation.

She pulled the door closed and sat back on the bed. Staring at the back of the door, she took some deep breaths. The surprise of seeing him had made the crying stop, at least, but now her heart was hammering in her chest. Rubbing her hands over her face, she wondered who that guy had been. She'd never seen him before. That wasn't common in Colmstock. Not just that. He didn't look like the other men in town. His face was so unusual, she wasn't sure what his ethnicity was, and he was wearing a T-shirt with a band's logo on it and blue stovepipe jeans that looked brand-new. Definitely not the usual uniform for the men around here. She crept over to the door again and opened it an inch, peering out, sure he was going to be standing there still. He wasn't. But she noticed a Do Not Disturb sign hanging from the knob of the other motel room. Of course, they had a guest.

Closing the door, she went into the bathroom to throw some cold water onto her face. She had been rejected before; she should know how to handle it by now. If she could make it through the rest of her shift, she'd figure everything else out tomorrow. That was all she had to focus on now, getting to the end of the shift. She stood still, centering on just the feeling of her bare feet on the carpet. Then quickly and cleanly she put the Band-Aid on her other heel and, gritting her teeth, pulled her shoes back on.

Back in the kitchen, Jean was flipping a burger on the grill. It sizzled and smoked. Rose's nose felt itchy with the acrid smell of burning, but she didn't say anything. She would never tell Jean how to cook and not just because she was her boss. No one would say a word to Jean even if their meat was as black and rubbery as a tire, which was often the case. Even though she was nearing sixty, no one would want to cross her. You'd know it if she didn't like you.

Rose still remembered the one and only time someone did insult one of Jean's steaks. Some dickhead friend of Steve Cunningham's had demanded a refund. He'd told Jean that if she wanted to cook bush tucker she should go back to her campfire. That man had never got his refund, and he had not been allowed to set foot in Eamon's again. Rose herself would have made sure of that if she'd had the chance, though Jean never needed any help. Even thinking about the guy now made Rose's blood boil. Steve was lucky; he'd apologized repeatedly to Jean, and Rose could tell he meant it, so eventually he was allowed back.

"Do we have a guest?" Rose asked as she bent down to install the keg she'd brought in earlier.

"Yep. William Rai." You could hear the pack-a-day habit in Jean's voice.

"What's he like?" Mia called from behind the bar.

"Quiet."

Rose wiped her wet hands on her shorts and went around to the bar. She put a jug under the beer tap and began running the froth out, happy to be away from the stink of singed meat.

"Have you seen him yet?" Mia asked, quietly.

"Yeah," Rose said. His eyes had looked so shiny, but surely that was just the light.

"And?"

"What? You think he might be your soul mate?" she joked.

Mia shrugged. "You never know."

Rose smiled and leaned back, watching the white creamy froth overflow from the jug as it slowly turned to beer.

"So I'm guessing you haven't heard back from *Sage* yet?" Mia said, looking at her carefully.

Rose flicked off the beer tap. "No."

"Don't stress about it—one more day won't make a difference."

Rose looked up at Mia and smiled feebly. She wanted to tell her, she really did, but she was afraid she might start crying again in front of all their customers. Just as she was opening her mouth to ask if they could talk about it later, the tavern went silent. It was the sudden, loud kind of silence that felt wholly unnatural. Mia and Rose looked around.

It was the guest. Will. He was paused in the doorway, every single pair of eyes in the bar on him. Rose had been right before—this man was not from Colmstock. He took the stares in, not appearing unsure or uncomfortable, and sat down at the far table. The cops turned back to their beers and the talking resumed.

"Wow. He's not bad," Mia said quietly.

"He's all yours," she told Mia. She could feel the humiliation crawling back. He must think she was such a weirdo, sitting there with the door open, crying. Hopefully he wasn't staying long.

Rose watched Mia peel a plastic menu from the pile. She walked swiftly over to Will's table and put the menu down in front of him. Mia put her hand on her hip and, even without being able to see her face, Rose could see that she was flirting.

The girl was hardly subtle. Will smiled at her, only politely, Rose noticed, and pointed at something on the menu. He didn't know yet not to order Jean's food. His eyes flicked away from Mia, and he looked straight at Rose, making her breath catch ever so slightly. She turned away and busied herself washing glasses.

By the time his meal was ready, Mia was on her break. She was sitting up at the bar, eating what she normally did for dinner: a burger bun, the insides slick with tomato sauce and nothing else.

"Order up," Jean called.

Mia shrugged at Rose, her mouth full. "I donf fink he fanfies me."

Rose looked around, trying to think of a way to avoid a second encounter with the stranger. Maybe she could ask Jean to do it? But she knew then they'd want to know why and telling them would be even worse.

Grabbing the plate, fingers below and thumb on top, she strode toward him. Looking down at it, she saw that he seemed to have ordered a burger without the meat, just limp lettuce, pale tomatoes and cheese on the white bun. He was leaning back in his chair, reading a book, but she couldn't see the title. As she stepped in front of his light, he looked up at her.

"Here you go," she said.

He leaned forward. "Thanks." He paused. "I wanted to ask...are you all right? Before I—"

"I'm fine," she snapped. "Why wouldn't I be?"

She looked him right in the eye then, daring him to mention what he'd seen. He didn't.

"Just checking," he said and half smiled, creating little crinkles around his dark eyes.

At closing time, when all the stools were on the tables and the floor was mopped and drying, Springsteen was singing about dreams and secrets and darkness on the edge of town, and Mia and Rose sat on the bar, drinking beers. Their aching feet feeling blissful now that they weren't on the hard concrete. Jean stood behind them, counting the money in the register.

"How long is our guest staying?" Rose asked, trying to sound casual.

"He's booked in for a week," Jean muttered, writing down figures on an order pad.

"You keen?" Mia asked.

"Nah, the opposite. He seemed like a dickhead. Really patronizing."

The sound of something banging on the window interrupted them. It was Frank, rapping his knuckles on the glass. He waved good-night, his brown eyes so hopeful that he looked more like a small scruffy street mutt begging for a scrap than a policeman in his thirties. They waved back.

"That man needs to take it down a notch," Jean said, slight disapproval in her voice.

Rose didn't respond.

"He's a nice guy," Mia said, pushing it.

"It's not about that," Rose said. "There's just no point. This won't be where I end up." She took a swig. Mia watched her, carefully.

"You heard back from *Sage*, didn't you?"

Rose didn't look at her; she couldn't.

"I was so sure you had this one," Mia said.

Rose felt warmth on her hand and looked down. Jean had placed her weathered palm on top of Rose's fingers.

"You're a fighter— it'll happen for you. It might take a while, but it will happen."

For the first time that night, the tightness in Rose's throat loosened.

Jean withdrew her hand and placed two envelopes between them on the bar.

"Patronizing or not, our guest tips well."

The air felt cooler as Mia and Rose stepped off the porch outside. The cicadas were trilling loudly. Despite everything, Rose felt a sense of victory. She'd done it. She'd got through the shift, and now she could go home to grieve, while she still had a home. She looked back at the tavern as they walked toward Mia's car, wondering again about the guest, Will. He must be a relative of someone, down for some family occasion. She couldn't think of any other reason someone would want to stay in this town for a whole week.

"Oh." Mia paused next to her.

"What?"

Mia ran to her beat-up old Auster and pulled a parking ticket from the windscreen. She looked at her watch.

"I was only three minutes late!"

"They must have been waiting for it to tick over."

They looked around. The street was empty. Getting in the car, Mia held the ticket up to the interior light.

"It's more than I even made on my shift."

Rose took her envelope from her bag and put it on the dashboard.

"You don't have to," Mia said, but Rose could already hear the relief in her voice.

"I know."

They didn't talk as Mia drove. The radio played some terrible new pop song that Rose had heard one too many times, but she knew better than to mess with the stereo in Mia's car. She stared out the window, looking forward to the oblivion of sleep. She slid her heels out of her shoes. Tomorrow, she decided, she wouldn't wear shoes at all. The tavern was closed on Tuesdays, so maybe she wouldn't even get out of bed.

The car went past the fossickers. At first it was just a few tents set up in and around a gutted old cottage that had been there for forever. Now it was a real community. People lived in cars; structures were set up. Some people just slept under the stars. It was warm enough. They kept to themselves, so the cops didn't seem to bother them, even though they all sported missing teeth and raging meth addictions. Rose hadn't known why they were called the fossickers at first, but then found a couple of years back that they fossicked for opals and sold them on the black market. That was how they got by. Her stomach clenched with fear and she looked down at her hands. She would never end up there.

"So, I heard some great gossip today." Mia couldn't stand to sit in silence for too long. No matter how miserable she was, Mia always seemed to feel better when she was talking. "Maybe you can write your next article about it? Working at a cop bar has got to be good for something."

Unlike Mia, Rose often craved solitude. She didn't need to answer anyway. Mia usually seemed perfectly happy to just listen to the sound of her own voice chirping away.

"Apparently someone has been leaving porcelain dolls on doorsteps of houses, and the dolls look like the little girls that live in the house. How freaky is that?"

Rose snapped her head around.

"The cops are worried it might mean something. Like maybe it's a pedophile marking his victims."

Rose gaped at her.

"What?" asked Mia.

Rose scrambled through her bag, trying to find her cell phone, the image of Laura in her mind, sleeping cheek to cheek with her tiny porcelain twin.

5

"Help! Stop it!" the child wailed.

Frank had tried asking nicely. Now he was prying the doll out of the little girl's hands. When he'd imagined being a cop, he'd never thought fighting kids for their toys would be part of the job.

"She's mine!" Laura yelled, just as Frank gave the thing a proper tug, released it from the kid's iron grip.

Laura stared up at him, looking more angry than upset, and kicked him right in the shins.

"Laura!" Rose yelled at the little shit as she ran out of the room and slammed her bedroom door.

Frank rubbed his shin. She'd got him right on the bone. Truth was, it was throbbing.

"Sorry," said Rose, looking him up and down. He stopped rubbing his leg and grinned.

"No stress," he said. He should have guessed Rose's sister would be like that. Cutest damn kid you ever saw but a real little fighter. When she grew up, she was going to break hearts. That was for sure.

Frank could see the worry in Rose's eyes, and if he were

honest, he liked it. Rose had never looked at him like this before, like he had something to give, like he could protect her. Ben Riley's mother and the arsonist felt a million miles away now.

"What do you think?" she asked.

"About what?" asked Bazza. Frank won the fight not to swear under his breath. That guy could be an absolute moron sometimes.

He put a hand on Rose's soft arm. Every part of him wanted to slide his hand up and down her arm, feel her warm unblemished skin. He wondered whether her whole body was that same pale honey, or whether the parts of her that didn't see the sun were still the color of cream. He could feel his pants tighten ever so slightly.

"I really don't think it's anything to worry about," he said, letting go of her before it really got out of hand. He was here as a professional.

"That's not what you said at the station yesterday," Bazza interjected from next to him.

"Shut up, Baz," he said out of the side of his mouth, his budding erection deflating instantly. He smiled apologetically at Rose. "You've told your mum about this, right?"

"Yeah, but she's doing a double today."

"We'll let you know if there are any developments, but if you're feeling at all worried, you can call me and I'll be here in a flash."

"What did we say about sharing police information?" Frank said to Bazza as they walked back to the car. The sky above them was overcast, but still it was hot and slimy. Half-moons of sweat hovered under each of his armpits.

"Sorry," mumbled Bazza.

Usually that would be the end of it, but not this morning.

"It's not okay. You've been a cop long enough now, mate. You should know better."

The guy was taller than him, and much broader, but Frank had never once felt threatened by him. Right now, he was giving Frank the round-shouldered, hurt look like you'd get from a kid caught stealing from the biscuit tin. Frank stared back at him like he was just a piece of shit on his shoe. Bazza's lip jutted out and he went to sit in the car to sulk. Good. Let him stew and think about what it meant to wear the badge.

Frank turned for one last look at the small white brick building. The lawn had not been cut for a long time. Around the side of the house were monstrous, spindly bushes growing around pieces of broken furniture and an old dog kennel.

To other people the place probably looked like a bit of an eyesore. Not to Frank. This was Rose's house, and he had been allowed inside. He could smell her everywhere. He'd thought that clean, spicy scent was unique just to her, but it must have been the detergent she used because her whole house had that same smell. It was heaven. Now he could imagine what her life was like when she wasn't at work. Everything in that house, even the toaster, had a strange erotic quality. He only wished that he had got a look at her bedroom.

God, he could do with a drink right now. Just to calm down. The day was only just starting and already it felt like too much. He was hungry for that look in Rose's eyes. That look like he could protect her from the filth of this world. It made him feel taller, broader, and he could, if she let him. He would protect her from everything. She would never have to pull another beer again.

Although his mouth was already watering, he banished the thought of beer from his mind and pulled the trunk open to grab an evidence bag. He flicked it to let the air in and then took the doll out from under his arm. God, the thing was freaky to look at. He had no idea why that kid had fought so hard to keep it. He was a grown man and it gave him the major willies. Its eyes were wide and glassy and its hair felt too soft. He hoped like hell it wasn't real human hair. Frank was used to wife bashers and drug addicts; he was used to the guy with bloody knuckles being the one who threw the punch. These dolls were something else completely. More than anything, it was bizarre. It wasn't only that he didn't know who the pervert was. He had no idea what on earth he was doing, and even less of an understanding of why. Hell, right now he'd take the arsonist over this case. At least that was cut-and-dried police work. Leaving anonymous little gifts for children wasn't something they'd ever covered in training.

He squeezed the awful thing into the evidence bag. The plastic stretched across its face, its open mouth gaping as though it was trying to breathe. Frank tried not to think about how much it looked like an asphyxiated child. Despite himself, he shuddered as he snapped the trunk shut.

6

Rose didn't have a chance to think while she got the kids ready for school.

"Shoes on," she said to Laura as she passed her bedroom. The little girl was sitting on her bed in her socks, arms crossed. She was still angry about Frank taking her doll away.

In the kitchen, Sophie was attempting to put peanut butter on bread, but somehow had managed to get most of it on her hands, cheeks and the bench. Their mother had recently given her the new chore of making the school lunches, but Rose always ended up doing it. She nudged Sophie out of the way with her hip; it was quicker just to do it herself.

The piece of sandwich Sophie had attempted to make had holes in it from where she'd pressed too hard with the knife. Rose folded it over and took a large bite as she lined up six slices of white bread. She chewed, enjoying the salty crunchiness, as she neatly spread each slice. The peanut butter had to reach each corner; she knew that from when she was a kid. She finished off her own mangled sandwich as she neatly cut each of the three in front of her into two even triangles. Behind her, she heard shrill giggles.

"What are you doing?" she said, turning to the twins. Sophie was lying on the floor and Scott was crouching over her. They stopped and looked at her, Sophie rubbing her wet cheek.

"He was hungry," said Sophie, and they burst out laughing again.

"Were you eating the peanut butter off her face?"

"Maybe," said Scott.

"Gross! Hurry up."

She quickly wrapped the sandwiches in cling film, then tossed them into the schoolbags that had been dumped next to the front door yesterday afternoon. She remembered Bazza tripping on them when he and Frank had come in this morning. The thought made her wince. She hated the idea that they'd seen where she lived. Somehow, with them standing there, the stains on the carpet and the crumbs on the bench top seemed magnified.

She picked up Laura's bag and went into Laura's seemingly empty room. Rose knew better.

"Don't leave without her!" she yelled, hearing the twins opening the front door.

"But she takes forever."

Rose placed the backpack on the ground and knelt down in front of the bed, taking the small scuffed-up shoes off the carpet.

"Can I have a foot?" she asked softly, and one of Laura's little socked feet emerged from under the bed. She slid the shoe on and gently did up the buckle.

"Are you angry with me?" she asked.

There was no response, but another shoeless foot was extended out from under the bed. Rose took it in her hand.

"Fair enough," she said as she slipped the white-socked foot into the shoe. There was no point in trying to explain to

Laura. Rose would prefer her sister feel angry than afraid of whoever had chosen her for that strange present.

She held Laura's ankles in her hands and carefully slid her out from under the bed. Laura ignored what was happening and stared at the ceiling, her cheeks blotchy and red from all the angry crying, her eyelashes still wet.

Rose took her under her arms and, pulling her up onto her feet, kissed her on the top of her head. "Off you go, then."

The twins banged and skidded out of the house, Laura trotting quietly behind them. Rose often felt sad watching her siblings walk to school. Laura was always left lagging behind. Like Rose herself. She closed the door against the heat and noise, and the house went totally silent except for the low hum of the refrigerator.

Rose padded across the carpet to her bedroom. Standing in the doorway, she didn't enter. Her suitcase was in the corner of her room. It was open, her best clothes folded inside. She'd packed. Actually packed. That was how sure she'd been about the cadetship. She was such an idiot.

There was no point in unpacking. Cadetship or not, her mother and Rob had told her she had to move out by the time Rob came home from his latest haul. That was in just one week. Part of her thought that maybe if she told her mum what had happened, if she asked for a bit more time, her mother would relent.

Really, though, she'd long stopped thinking of this place as her home. She had to start looking for a rental, but even the idea of it made her exhausted. Her sleep had been hollow, never dipping far from the surface of consciousness. Frank had promised he'd come over first thing the next morning when she'd called him in a panic from Mia's car last night. When she did get home she had quietly pulled the doll out of Laura's sleeping fingers and put it on the highest shelf, its glass eyes staring at her.

The strangeness of it, her own inability to understand what the implications were, meant that no matter how tired her bones felt, her mind had whirred on. She had listened to her mother get up at 5:00 a.m. to go to work. Heard her soft footsteps down the hall, her sigh, barely audible, from the dark kitchen. She hadn't moved. She'd remained motionless in her clammy sheets, listening as her mother's car backed out of the driveway, the headlights illuminating her bedroom. Then her thoughts turned to dreams and she was asleep without even knowing it. Soon after she had awoken sharply to Laura's screams.

Jumping out of bed, she'd realized the screams were out of anger, not fear. Laura had found the doll eventually and was almost crushed in the process by climbing up the bookcase. She only had the thing for about fifteen minutes when Frank and Bazza had pulled up.

Rose was still hovering in her doorway when the home phone rang. She ran back into the kitchen and snatched it up.

"Rose?" It was her mother, sounding breathless. "I just got your message. The police were at the house? Is everyone okay?"

"Yep, but everything's fine. They just came because someone left Laura a doll."

There was silence down the line, and Rose braced herself.

"You called the police because of a toy?" The panic was totally gone from her voice now.

"The police were worried, Mum. They say that there's been a whole bunch of kids getting dolls and—"

"Rose." Her mum's voice was quieter then. Rose imagined her in the break room at the poultry factory, her hairnet still on, her body turned away from the rest of the workers' pricked ears. "We'll discuss this when I get home."

The line went dead. Rose slammed the phone back onto the cradle. Her mum never listened to her anymore. Rose ignored the peanut butter smeared across the counter and went back to her room, diving onto the bed. Turning away from the suitcase, she squeezed her eyes shut. The sheets beneath her felt sticky from her restless night.

Rose knew the conversation that was going to happen with her mother when she got home. She knew the way her mum would look at her too, like she was an inconvenience, like she was just another frustration on an already-long list. It hadn't always been like that.

It was less than a month after the rumor began that the Auster Automotive Factory would close that her mother had started seeing Rob. He was a long-range trucker, and looked the part. Rob was someone her mother would never have fancied before. But when a steady wage became a rarity in the town, Rob became a catch. Back then, Rose didn't even care. She didn't care when he moved in, or even when they announced that her mother was pregnant with twins. Rose was seventeen, almost finished high school and stupid enough to be excited about the future. The idea that she would fail to get a scholarship, and what with no savings and no financial support wouldn't be moving out of town anytime soon, hadn't even crossed her mind. Ever since then she'd been living on borrowed time.

She pulled her curtains shut and put on the fan. She could smell the ripe stink of her own sweat and it made her even more frustrated. She had been totally right to call the police, and now her mum was angry with her.

Again, the memory of the last time she'd seen Rob surfaced. She'd come out of her bedroom, where she basically lived these days, and her mother and Rob had been sitting in the living room. They'd asked her to sit down. Rob had actually said the words *our home*, when he'd told her it was time for her to get her own place. Rose was no longer part of the "our," even though she'd lived in the house for seventeen years longer than he had. Her mother had said nothing, but she'd nodded along with him and hadn't looked Rose in the eye.

The fan whirred, blowing cold air onto her sweaty neck and making her hair flutter around her face. The pillow felt soft against her cheek. She closed her eyes, relishing the silence and the dark, trying to let herself dissolve into it. To forget her life, just for a moment. But she couldn't. Every time her mind felt clear, she'd see that porcelain face. Or Will's expression when he'd caught her crying. Or, worst of all, she'd see herself, staking a claim to some earth near the fossickers. She opened her eyes. It was too stuffy for this. Sitting up, she pulled the window ajar, letting some air in. Fuck it. Just because her life was depressing didn't mean she had to be. She was going to figure this out. Besides, it wasn't like she even had a choice. She had to do something.

She slipped on some sandals and put her phone and notebook in her pocket. She left the house, banging the screen door shut behind her. The air was heavy with humidity. Listening to the slap of her shoes against the road, she walked briskly down the street. The tiredness lifted off her like a blanket. It was good to get outside. The morning was getting hot, but at least there was movement in the air. Sitting at home in the house where she grew up, but where she no longer felt welcome, was hardly comforting. From a distance, she heard the echoes of children squealing and laughing. They must have been stragglers, late to school, or perhaps playing truant. She and Mia used to do that sometimes, she remembered, back when there was a high school in Colmstock. Things were so different then, it was hard to believe it was the same place. They'd had a whole group of friends. All of them, except for Rose, had their futures mapped out perfectly. They'd graduate high school and then go to work at Auster's. It wasn't a bad job, and the pay was good. High school had felt like their last chance for freedom.

Walking past the football oval, Rose remembered what it used to look like. It had been perfectly green, and one night, they'd done doughnuts with one of their fathers' pickup trucks. Rose and Mia had lost touch with their friends very quickly after their final year. Two of them had married each other and were on to their third kid, Mia's boyfriend had killed himself, and one of them, Lucie, had moved out of town for three years only to come back to Colmstock pregnant and alone. Rose had tried calling her, but she'd never called her back and so that was that. Looking out over the field, where the dead yellow grass was coming up in clumps, it seemed incredible that it could be the same place. The stands were covered in graffiti, and the seats were broken. But she could almost still feel the wind in her hair, still hear Mia's and Lucie's squeals of delight echoing in her ears.

Colmstock had once thrived as a farming area, but in World War I, more than two-thirds of the young men who left didn't come back. The town had almost been deserted then, and Rose wished it had. It would have saved them all a lot of disappointment. But it hadn't, because someone had stumbled on deposits of oil shale in the late 1930s. The rest of the country was still recovering from the Depression, so people flocked to the middle-of-nowhere town to work in the mines. The car factory was built around then, and Colmstock had become a very wealthy town. You could tell which buildings were from that period: grand white facades that were now cracked and weathered.

The mine closed in the eighties. Something to do with cheaper alternatives being discovered, but Rose couldn't quite remember what they were. The mine entrance was still there. A wide black mouth leading into oblivion. It wasn't too far from the lake near Rose's house. When she and Mia had been bored kids they used to sneak under the fence around it and dare each other to jump inside.

The council building was one of the big white buildings, but more important, it was one of the few places in town with air-conditioning. An old woman with a hunch and thick Coke-bottle glasses was sitting on a bench out the front; she smiled hopefully at Rose, who nodded in return. This woman was often hanging around, and if you weren't quick you'd get stuck listening to her rattle on all day about her cat. Rose stepped inside, and her skin prickled cold. It was a lovely feeling. She stood in front of the notice board, her eyes closed, feeling her blood cool.

This was where the office for the local newspaper used to be. *The Colmstock Echo*—Rose had done work experience there when she was in high school. Everything about it had felt so right. Going out and finding the real story. The smell of ink on printing day. She'd started working there during the day after she'd been rejected in her university scholarship applications. It had only been for six months, and she'd been at Eamon's at nighttime, but Rose had been okay. She'd almost been happy. It hadn't been long until they could no longer afford to pay her, but she'd stayed on anyway. Most of the other staff had left, so Rose had become the deputy editor. Eventually the funding was cut completely. That was when Rose had done the stupid thing. The dumb, reckless thing that had really sealed the deal on her crappy life. The idea of the newspaper closing, of her life just being about Eamon's, killed her. So, big ideas in her head, she'd got a small loan from the bank. She had been sure if they could just hang on until they had some advertisers, she could save the *Echo*. It hadn't made any difference; the newspaper had barely lasted another month. Rose's loan had grown steadily, and now she wasn't even managing to pay off the interest each month.

"Rose?"

Steve Cunningham came to stand next to her.

"I thought that was you," he said, smiling. "How are you?"

"Fine." She felt caught out; she didn't want to have to explain to him that she had nowhere to live. He looked up at the board, but didn't ask her about it.

"It's quiet around here," she said, and it was true. They were the only people standing in the corridor.

He shrugged. "I'm used to it."

Steve was looking terrible; he was pale, which was making the shadows under his eyes appear deep and purple, but his smile was real. She had always suspected Steve might admire her, not in the ogling bad-joke way that some of the other punters did, but like he actually thought there might be more to her than her arse.

With a swish from the doorway, his smile fell instantly from his face. She followed his gaze. Mr. Riley was opening the building's front door for his wife, his hand on her lower back as he steered her through it. Rose looked away quickly. Since the fire, the Rileys had become almost famous in town, triggering silence and averted eyes wherever they went. Their grief followed the couple like a cape.

"Hi," Steve said, walking toward them, hand outstretched. "Good to see you both."

He escorted them past Rose and into one of the rooms beyond the staircase. Rose watched them go, trying to imagine how it would feel to have both your child and your business disappear all at once.

She swallowed and looked back at the board, oddly grateful she definitely wasn't the least fortunate person in town. She looked for rooms to rent among the badly photocopied posters advertising secondhand cars and used baby cribs for sale. There were two advertisements for tenants. One was so far out of town she had no idea how she could get to work, and the other was a room share, but she wrote both numbers down in her notebook. Neither was appealing, but both were better than sleeping under the stars with the fossickers.

As she stood thinking of how the rent per month added up against her income, she felt a movement behind her. Nothing touched her, but the hair on her arms prickled and stood. Turning, she saw the back of a man walking up the stairs. Will. Without thinking, she began to follow him. She wanted to know more about him, understand what someone like him, someone with new clothes and no apparent connections with the town, was doing here in Colmstock.

Rose waited until he reached the crest of the stairs and turned down the corridor before she began quietly climbing them herself. When she reached the top, he was gone. He must have entered one of the offices. Rose looked into one. A woman sat glumly behind a computer, barricades snaking around the room in preparation for a long line, but no one was waiting. The woman straightened when she saw Rose but Rose just smiled at her and kept walking. The next room was the public records. You were meant to register yourself at the station and ask the attendant to find records for you. Rose had done research for stories here a couple of times. There was no one behind the desk now. Looking at the logbook, she saw that the last entry was for over six months ago. There'd been layoffs at the council around then.

She was about to turn when she heard a sound of a filing cabinet drawer squeak open. Leaning across the desk, she looked into the archives. There was Will, flicking through a drawer like he was perfectly entitled to be there.

"Hey!" she said. "What are you doing?"

He looked up at her and smiled. "Hi," he said. "You're the waitress from Eamon's, right?"

As if he didn't remember who she was. She narrowed her eyes at him. "You know you're not allowed to just look through this stuff yourself."

He shrugged. "Are you going to help me?"

"No," she said. "I don't work here, you know."

He didn't answer but began flicking through the records again.

She came around to the other side of the desk. "What are you looking for?" she asked.

He stopped, turning around completely this time, and fixed her with a blunt stare. She found herself taking a step backward.

"If you don't work here," he said, not smiling anymore, "I don't see how it's any of your business."

He stared at her, waiting for her to leave. And she did. As she was turning to walk out of the room, she wondered why she was doing it. She never, ever let people talk to her that way. If they did she was quick to tell them to bugger off. But something about the way he'd looked at her, about the severity in his voice, had made her falter.

She was almost home, replaying the encounter over and over in her head, when she remembered the reason she'd gone out in the first place. She took the notebook out and flicked to the page where she'd written down the phone numbers and prices for the rentals. Wishing she'd paid more attention in math, she divided the monthly amounts by 4.3 and then put together a rough estimate of her weekly wage. Snapping the notebook shut, she felt the all-too-familiar lump rise in her throat again. There was no way it would work. She'd have to get a second job, like most people in town.

Walking in through the front door, she imagined it. The

only jobs around were at the poultry factory. She desperately didn't want to work there. Her mother's job there was de-beaking. Rose remembered the way she'd looked after her first day. She'd come home so pale she looked sick.

Rose had poured her a glass of water and asked her what had happened. She hadn't really wanted to know, not at all, but she wanted her mother to feel better. Her mother told her about how she'd had to use a dirty pair of scissors to cut the end of chickens' beaks off so they didn't peck each other in the battery cages.

"The noise they make," she'd said. "They're in agony."

She had to do one hundred a day; if she didn't reach the target she'd get her pay docked. Rose had told her not to go back, that she was sure there'd be another job she could get. But her mother had gone back. That was five years ago.

Rose sat down on the end of her bed and looked at her suit-case. If she worked at the factory, she'd give up on ever getting out of town. There wouldn't be time. Slowly, she shut the lid of her suitcase with her foot and pushed it under her bed, her good clothes still folded inside. She was going to ask her mum for a month, just one month, and in that time she was going to make her dream happen. She was going to get out of here.

7

"So Frank wasn't worried?" Mia asked, as they laid towels down on the carpet of her bedroom.

"He said he wasn't, although Baz said he was. It is just a toy though, right? It can't be anything too bad," Rose told her.

"How did Laura handle having to let it go?"

Rose smiled. "I don't know if she'll ever forgive me."

"I'm sure they'll give it back to her when it turns out to be nothing."

"Hope not—I don't think I'd sleep with that creepy thing in the house."

They sat down on the coarse gray towels, the bristles rough on their bare legs.

"If I tell you something, you won't laugh?" asked Mia, who was stirring the wax that they had heated up in the microwave. The two of them were sitting on the towels in their undies, a half-empty bottle of Bundy between them.

"Maybe, but tell me anyway."

"My aunt Bell said she's going to give me her old tarot cards."

Rose snorted. "You're going to be a fortune-teller?"

"No!" Mia hit her playfully. "I don't know—it's stupid, I guess. I just find it interesting."

"It's not stupid! You should do it. You're good at that stuff. Your beer-foam readings double our tips."

Mia smiled into the wax tub.

"Maybe we could get in touch with the ghosts of the Eamons?" Rose said, poking Mia in the side.

"They're tarot cards, not a Ouija board!"

"Same thing though, right?"

Mia opened her mouth to retort, then saw Rose's smile.

"But seriously," Rose said, "I think you could do the tarot thing and charge suckers a mint. People in the city love that shit, and I won't be able to pay the rent on my own."

"The city?" Mia asked. "I thought, you know, without the cadetship…" She trailed off.

Rose leaned back against her bed. "I'm going to work it out," she told her. "I've already sent in a bunch of job applications. Just for crappy temp jobs and call centers, but something has to come up, right? And once I'm settled, you can follow. We can still do it."

"Cool. Okay, are you ready?"

"Ready."

They repositioned themselves so their bare legs were laced together. It was always easier to do it to someone else. One time, when Rose was about fourteen, she had been too afraid to pull the wax strip off and had left it on for a full twenty minutes. When she had finally worked up the courage to do it, it had hurt like hell. The thing had pulled off a layer of skin. For the next week, Rose had a raised pink rectangle on her calf that was so tender she could barely even touch it.

They'd been doing this together for ages, thinking it was easier if someone else was the one to pull the strip off. Sometimes, Rose worried that their friendship was a little stunted.

She loved Mia, but it was like they both reverted back to being teenagers again when they were together. Like neither could really grow up with the other around.

Swirling the wax with a Paddle Pop stick, Mia scooped up a globule. It felt warm and nice on Rose's thigh and smelled like honey. She rubbed a bandage down on top of it. They both took a swig of Bundy, enjoying the burn of it in their throats.

They nodded at each other and Mia pulled Rose's strip off at the exact moment that Rose pulled off Mia's.

"I always forget how much it hurts," Rose said.

They both took another swig.

By the time they'd finished they each had shiny, hairless legs. They were also a bit drunk. They lay on the floor giggling, staring at the cracks in Rose's ceiling. Slowly, the giggles subsided and their breathing became even.

"My mum will be home soon," Rose said, the impending argument playing out in her head. "I'm going to ask her if I can stay a few more weeks. She won't be happy."

Mia propped herself up on an elbow.

"One of the *Friday the 13th* films is on telly tonight. Do you want to come to mine?"

They decided to stop off at the gas station for snacks. Rose was in the mood to really gorge. She was sick of planning and worrying. Watching a shitty movie and eating junk sounded like absolute bliss.

Rose rolled down her window, and they turned up the radio, letting the girlie pop song blare. Turning the corner, Mia braked hard for some kids crossing the road.

"Paper-plate kids never even look," she said, shaking her head.

One of the kids poked his tongue out through his mask at them. Mia, like most people, thought they were cute. Rose found them disturbing. There were around ten of them, both boys and girls from the local primary school. They wandered around together, sometimes even at night, wearing those dumb masks they'd made in class. Paper plates with eye and mouth holes cut out of them and silly noses and eyebrows painted on. They wore them constantly, the strings tied tight around the backs of their heads.

"So creepy," Rose said.

"You just think that cos they got you!"

"Shut up!"

It was true. The kids played a game where they'd hide around corners and jump out at people, yelling *boo*. They scared Rose so much one day she'd actually screamed. Mia didn't understand how Rose could hate the poor kids. Really she should hate their parents for kicking their children out for the night while they got loaded.

Mia pulled in to the pumps slightly too fast; the brakes squeaked when she stopped.

"Whoops!" she said. "Usually I'm a good drunk driver."

Rose laughed and they got out of the car, snapping shut the doors. Mia left the keys in the ignition so the pop song would continue playing. She hummed along as she unscrewed the lid to the tank, pulled a ten-dollar note out of her pocket and flicked it to Rose. It seemed to hesitate in the air for a moment before floating down into Rose's hand.

"Thanks."

Dusk hung heavily around her. The air retained the heat of the day and felt sticky against her bare skin. Walking toward the service station, she breathed in: freshness, mixed with the tang of petrol and hot cement. The automatic doors opened for her and goose bumps rose on her arms as she walked into the air-conditioning.

There was a line, as usual, at the counter. Since the grocery store had burned down, the service station had been doing great business. Of course, the place was a chain, so the profit it made was being filtered straight out of the town. To another country, probably. Rose plucked two large packets of corn chips, a jar of spicy salsa and a family-sized block of Dairy Milk chocolate from the shelf. Holding the bundle, she grabbed a large plastic cup and put it on the grille of the frozen Coke machine. She watched as the shiny brown icicles filled the cup. Really, she should have picked savory or sweet. They'd probably both feel ill later, but oh well.

"Pump four," she said to the clerk when she reached the front of the line, "and these." She dropped the packets and a frozen Coke she'd been awkwardly cradling onto the counter.

"Having a big night?" a voice behind her said. Bazza. He was smiling at her and eyeing the assortment of snacks.

"Yeah," she said, putting down Mia's note and matching it with one of her own, feeling a twinge of guilt like she always did when she spent money unnecessarily.

"How's your sister?" he asked.

"Cranky, but fine."

"Frank had my bollocks for telling you we were worried at the station." He laughed, but she noticed a sour note in his voice.

She smiled at him, then took her change and the bag from the cashier.

"I appreciated you telling me," she said, waiting while he took out a credit card to pay for his milk, bread and chocolate biscuits. Now that Frank wasn't here, maybe she could get a bit more information out of him.

"So," she said casually, "how many other families got dolls?"

He thought about it as he put the card back in his wallet. "The Rileys, the Hanes and the Cunninghams... So, just three."

Rose half expected him to count on his fingers, the idiot. He'd just told her the names of the families without her even having to ask. They walked out of the service station together, Bazza holding his plastic bag in one hand and swinging the large bottle of milk in the other.

"Are you with Mia?" he asked, looking over at her car. Rose was just about to snigger, there was a definite eagerness to his voice, when she saw Mia's face drop as she spotted them. It took all of three seconds for Rose to grasp how stupid she was being. Mia was more than tipsy, and they both probably stank of rum. Bazza was off work, but he was still a cop. Rose had been so focused on trying to get a lead she hadn't even thought of it.

"I'll come say hi," he continued.

"Sorry, I forgot we were in a hurry. See you later!" she said and ran back to the car, pulling on her seat belt and waving at Bazza. They drove very carefully out of the gas station and then veered quickly around the corner. Mia's house was only two streets away.

Rose had met Mia on the first day of kindergarten. She'd been wandering around at lunchtime, looking for a good place to eat her lunch alone. Even as a five-year-old, she hadn't been great at niceties, so meeting new people hadn't come naturally to her. Holding her lunch box, her backpack a strange new weight on her back, she'd staked out a small flowering bush. If she sat behind there, she'd been sure no one would bother her. But as she turned the corner, she saw that there was already a little girl sitting behind the bush. She was crouched on the ground, holding her arm up at a strange angle, staring at it.

What are you doing? Rose had asked.

Mia had smiled. *Look*, she'd said.

Rose had got down onto her knees and looked at Mia's arm. There was a tiny red ladybug on her wrist.

Fairies, Mia had whispered.

No, they're ladybugs, Rose had said.

Mia shook her head solemnly, looking at Rose as though she was the silliest person in the world. *Ladybugs are fairies. Didn't you know?*

Rose had looked from the ladybug back to Mia. *Really?*

Yeah, and if you sit here long enough, they'll climb all over you, Mia said. *I already did it this morning. This is their fairy house.*

So Rose had sat. They'd sat in silence to begin with, watching as the beautiful little red bugs timidly made their way onto Rose. It tickled a little bit. Eventually they'd started talking, and upon finding out that Mia had no mum, and Rose had no dad, they decided they should be best friends.

"You'll have to feed me," Mia called from the couch. She was lying on her back, arms above her head, eyes closed.

Mia's house was even smaller and shittier than Rose's, although it was always impeccably tidy. The place sort of resembled a caravan, without the wheels. Her kitchen cupboards and small table were covered in laminate, printed with a fake wood grain. The couch, which doubled as Mia's bed, was squeezed tight in the small lounge room, the main room of the house. On the left were two doors. One to the bathroom, the other to Mia's father's room. Both were closed.

Rose took out two bowls from the cupboard. She opened the chip packets, the plastic making loud squeaky sounds, and threw a chip toward Mia. She opened her mouth wide, but it missed, landing on her forehead. Rose emptied the rest into the bowls.

The squeaking sound of bedsprings moving sounded from the other room.

"He must be awake. Back in a sec." Mia slid off the couch, munching on the chip, and went into his room. Rose could hear her talking quietly from inside, her voice soft and gentle.

Rose put the bowls on the coffee table and sat down on

the couch, still feeling the heat from Mia's body on the backs of her thighs. She switched on the TV and opened the chocolate. Tossing a square into her mouth, she wanted to close her eyes, the rich sweetness tasted so good. She'd forgotten to have lunch today and she was starving.

"It's starting!" she called. A girl was walking around her apartment, creepy music playing in the background. Rose knew she was probably going to die within the next five minutes, but she still couldn't help feeling jealous that the girl had her own place. This girl had a cool Japanese-style dressing gown and could wander around in it and make tea whenever she wanted.

Mia ran back in and sat on the couch. "What did I miss?"

On the screen, a cat pounced through the window and they both jumped. Laughing at each other, they settled back on the couch, passing the frozen Coke back and forth between them. Soon, the murderer appeared. A sack over his head. They tried not to scream out loud and bother Mia's dad.

"Isn't he meant to be wearing a hockey mask?"

"I think that comes later."

Rose thought a sack was probably creepier anyway.

"The hockey mask would make him look like a paper-plate kid."

"Awww," Mia cooed.

"Why is he doing it again?" Rose asked when it cut to commercials. She wasn't sure if she'd ever seen the first one.

"Killing everyone?"

"Yeah."

Mia leaned back, stretching out her feet on the coffee table. Her toenails were painted a dark purple. "Something to do with teenagers having sex instead of taking care of him when he was a kid."

"So stupid," Rose groaned. Somehow, giving someone a good reason for mass murder made it so much more fascinating. She wondered what reason the person would have to leave dolls on kids' doorsteps. It really was such a bizarre thing to do. Mia squealed from next to her; Rose hadn't even been watching. She got comfy, nestling her bare feet underneath herself.

By midway through, the violence had lost its shock. They were both sleepy and covered in crumbs and their stomachs swirled. They were lying down now, Rose's head on Mia's hip.

"I should go," she said.

"Yeah, I'll drive you."

"Okay."

Neither of them moved.

By the time Rose got home she knew she had left it too late. She shouldn't have gone to Mia's house. She should have been here when her mother got home, not left her mother's anger to stew even more.

"Hi," she said.

Her mother just looked at her, exhausted, from her place in front of the television.

"Listen," she continued, "I know it sounds like I was overreacting this morning—"

"I don't want to talk about it, Rose. I've had a long day."

"Sorry," she found herself saying. She took a breath; this was going to be a hard conversation.

"So I know Rob's coming back next week—" she began.

"You're not going to ask me for more time, are you?"

The way her mum looked at her told her the answer, and not only that, it told her that her unhappiness, her pain, was just another burden. Something to be endured like the sound of screaming chickens.

"No," she said and left the room.

PART 2

The day you give up on your dreams is the day you give up on yourself.

—Unknown

8

Pulling her hair into a knot on top of her head, blowing a few loose strands out of the way, Rose turned on her computer. It was an old PC, its fan was loud and hot, and it took a full five minutes to load. She was afraid that one day, it wouldn't turn on at all and then she didn't know what she would do. You could hardly mail newspapers handwritten articles. That definitely wouldn't be considered professional.

She'd slept better last night, maybe because there was too much to think about, too much to worry about to even bother. Her exhaustion was stronger than her anger and frustration, and so when she went to bed she'd fallen unconscious almost instantly, waking up with a claggy mouth. She hadn't even brushed her teeth. But the rest had given her a new sense of determination, something that even the two rejection emails she'd received from the jobs she'd applied to yesterday couldn't shake.

She took a swig of Coke, the cold bolt of flavor pushing back against the sleepy heat.

When her computer was finally on, she linked it with the Bluetooth on her phone. She tried to use as little of Rob's resources as possible. She bought her own food, used her own internet plan and never used the home phone. It wasn't just that she didn't want to be indebted to him. She also hated the idea of touching anything he used; she despised everything about him. Not that it mattered much anymore.

All morning she had replayed last night's conversation with her mother. Rose wished she had made it clear, at the very least, that she hadn't been stupid in calling the cops. Say the word *pedophile* and she was sure she could get that breathless panicky quality back into her mother's voice. The idea did something strange to people, especially parents. Everyone agreed that pedophiles were the lowest scum on the planet, yet people also seemed weirdly fascinated by them. Their stories were always in the news the longest, front page after front page of disturbing stories in sickening detail. Maybe people enjoyed feeling horrified.

The screen lit up and, already, she felt a little wired. She'd dismissed the idea of writing about the dolls almost immediately. Dolls on kids' doorsteps was hardly a story.

But maybe it didn't even matter.

She opened a blank Word document and typed the title in, just to see how it would look: *Porcelain Terror in Colmstock*.

Everyone loved a good mystery. Her fingers started flying across the keyboard, trying to shape the strange truth of what had happened into something more menacing. Trying to make it into a story.

It wasn't the sort of thing that would ever stand a chance in the *Sage Review*, but maybe it would be possible in the *Star*. She and Mia only read the thing for laughs, and because it had the most ridiculous star-sign predictions. The tabloid was always filled with tacky sensationalist articles, like how a suburban man had made his wife swallow an entire live snake as part of a voodoo ritual or how a mother was addicted to eat-

ing her children's glue sticks, in between full-page advertisements for diet pills.

It was fun writing something dramatic and salacious. By
the time she had to leave for work, she'd emailed the article
to the *Star*. Usually, she would spend at least a few weeks on
a piece, but this one she kept short and to the point. If they
didn't like it, they could go fuck themselves.

PORCELAIN TERROR IN COLMSTOCK
By Rose Blakey

Mystery dolls threaten children of small town.

A mystery is an unusual thing in the town of Colmstock, which all but disappeared from the map
after the closure of the Auster Automotive Factory. Now, to add insult to injury for the residents
of this forgotten place, a bizarre case has emerged
that has the local police baffled.

Multiple families have made the terrifying dis-
covery of old-fashioned porcelain dolls on their
doorsteps. Most horrifying of all, the dolls are the
spitting images of their young daughters. Hair and
eye color of these unwanted gifts exactly matching
the scared little girls.

Local police have attempted to calm the victims.
However, these families may be right to be frightened for the safety of their youngest daughters.
Inside sources have revealed that possible links to
child molesters and pedophiles are being investi-

gated and that the dolls are marks of this anonymous sicko's intended prey.

With the limited resources available to the impov-
erished Colmstock, the community fears the of-
fender may not be apprehended until it is too late.

Rose leaned into the wide freezer in the storage room of
the tavern. She stroked the back of her head, combing her hair
with her fingers so that it came off her sweaty neck. She let it
dangle around her face like a veil.

Today had been an especially hot day, the humidity making the air a sweltering, oppressive weight as she'd walked to
work, her shoes banging against her bandaged heels. The road
had felt like it had been sizzling. Her head was full of dolls,
although as soon as she'd started walking she'd realized what
she'd written was crazy. It didn't even really make sense.

The freezer reeked. It was as if something had died in
there, froze, then thawed, rotted a bit and then froze again.
Still, the cool air on her skin was worth it. It felt like little icy
pinpricks on her face and neck. She could happily stay there
all day, but Jean would notice her absence soon enough and
come to find out why she was slacking off. Reaching into
the freezer, she pulled out a hunk of frozen meat wrapped in
plastic. It was wedged in there, and the sound of the icicles
squealing against each other as it scraped against the side of
the freezer made her wince. It was heavy; she held it tightly
with one trembling arm as she slammed the lid of the freezer
closed with the other.

The meat started to stick to her forearms as she walked up
the corridor. She passed Will's room. The light inside was on,

but the Do Not Disturb sign was still plastered to his door. Rose dropped the hunk of meat down on the kitchen bench.

"Thanks," Jean said from the stove; her white shirt was damp with sweat. Rose couldn't imagine trying to cook on a day this hot.

"Look at her go." Jean pointed her chin toward the bar, a smile playing on her lips.

Mia was flirting with Bazza outrageously. She was leaning against the taps, literally twirling her hair. It was almost laughable, but Bazza was eating it up.

"I'll give them a few minutes," she said to Jean and went over to the bin. It wasn't completely full yet, but Rose didn't really want to go back to the bar. It was only a matter of time before Frank asked her about the cadetship, and she'd have to tell him that she hadn't got it. She didn't want pity, not from him or anyone else. Plus, the longer you left the bin, the more likely it was that you'd leak foul-smelling bin juice down the corridor. She tied the black plastic rubbish bag into a knot at the top, then slid it out of the bin; it was already heavy.

Holding it in one hand, as far away from her body as possible, she walked quickly down the corridor. The back door to Eamon's, past the keg room, was propped open with a brick. They always left it like that when the pub was open. People went into the back alley for cigarettes sometimes, or, very rarely, for make-out sessions. Rose couldn't imagine anything less romantic. The concrete was cracked and uneven, and the large metal Dumpster stank, even when it was empty. The thing had probably never been cleaned. It smelled like sweet, rotting rubbish and made her want to gag. There was no light out there except for the streetlights around the front and the light that spilled from the open door down the four cement steps. Rose let the bag slide down the steps next to her, then picked it up and hurled it into the Dumpster. She heard it hit the bottom with a heavy thump like a bag of flour, or a dead body. Rose wanted to laugh. It would be great for her career if she found a dead body out the back here, but unluckily for her, it hadn't happened yet. Although, Jean had told her she'd found a dead cat in there once. She'd said that when she picked it up it was as stiff as a brick. Rose slapped her hands together and walked back inside.

As she passed Will's door, her curiosity overwhelmed her. She knocked, wondering if he was even inside. The squeak of the bedsprings told her that he was. She thought about running. It was too late. He opened the door a crack, smiling slightly when he saw her.

"Housekeeping," she said, sarcastically, trying to look past his head into the room.

"I'm fine for now, thanks." He smiled and went to shut the door in her face.

"Are you sure?" she said, before he could.

"Yes." His smile widened. "You know, I can't decide if you are trying to be very helpful, or if I've done something to piss you off."

She blinked. Usually she was the confrontational one.

"Just trying to be helpful," she said, shooting him a huge, fake grin, then turning to walk away. He might be the weirdest guy she'd ever met. The way he'd hidden his bedroom from her, it was like he didn't want her to see past him, like he was hiding something. She imagined his room was filled with porcelain dolls and snorted back a laugh as she walked back to the bar. The dolls had only started appearing when he arrived. It was definitely possible, although not very likely. Journalist Uncovers Weirdo Doll Lover Tormenting Town. Now, that would be a good story.

9

"I'm seeing something really special here," Mia said, staring at the leftover foam in Bazza's empty beer glass.

"Really?" He leaned forward. She showed him, and his face screwed up as he looked inside. She noticed the way the light lit up the fine hair of his eyelashes.

She leaned closer. "See that line of foam across there." She pointed at the line near the top of the glass.

"Yeah."

"That's your heart line."

"Really?"

"Look." She let her voice go really quiet so he'd get closer. "It's unbroken."

"Is that good?" He looked up at her.

"It's really good. It means you're going to find love. Soon."

He looked between the line and her. She grabbed an empty glass and flicked on the tap, smiling at him, trying to beg him with her eyes to ask her out. He didn't seem to notice.

"Thanks," he said, when she put his beer in front of him. "I wonder what this one will say."

He left her a tip and went back to his seat next to Frank.

Her heart sank a little bit. Had he seen what she was doing and not asked her out anyway? She wasn't sure if her advance had been rejected or not, but either way she could feel the sting.

"You know, I think he does like you," Rose said, coming up next to her. "He looks at you like you're beautiful—he was doing it last night at the gas station too."

"What, like that?" Mia said, and they both looked to Frank, who was staring at Rose, his eyes soft.

"Yeah," Rose said and turned away defensively.

Mia sighed and propped herself up on the bar. "Bazza's dumb but so hot. It's the perfect combination," she said wistfully. "I think he'd make a great husband."

"You're kidding, right?" Rose said with disgust.

"Nope," she said, then flicked Rose with the wet, dirty rag in her hand. It left a gray smear on her thigh.

"Yuck!"

"Streets of Fire" came on and Mia started humming along under her breath. She didn't understand why Jean didn't play a more varied mix of music, but she didn't question it. If Jean wanted to listen to Bruce Springsteen every single night, then that was her choice. It had irritated her at first, but after a while she'd begun to enjoy knowing exactly what to expect out of her evenings. Unlike Rose, she quite liked working at Eamon's. When she was here, she could just focus on each task: pouring beers, serving meals, mopping the floor, and not worry about the past or the future.

Wringing out the cloth in the sink, she watched the gray water squeezing out from the fibers. She rinsed it, letting the water absorb, wrung it out again and then hung it over the tap to dry. The detergent and grit made the skin on her hands feel tender. She wiped them on her shorts, trying to push herself to remember to put on hand cream before she went to sleep.

She was always forgetting, and her flesh sometimes got so dry that the skin around her fingernails would crack.

She watched Rose out of the corner of her eye as she dried glasses, the cloth squealing against the glass. Rose never had problems with dry skin. For the tiniest of moments, she felt a pang of jealousy. Rose was so beautiful. If she wanted to, she could get any guy she liked. She could quit this place and start a family and be looked after. But Mia wasn't a jealous person. She hated negativity, especially in herself, and she loved Rose more than anything. She put the glass down and went over to her, resting her head on Rose's shoulder. Rose gripped her in a one-armed hug. Their skin stuck together slightly from sweat but Mia didn't mind. She loved being close to Rose. It held the darkness that she sometimes felt at bay.

"I'm going to miss you when you're famous."

"Shut up," said Rose, but she squeezed her tighter.

They laughed and Mia picked up her rag again. She sprayed down the counter, the bleachy disinfectant stinging her nostrils, and wiped away the beer rings that had dried and gone sticky.

Steve Cunningham came in, a huge grin on his face. This was unusual.

He walked straight up to Mia and slapped a fifty-dollar bill on the bar. "A round for the boys on me."

A low cheer came from Bazza's table, and Mia began pouring the drinks, lining them up next to Steve's note. Steve awkwardly gripped three in his hands and brought them over to the table.

"Is there something to celebrate?" she heard Frank ask.

"Not yet, but maybe," Steve said, leaning with both hands on the back of a chair. "My application for a review of the shale mine's gone through. They're sending someone next month to survey it."

"Great job, mate," Bazza said.

"Knew you'd come through."

They cheered their drinks, glass clicking against glass, and Mia turned away from them.

"Do you remember how we used to play at the mine?" Mia asked. "It's weird that it used to be a fun place."

"Yeah," Rose said. "Are you thinking about him again?"

"No," Mia told her, "not really. It's just weird to think about what that place was like before."

"It was always pretty horrible."

Mia wasn't sure if she agreed. She'd go visit the place sometimes, think about his final moments. Right after graduation, her high school boyfriend had disappeared for three days. They found his body at the bottom of the mine. He'd jumped.

"Cover for me," Rose said from behind her.

Rose was looking at her phone, a shocked look on her face as she rushed out to the back hallway.

For a fleeting moment, Mia wondered who it could be to warrant that look of exhilaration. Her fingers went to the rose quartz that she wore on a chain around her neck, holding the cold rock, trying to find comfort.

"Tell Steve," she heard Baz say to Frank. Then he turned to Steve. "Honestly, you won't believe this one."

"Why don't you tell him?"

"You tell it better."

"All right," Frank said, and Mia leaned forward to listen. She'd heard them all laughing about something before, but hadn't caught what it was.

"So we get a call out to the wildlife sanctuary out in Baskerton."

"Yeah?"

"When we get there it's bloody mayhem. Ambulances,

Japanese tourists running around screaming. It's nuts. So we find this kid."

"That poor kid," Buddy added.

"He's got his uniform on, probably only fifteen, and he's just standing there, walking real slow in the grass. We make him give us a statement. He tells us a group of Japanese businessmen had come in from the city, wanted to see some real deal fauna.

"So he's showing them around. Telling them all about the mating practices of tiger snakes, or some such shit. But all they want to see is the kangaroos, you know?"

Steve nodded, already smiling, waiting for the punch line.

"So he brings these bloody idiots into the field where the roos are. They've got a red one there. Huge. Taller than Baz here. So the boss is trying to be the big man, you know. So he gives his camera to this poor kid and keeps going." Frank put on a terrible Japanese accent. "Hoi take my photo, hoi!

"The kid is telling him not to get too close," Frank continued. "But he wants his picture, you know?

"So he gets real close to the big red. Puts his fists up, posing, like he's fighting it. The red's not bothered, just chewing away, ignoring him. The kid's telling him to keep his distance, but the guy keeps saying 'Take my photo, take my photo,' and all the other guys are laughing along. They'd probably been drinking.

"The guy gets even closer, fists in the air, and the roo, he doesn't even look at him, just swipes. Just one swipe."

"And?" said Steve.

"Pulled his eyeball out."

The guys cracked up laughing.

"That's what the kid was doing. The red had jumped off when everyone started screaming. He was looking for it in the grass. The eye."

Frank banged on the table and took a swig of his beer, and all the men started snorting with laughter again.

"So did you find it?" Steve asked.

Mia went back to drying glasses; the image of a bloodied eyeball in the dry grass was enough. She didn't want any more details to add to the visual.

Father came up to the bar, looking a bit white. He annoyed Mia, although she would never admit it. He was a really friendly man with the kindest eyes she'd ever seen, but he was just too damn nice. It made her feel guilty for everything unchristian she had ever done, or even thought. It was as if he could sense her jealousy and that was why he'd appeared. To remind her that it was a sin.

He put five empty beer glasses on the bar. He always did that, collected the glasses from the other guys so that she and Rose didn't have to.

"Thanks," Jean said, coming in from the office and picking the glasses up between her fingers and taking them to the dishwasher.

Mia began pouring him a soda, the spits of fizz hitting her fingers as it reached the top. The guy spent so much time in the tavern, yet he never drank alcohol.

"Are priests not allowed to drink?" she asked.

"Mia!" Jean turned around and looked at her sharply.

"I've been dying to ask!"

Father just smiled. "It's not prohibited, but I prefer not to. Plus, one of the boys usually needs a lift home."

She smiled at him as he took the soda and returned to his seat. He was so charitable; it was next level. Although part of her thought maybe he just got a bit lonely hanging out in the church by himself. She imagined it would be pretty creepy there alone at night.

Jean stood close to her, her bosom pushing warmly onto Mia's arm.

"I've been dying to ask too," she said quietly, in that scratchy voice of hers.

Mia suppressed a giggle as Jean went back into the office. She pulled the wet, fogged-up glasses from the washer, shutting the lid with her foot. Bazza caught her eye and smiled at her, warmly. Why had it taken her so long to notice what a great guy he was? Maybe it was because of the way Frank talked about him as if he was an idiot. Rose as well.

Mia used to have a crush on Jonesy. He was a cop too, on highway patrol. He was a tall, thin guy, his clothes always looking too short at the ankles but too wide at the waist. Somehow, he always gave Mia the impression that he was laughing at her. One drunken night, she'd given him a blow job around the back of the tavern. He'd gone out for a smoke and she'd pretended that she wanted one too. When she'd taken a puff she'd started coughing. He'd raised his eyebrow at her, told her she was cute and somehow they were kissing before she even knew it. The taste of tobacco in his mouth made her eyes water.

Desperately, she'd wanted to impress him. To show him that he had underestimated her. That was why she'd given him the blow job, just to see what he'd do. But as soon as his dick was in her mouth she wished she hadn't started it. She didn't feel as powerful as she'd thought she would. Afterward, he just zipped up his pants, went back inside and still talked to her in the exact same dismissive way he always had.

Bazza was different. She had never even noticed him until the night of the big fire. She remembered it vividly. The acrid stink of smoke, the windows of the courthouse exploding, one after another. She'd stood there, hands over her mouth, trying not to cry. Out of nowhere, Baz was beside her.

"You okay?" he'd said.

She had just looked at him, and then his big arm was around her. Immediately, everything had felt a little easier, just like when she was with Rose. Every time she thought about him, she could still feel that warm, heavy, protective arm across her shoulders.

Rose came back into the bar, her hand over her mouth.

"What?" Mia asked, but Rose didn't reply. Instead, a small smile crept out from under Rose's hand.

"Who was it?"

"Don't laugh," Rose said, and her eyes were all lit up in a way Mia hadn't seen for a while. Not since she'd told her about being short-listed for the cadetship. Something cold gripped Mia's stomach.

"Just tell me."

"I sent an article in to the *Star.*"

"The *Star*?" Mia asked, both desperately wanting to know what Rose would say and also frantically trying to put off knowing. "Don't you think they're a joke?"

She wasn't ready for Rose to go. Not yet, not quite yet.

"I do, but who cares? I've got to start somewhere. I sent them an article this morning. They're going to publish it!"

"What article?" Mia asked. "You didn't mention it."

Rose looked at her, and Mia knew her reaction was all wrong. "Just something stupid about those dolls," Rose said. "It doesn't matter though—it's my first byline."

"That's fantastic!" Mia grabbed Rose's hand and grinned. "I knew I could see your success in the stars."

"I guess you did!" she said gleefully.

"This is so great," Mia said, letting go of Rose's hand and turning to put down the tea towel so that she could let her smile drop.

"And they said they want me to write a follow-up piece and they'll publish that too!"

It was happening; Rose's big breakthrough, her ticket out of Colmstock. Rose was always saying they'd go together, but Mia knew it would never happen. She couldn't leave. She turned back around and threw her arms around Rose.

"Congratulations," she said, squeezing her tight and trying her hardest to focus on Rose's happiness and block out the fear of what her life would be like without her.

10

Rose had never experienced happiness like this before. It was just the *Star*, which she knew was a pretty crappy newspaper, but still she felt giddy. It made her want to smile at people on the street; it even made church slightly more bearable. Slightly.

The pews were full today. Father stood at the altar, giving his sermon. Usually, Rose didn't even bother to look interested, but today she tried her hardest to actually listen.

"'Now have come the salvation and the power and the kingdom of our God, and the authority of His Christ,'" he read. Rose wished they had one of those young, hip priests she'd heard about. Someone who made their sermons relevant to people's actual lives. She looked around the room, wondering if it was someone here who had left that doll on her doorstep. Should she hate them or thank them?

Rose was squeezed tight between Scott and Sophie. She always chose to sit between them. It was easier than trying to get them to stop squabbling if they were next to each other. Next to Sophie was Laura, who was leaning against their mother. Last Sunday, Laura had started crying because their mum would not let her sit on her lap. It was loud and embarrassing. But now she seemed happy enough, sucking her thumb with her eyes taking in the room. Church was the one time you saw everyone with their families. She could see the back of Frank's head. He was sitting near the front with his elderly mother listening intently, as he always did.

"'For the accuser of our brethren is cast down,'" Father continued, "'which accused them before our God day and night.'"

Bazza was sitting in a row with his three brothers. They looked very alike, with their broad shoulders and dumb eyes. Not that you could have seen their eyes today, or any other Sunday. All four of them were asleep in a line, their chins lolling on their chests.

"'They have gained the victory over him by the blood of the lamb and of their testimony; and because they held their lives cheap and not shrink even from death.'"

Rose wondered what kind of dreams they would be having. She noticed Mia was watching Baz too. Rose caught her eye and made a dumb face, pretending to drool out the side of her mouth. Mia snorted as she tried to hold in her laughter. Mrs. Cunningham, the councilman's wife, shot her a disapproving look.

Father hesitated, looking around for the source of the laughter. It was so quiet you could hear a pin drop. Mia and Rose stared back at him innocently, just as Bazza let out a loud snore.

Suppressing her own rising giggle, Rose looked over to see what Mrs. Cunningham would do. But she just continued staring at the Father, sniffing with disapproval. Unlike her husband, Steve, Mrs. Cunningham was a pain in the butt. It was only Steve who was from England originally, and although she was born in Colmstock, Mrs. Cunningham often mimicked his Pommy accent. Rose guessed she thought it made her sound posh. Really it just made her sound like a fake.

As soon as the sermon had finished, everyone was on their feet. Rose ducked and wove between people to get to Mia.

"Nothing to worry about—that's what you keep saying. But I am worried, Frank."

It wasn't the words that made her hesitate, but the way they were said. There was enough emotion in them to make her head snap up, looking for the speaker.

"Honestly, mate, there's nothing to suggest—"

"Have you read the paper this morning?"

"What do you mean?"

Rose felt her face color.

"I want to know who left that thing on my doorstep."

"We're looking into—"

"Yes, you've said that before. But whoever killed my son is still out there too."

Rose took a step closer. It was Mr. Riley.

"This guy killed our boy, burned down our livelihood— we need to know why."

"We are doing everything—"

"And now we have to worry about our daughter as well? Is that what you're telling me?"

Frank didn't say anything this time. Poor Mr. Riley. The last thing Rose wanted was for her article to upset him. Their family had been through enough.

Rose inched closer. Frank looked around, noticing the movement. He locked eyes with her and she ducked away, running out the front doors of the church. Mia was already there, waiting for her. She had leaned against the wall, the morning sun making her look like an oil painting of gold and bronze. For a moment, she looked sad, but when she saw Rose her face changed.

The bell on the door of the post office chimed when they bounded inside. Rose ripped the *Star* off the shelf and began flicking through the pages. Looking for her name, part of her still not really believing she would see it.

"Look!" Mia said, stabbing the page with her finger. There it was. Her name in black and white. Her insides glowed.

"Page ten," she said. "Not bad!"

"Page ten is excellent! I'm framing it," Mia said, grabbing another copy of the newspaper. She put it on the register and plopped a chocolate bar on top. Rose listened to Mia's small talk with the clerk, staring at her article. Grinning, she folded the newspaper under her arm. On the shelf next to the papers was stationery. A pale blue notebook caught her eye. Rose had this thing about notebooks. She loved buying them, like if she got a perfect one the ideas she wrote inside would be perfect too. She flicked through the pages. Each page had faint gray lines and the corners were rounded. The white notebook she had now wasn't even half finished, but she could always buy this one now to use after it was. It would be something to mark the occasion. After all, it was her very first publication.

Rose smiled at the cashier and put down the notebook on top of the *Star*.

"You should get her to sign this," Mia said, tapping the paper. "First publication of the most famous journalist of our times."

Rose cringed with embarrassment as Mia laughed and the cashier smiled and nodded politely.

"Breakfast of champions." Mia broke the chocolate bar in two as they left the store. She gave half to Rose as they walked back toward where Mia had parked outside Eamon's.

They passed the Rileys' grocery store, or what had once been their grocery store. It was half burned now, the whole side of the building black from where the flames had licked it. The courthouse was worse though. The building, which had once been one of the nicer-looking ones in town, was now a mess of charcoal.

"You know, the Rileys' daughter got a doll," Rose said. "Baz told me."

"God. That poor family."

"Mr. Riley was angry with Frank in church—I overheard him."

Mia shrugged. "I bet he was. But it's not like it's Frank's fault."

Rose looked at the charcoal. "They've got the worst luck."

Mia and Rose had been at Eamon's when it had happened, just one month ago. Everything was normal. Just another slow Wednesday shift. Then out of nowhere, phones started beeping and ringing. Within an instant, the cops were on their feet and running out the door. Something was happening. They had looked at each other, mouths open in question, and then Jean had come out of the office and walked straight to the doorway. Through the windows next to her, they could see the glow of it. Orange against the black night.

"What do you want to do today?" Mia asked, very forcibly changing the subject. The chocolate in Rose's hand was starting to melt. She put it in her mouth and then licked the brown drip from the side of her wrist.

"I need an interview," Rose said after she swallowed, enjoying the feeling of the sugar hitting her empty stomach as she chewed the melting chocolate.

"Frank?"

"Nah, I doubt it. He doesn't want anyone worrying about it," Rose said slowly as they walked down the pavement.

"Do you think he'll be angry about what you wrote?"

"Hope not." The truth was, Rose hadn't even considered what Frank would think until she'd seen how upset Mr. Riley was outside church that morning.

Passing Eamon's, Rose looked inside at the darkened bar. It was strange to imagine that Will was inside there right now, alone.

"Will's weird, don't you think?" she asked Mia.

"Who's Will?" Mia said, licking her fingers.

"The guest."

"Oh, yeah. I forgot his name. Yeah, I guess. Why?"

"I just don't understand why he's in town—it doesn't make sense."

"He's visiting family," Mia said.

Rose stopped and looked at her. "How do you know that?"

Mia laughed. "Because he told me, idiot."

"Why?" Rose pressed.

"What's with you? Do you li-ike him?"

"No," Rose said. "You know I don't!"

Mia raised her eyebrows and they kept walking toward her car.

"So, why did he tell you?"

"Rose," Mia said, grinning, "I know you're not one for polite conversation, but I am. When I served him the other night I asked him what he was doing in town. It's just good manners."

Rose thought on that for a second as they reached Mia's car. Rose pulled open the passenger-side door.

"And he said he was here to see family?" she asked, but Mia wasn't even listening to her anymore. She was looking over at the police station. There was a commotion going on; four women were standing out in front, talking loudly.

"There she is!" one of them called.

The four of them turned, staring at Rose, then walked down toward them, copies of the *Star* under their arms.

"Uh-oh. You're in trouble," Mia whispered.

The four women were middle-aged, and still in their church

clothes. Rose recognized one of them as her former year-six teacher, Mrs. Scott. Beside her stood two women with matching blond bobs and black regrowth and a doughy-looking woman with tears running down her cheeks.

They watched the women approach, the sun bouncing off the concrete around them. Rose swallowed her last bite of chocolate.

"Are you Rose Blakey?" the doughy woman asked.

"Yes."

The woman reached out and touched her arm. "Frank says that he never said anything about...about..."

"Pedophiles," one of the blonde women finished. Rose noticed the gleam in her eye. Her expression of concern was forced. Rose could tell this was the most excitement she'd had in years.

The doughy woman began letting out loud, snorting sniffs.

"Mrs. Hane," Mia whispered in Rose's ear. "She lives on my street."

"Your daughter got a doll too?" Rose asked.

Mrs. Hane nodded sadly.

"My sister got one."

"Laura?" asked Mrs. Scott.

"Yeah." A twinge of guilt pulled at Rose's stomach. "Listen, what I wrote in my article was really just a theory—it doesn't mean—"

"See, that's exactly what Frank said," the second blonde woman butted in. "He's a great police officer and an honest man. Not a lie comes out of his mouth."

"If Frank says there is nothing to worry about, there isn't." Mrs. Scott rubbed Mrs. Hane's arm. "He's our protector—nothing bad will happen to any of the children while he's around."

Rose was shocked at how much faith they had in Frank.

It was true, he knew everyone in Colmstock, and everyone seemed to know him. But the way they talked about him, it was like he was some sort of messiah. Rose could never think of him that way. Maybe she'd seen him drunk one too many times.

"Listen, Mrs. Hane," Rose said softly. "I think it would be great if I could speak to you and your husband later about all this. Get the full story for my next article."

Mrs. Hane sniffed, "Do you think it would help?"

"I'm happy to make a comment if you need," one of the blonde bobs butted in.

"I'd like to hear your opinion on all this," Rose said, ignoring the other woman.

Mrs. Hane looked unsure. "Honestly," Rose added, "it would just be great to talk to someone else who's been affected."

Mrs. Hane looked at her friends, then back to Rose. "And our picture would be in the *Star*?" she asked.

11

Mia sneaked little looks at Rose as she drove. She was gripping the *Star* tightly in her hands like she was afraid that somehow her article would disappear off the pages if she gave it the chance. Her face was thoughtful. She was probably planning her questions for the Hanes. Mia hoped they wouldn't get angry. After all, Mia had never even spoken to the round-faced family even though they had lived on the same street for her whole life. She had seen them pile their kids into the car a few times. The mother had even nodded hello to her once, but that was all the contact she'd had with them.

Mia was trying her hardest to shake off the groggy feeling she'd had all morning. She couldn't really sleep when she'd got in from work at 1:00 a.m. Then she'd had to get up at eight o'clock for church. She could feel herself slipping into a dark mood and she didn't want that. Her dark moods could get really bad sometimes; she'd feel like she was drowning. She thudded the steering wheel with her thumbs in time to the radio.

"Are you worried about what Frank is going to say?" she

said, not being able to bear the sound of her own pounding thoughts.

Rose turned to look at her, eyes clearing. "Nope."

"Really? He's going to be piiissed." Mia drew out the word, trying to show just how pissed off Frank would be.

Rose laughed and already Mia felt herself floating back up to the surface.

"It'll be worth it."

Rose looked back at the paper. Mia knew Rose well enough to know exactly what she was thinking: this was it. That it didn't matter if she pissed off Frank; soon she would be out of here. The darkness closed over Mia again. Too much was going on. As soon as they were done with the Hanes she'd go home and have a shower. It was her little ritual. She'd lock the door and turn the shower on, making sure the water was the perfect temperature. Then she'd dim the lights. Take off her clothes and sit down naked on the porcelain floor, pulling the curtain closed around her. It was one of the few things that made Mia feel better when she was totally overwhelmed like this. The gush of the showerhead blocking out all other sounds. The rich black around her. It felt like she was engulfed in darkness and water. She'd let herself prune, put her arms around her knees and try to sort her thoughts out. Sometimes she'd even speak out loud. Hearing her own voice soothed her. Sometimes she'd cry. When she came out of the shower, pink and clean, her head would be clear. It was her own sort of therapy. After, she'd feel better and she could go back to being her sunny, happy self. Even the idea of it made her feel brighter.

It was her secret. If anyone found out she would be in so much trouble. There'd been water restrictions in Colmstock for as long as she could remember.

"Are you sure about this? I feel like we're intruding," she asked.

"Yeah. Or would you prefer to go to the Cunninghams' instead?"

"The Cunninghams got one too?"

Soft-spoken Steve Cunningham was nice enough; Mia liked his accent. His bustling loud wife, Diane, however, was a force to be reckoned with. She'd given Mia an absolute death stare when she'd laughed in church that morning.

"Yeah," Rose said, sniggering.

"Did Bazza tell you that too?"

"I can't reveal my sources." Rose smiled.

Mia turned onto the street, passing five For Sale signs in a row, all in different stages of decay. The last sign was so faded you could barely even see the pictures on it anymore. About a quarter of the houses in Colmstock were empty. Once in a while a hired thug from the real-estate agency in the city would be sent down to throw out the squatters.

"Is this it?" Mia asked, as they stopped outside a well-kept white house.

"Yeah. Look, there's their fugly car," Rose said, pointing toward the burnt-orange Auster they'd seen Mrs. Hane get into earlier.

"Do you think we've given them enough time?" Mia asked, idling.

"Yeah, I think she probably just wanted to clean up a bit. Hope she knows there aren't going to be any photos."

"She probably just wanted to talk to her daughter, make sure she's all right with it."

Rose snorted. "Come on—she's just excited. Probably thinks this will be her fifteen minutes of fame."

"You always think the worst of people," Mia said, laughing, although deep down she thought Rose was being overly harsh.

"And you always think the best of people, so together we're even," Rose said, smiling.

Mia pulled in to the curb, the car braking with a squeal and clunk. She loved her rusty old car, but even she could see it didn't have a lot of life left in it. She patted the bonnet softly as they got out, feeling the hot steel under her fingertips.

The Hanes' place looked like most of the other houses on the street, except for a few toys scattered in the front yard. They walked up the drive shoulder to shoulder. Mia had no idea why Rose wanted her there, but she could never bring herself to say no to her.

Rose knocked. No answer.

"Maybe no one's home," Mia said quietly, just as the door swung open.

To some, the interior of the Hane residence might look like a sort of domestic bliss. Everything was warm and homey from the family portraits to the worn-out floral sofa. To Rose, it looked like some sort of hell. They sat on the sofa, staring at the Hanes. Mrs. Hane looked a lot like her husband. They were both flabby with short limbs, like two panting corgis. Dopey eyes and big dumb smiles. Somehow, they had managed to conceive an angelic little daughter, Lily, who sat between them staring at her lap. Behind them was a snotty-nosed little boy, Denny, they'd said his name was, who lay on the floor playing a particularly violent video game.

"We were very surprised, weren't we, hun?" Mr. Hane was saying.

"Very surprised," Mrs. Hane added. "Last thing you expect to see on your doorstep."

Rose looked down at her notepad for her next question. "You called the police right away?"

Mrs. Hane thought about it, her ugly little face squishing up like a fist. "Not till we heard from our friend Liz, right, hun?"

"That's right. When we heard that the Rileys' kid had gotten one too, we thought it was odd, didn't we?"

"We thought it was strange."

If her life ended up like this, Rose thought, she'd kill herself. She stared behind them at that little shit Denny. He was bashing a man to death on whatever game he was playing.

"So when she wanted to call the police, we thought it was a good idea," continued Mr. Hane.

"And we're glad we did. The thought of that thing in our house all week. It's enough to make you sick, isn't it?"

"It is, hun. You're right about that."

Rose tried to make her face look calm. She didn't want her growing irritation to show. She forced herself not to look over at Mia. If she did she was sure she would start laughing.

"Okay, great." She may as well just cut to the chase—she needed them to say something with a bit more bite. "And do you feel like the police are doing enough?"

"Well, no, not since I read your article this morning," Mrs. Hane said, her brow furrowing in concern, looking like a row of sausages.

"It really knocked us for six."

"But you've already called some other fathers, haven't you, hun?"

"I've been talking to every bloke I know who has a young girl." His voice was low and serious. "I mean, these are our children."

"Our children!" wailed Mrs. Hane.

"I was telling your stepdaddy just last night, it's us fathers who are going to have to get this sorted."

Her stepdaddy? "Rob? He's on a haul," Rose said, confused.

Mr. Hane looked at Rose before his eyes slid away. "Yes, that's right."

He was lying. Badly.

"Did you run into him at the pub?" she fished.

"That'll be it. Had a pint together there last week."

Rose knew she should stop asking him about this; it wasn't why she was here. But what he'd said made no sense, and she wanted to know why he was lying to her.

"But Laura hadn't even gotten the doll last week."

Mr. Hane put his hands up in the air and smiled. "I guess I had a few too many that night—I can barely remember it."

If Rob was cheating on her mum, she'd kill him. Although that would definitely help her housing problem. Behind them, Denny was shooting a lifeless body on the ground in his game.

Before Rose could aim another question at Mr. Hane, Mia leaned forward next to her. "What about you, honey?" She looked into Lily's eyes. "How do you feel about the doll?"

That was good thinking. It could be great to get a child's perspective. Rose needed to focus on why she was here; Mr. Hane definitely didn't seem like he was going to spill the beans on Rob. She smiled at the little girl, waiting for her to answer Mia's question. Rose was fairly sure the *Star*'s editor would eat up a little kid saying she was scared. But Lily said nothing.

"Oh, she can't hear you, honey," Mrs. Hane said lightly.

"She's deaf," Mr. Hane added, just in case they didn't get it. "We've been saving for one of them cochlear implants."

"Every dime," said Mrs. Hane and patted Lily lightly on the head. "First sound she's going to hear is my dulcet tones."

Lily turned and looked at Rose right in the eyes, as though she knew exactly what was in store for her.

"Well," Rose said, standing, "thanks so much for your time."

Mrs. Hane heaved herself up to walk them out.

"Anytime, honey. We all want the same thing here."

Denny looked up from his game as they passed. He shot Rose a dirty look, and she shot him one right back. Mrs. Hane opened the front door.

"Say hello to your father for me," she said to Mia, patting her arm. "Poor man."

"Okay," said Mia awkwardly.

"You are doing right by him. You're a good girl."

"Thanks," said Mia, looking at her feet.

"We hope our kids will do right by us when our time comes," she said, then called, "Don't we, hun?"

Rose stepped outside into the air. She could not bear one more second of that stifling house.

12

Since she'd got the email from the *Star*, Rose's shifts at Eamon's had felt even longer than before. They seemed to drag endlessly. This was probably because she felt so different now. She was bursting with excitement and energy. The chicken factory and the fossickers shanties seemed laughable. It was crazy to think that just a few days ago they had felt like the only two options.

On the inside, she was dancing. But on the outside, everything was the same. The same heat, the same aggravating customers and bad tips and sticky bench tops. Mia yabbering on as usual by her side in that unbreakable sunny demeanor she had; Jean barking orders through small smiles. It was as though no one could see that she wasn't the same Rose anymore, that everything had changed.

Her feet dragged walking to work. She knew it would be the same tonight. Already, she felt tired and she hadn't even started the shift. All day at home she'd typed frantically at her computer. She'd transcribed the Hanes' interview carefully, trying to remember everything. Hoping there would be something interesting she could cobble together out of their stupid quotes. She needed a new angle, a new way to make what had happened seem compelling. But all she kept thinking about was what Mr. Hane had said about talking to Rob. The more she thought about it, the more strange the whole conversation was. It didn't really make sense. He had definitely been hiding something.

The air blew hot against her skin, the decaying smell of the courthouse riding on it. Her bag slipped off her sweaty shoulder, and she hiked it back up, quickening her pace so she wouldn't be late. She put up a hand to shield her eyes; the wind was blowing dried leaves and bits of fluff at her, flicking against the bare skin on her shoulders. The lake stank particularly badly today, blowflies buzzing around its surface. Soon she wouldn't have to look at the ugly scene every day. Soon she'd be walking through the city, skyscrapers on each side, and she'd leave this place to its steady decay.

As she reached Union Street she checked her watch. She was actually going to be a few minutes early for once. Although, as she waited for the traffic lights to change, another idea came to mind. The lights to the pub down the road were on; she could see them from where she stood. It was a bit of a long shot, but perhaps worth a try.

Inside, the pub made Eamon's look like a palace. It stank of vomit, the sound of the dog races drowned out the commercial playing on the radio and the men who looked up when she entered appeared as though they'd been sitting there so long their ample arses had fused with the stools.

"Hey," she said to the barman, "how's it going?"

"All right," he said, as he wiped down the counter. "You here to scope out the competition?"

She smiled at him. She was pretty sure he was one of Bazza's uncles. She'd seen them chatting before at church. Plus, he had the same broad shoulders and dumb eyes.

"Nah," she said, leaning onto the bar, "I'm looking for someone. You know Rob James?"

His smile disappeared, and he turned to restock the pint glasses. "I have nothing to say about all that. You're barking up the wrong tree."

"What?" she asked, but he didn't turn around.

"Look," she said, "Rob's my stepdad—I'm just trying to get ahold of him because his mobile's off."

He looked over his shoulder at her, his face softening again. "Sorry, darl. Didn't realize that."

She shrugged. "Has he been in here the last couple of weeks?"

"Nah," he said, "haven't seen him in yonks."

He turned back to the glasses. She looked around; all the men in the bar weren't even bothering to hide their gawking. All except for one man, right in the corner, who was closely surveying his beer. It was Mr. Riley. She turned back to the barman.

"Well, if he comes in—"

"Sure, sure, no wukkas," the bartender said. She stared at the back of his head for a second, trying to think of a way to make him tell her what he obviously didn't want to say. She couldn't, so she left, feeling all the men's eyes prickle into her back.

Pulling open the door to Eamon's, she felt her frustration mount a little. Mia was clicking on the taps, singing along to "The Promised Land"; Jean was emptying change loudly into the register. The beer signs were flickering on, the sky was beginning to darken and it was going to be another shift just like yesterday's.

"Hey, girl," Mia said, smiling up at her, happy she was there. Rose felt like a real bitch.

"Only five minutes late," Jean said, eyes on the clock. "Must be a record for you, Rosie."

She smiled back, resigning herself, and went back to the storeroom to get a fresh keg ready for the night. As with every shift, when she first arrived at Eamon's the whir of the fridges was loud. By the end of the shift, her ears would get used to the noise. She wouldn't be able to hear it even if she listened for it.

She threw her bag into the tiny office next to the toilets on the way, walking past Will's room without a glance at his door. It was unspoken between the three of them that Rose did most of the behind-the-scenes work, while Mia focused on the bar. This suited her fine; she'd prefer heavy kegs to drunk men any day.

The hot wind had blown some dead leaves from outside into the hallway, and they crinkled under Rose's shoes as she went to the storeroom. They'd only be replaced with more if she swept them back outside. She pulled a keg onto its side and began rolling it out of the tight space at the doorway.

She heard a crunch as it went over something in the corridor, something that felt more solid than a dry leaf. She pulled the keg toward her and looked over the top of it.

"Fuck!"

It was a rat. Its fat belly exploded and flattened against the cement. At least it wasn't squished into the carpet.

"What's up?"

It was Will, standing in his doorway, trying to see what she was looking at. She rolled the keg back over the rat to hide it, wincing at the wet sound of its tiny bones crackling.

"Nothing."

He laughed. "Then why'd you swear?"

She straightened up, keeping one foot on the keg so it wouldn't move. "I didn't."

"Okay." He was still grinning, and she found herself grinning back.

"This place is haunted—maybe it was a ghost you heard."

"Haunted?" He laughed.

"You haven't heard?" She looked at him as if it was the biggest surprise of her life.

"No," he said, then, playing along, "Did something bad happen?"

"I shouldn't really be talking about it."

"I won't tell." Will leaned against the doorway and crossed his arms.

"All right, since you insist. Did you know that before it was a tavern it was owned by the richest family in town? The Eamons."

"Them?"

He looked over her shoulder, at the framed photograph that she'd cracked.

"That's right."

She waited for him to ask her to continue, but he didn't. He just watched her, still grinning.

"Round here, wealth can rub people the wrong way," she started, "but not the Eamons. Their children were the cutest, sweetest kids. The mother made blankets for the poor. And the Colonel, he was a war hero."

"So they died here?"

Rose let her voice go dark and somber. "They were murdered."

"Really?"

"The Eamon house always had people coming and going. After three days, when no one answered the door, people started to worry. They cracked the locks with a sledgehammer. What they saw was so barbaric, at first they thought it was an animal that had done it—but it wasn't. It was the Colonel. He'd come back from the war not quite right. Mrs. Eamon and the kids had done everything to hide it, to pretend all was normal. They had played happy families right up to the morning that he ripped them apart, one at a time, trying to find their souls. But he didn't find anything. Only blood and brains. So he ate his own gun."

"Wow. That's pretty intense," Will said, but he didn't look worried in the slightest. In fact, he was still smiling. Was he some sort of psychopath? Usually people flinched at that last line, asked if it was really true. Sometimes they even looked around the tavern like a ghost was about to jump out and yell *Boo.*

"I guess," she said, shrugging and making sure her foot didn't move at all on the keg.

"Oh," he said, "that reminds me. I wanted to ask you something. Hang on."

He disappeared back into his room. Even the way he moved was different from the other guys in town; he didn't have the same heaviness to him. Those guys looked like they had a weight permanently strapped across their shoulders. She peered around to see if she could peek into his room. She couldn't, and she wasn't taking her foot off the keg. If he saw the squished rat he'd think Eamon's, and probably Rose herself, was disgusting. She wouldn't blame him. But for some reason she didn't want him thinking that.

He came back out holding a copy of the *Star.*

"Do you read that shit?" she asked, raising her eyebrows.

"Not usually, but it seemed to be all anyone was talking about today."

"Who?" she asked. "Your family?"

He began flicking through the pages until he came to her article. "Did you write this?"

She shrugged, not sure whether to be proud or embarrassed. She tried to go for nonchalant. "Yeah."

He looked at her, more carefully now. "Is it true?"

"What?"

"Are the police really thinking that?"

"That it's a pedophile?" she asked, and he seemed to wince at the word. "Why do you care?"

He cocked his head. "Why don't you answer my question first."

She flinched. The warmth was gone from his tone and he was looking at her dead in the eye. All she wanted to do was tell him to fuck off and walk away, but then the keg might move and he'd see the rat.

"Why don't you ask them yourself," she said. "This place is always full of them."

"I'm asking you," he said.

"I don't know!" she said, irritated now. "That's what the rumor is."

He nodded.

"Well, thanks for the inquisition, but if you don't need anything—" she let her voice drip with contempt "—then I have work to do."

"Nope, don't need anything," he said, smiling again. "Thanks for checking though." And he withdrew back into his room and shut the door.

As the sky darkened and the humdrum of the evening began—Jean in the office, Mia reading star signs aloud and talking to her about everything and nothing, the regular punters trickling in—it occurred to Rose that something was off. She didn't identify it straightaway, but then when she did it was obvious. It was Frank. He always sat in the same chair. But tonight he wasn't in his usual spot. At first she thought that maybe he hadn't turned up for his usual piss-up. But no, he was there after all. He was sitting with his back to her. Frank never sat with his back to her. He'd always sit in the same seat, the one with the best view to watch her while she worked. She hated it. It was like having an audience. But somehow, tonight, the back of his head felt even more intrusive.

She felt bad. He'd been kind to both her and Laura when he'd come over to collect the doll. Still, maybe his anger over the article would mean he'd stop staring at her. She hoped he'd realize that she didn't invite the attention he gave her. But she also wanted him to know she hadn't meant it to be malicious. He was a customer, after all, and she didn't like the idea of the tension going on longer than it needed to.

She'd have to say something. Clear the air.

But now she actually wanted to catch him alone, she realized how difficult that would be.

"Do you think he even notices?" Rose leaned on the bar next to Mia to watch the men.

"Notices what?"

"That he's the center of his little group," Rose told her, as Mia leaned on her shoulder. "Baz hangs on his every word. Sorry, but he does."

Mia shrugged.

"And look at the way Steve looks at no one else. It's Frank he smiles and nods to. Even Jonesy."

"Dickhead Jonesy."

"Yeah. But he's such a dickhead that it's only Frank he thinks is worth making an effort around."

They watched them. Rose couldn't believe she had never noticed it before.

"Even Father," Mia added. "It's always Frank he's trying to give his advice to."

Rose nodded, watching the way they all looked at him.

"You were right," she said eventually. "He's really angry with me."

"I know."

"What do I do?"

Mia nudged her with her shoulder. "Two words... First one is *I'm...*"

"But I'm not sorry."

"So what? It's just something you say so everyone feels better."

Rose groaned. Guilt didn't sit well with her.

"Fine." She grabbed a dish towel and flung it over her shoulder. If she waited to get him alone she'd be waiting all night. Worrying about Frank was only making her shift drag even slower.

"Go on," Mia said, flicking the rag at Rose as she walked away.

When Rose approached, cringing inwardly, the chatter at the table stopped. She began stacking their empty pints. The clang of glass on glass sounding obnoxious in the stilted silence. Frank avoided her eye.

"So I guess you're pissed at me?" she said.

He looked up at her, but not in the way she'd been expecting. He didn't look hurt; he just looked annoyed. It made her feel small.

"Yes" was all he said.

"I'm sorry, all right? I didn't think—"

But he'd already looked away, back to the table of men who were all trying hard not to meet her gaze.

Rose brought the glasses up to the sink. She washed them angrily, soapsuds flicking onto her singlet, leaving dark pinpricks on the cotton. He had no right to make her feel bad. What was with the men tonight? Between him and Will she was really starting to feel like crap.

"It's all right. Deep breaths," said Mia, smiling at her.

"I don't know why he's angry at me—I'm just reporting what happened."

"I thought you said you didn't care."

"I don't."

"Seems like you do."

Rose looked up at Mia, catching the teasing tone. "Come on. You know it's not that."

"Come on, yourself. I'm just saying it seems like little Frankie might have had more of an effect than you think."

"Little Frankie?" Rose scoffed, but Mia just raised her eyebrows and grinned that annoying knowing grin even though she didn't know shit.

They stopped talking as Will walked past and out the front doors.

"Where do you think he's going?" Rose asked.

Mia leaned forward, whispering. "Probably sick of Jean's cooking."

"Yeah, but it's not like there are many other options." The only food around that wasn't sticky takeaway was at Milly's Café, but that was over thirty minutes' walk without a car.

Rose wanted to follow him. To run out the front door, just to see where he went. If the place hadn't been full she might have. It wasn't just that she wanted to see where he was going, but she was feeling so restless. She needed something, anything, to make this shift go faster so she could get back home and turn on her computer and write. And so she didn't have to stare at the back of Frank's angry head, or need to think about the ache in the arches of her feet, the stiffness in her back, the tiredness that was always one step away.

"Have you cleaned his room yet?" she asked Mia, despite knowing the answer.

"Nope. Do Not Disturb is plastered on his door, which is awesome."

"Aren't you curious about him?"

"Not curious enough to want to clean the skid marks off his toilet bowl."

"Yuck." Rose pushed her. "Hey, want to do something?"

"Oh, no. I know that look."

"I'm just going to have a little peek."

"What, right now?"

"Yep. Got to get the scoop!"

Mia looked at the door. "What if he comes back?"

"You'll be my lookout." She smiled at Mia and patted her on the shoulder.

"Wait—hang on," Mia started, but Rose had already slipped the spare keys off the hook and begun walking toward the back rooms. Something about Will didn't add up, and she was going to find out what it was. She was going to find out why he had been so rude to her before and make him see that even though she had a shitty job he couldn't treat her like she was beneath him. All the giddiness from her success with the *Star* was pumping through her again, making her feel invincible.

The guy was acting weird, hiding something, and she was going to find out what it was. She checked the silent corridor, trying not to look at the still-damp patch of concrete where the rat had exploded, then slid the key into the lock, metal clicking against metal.

The light to the room was off. Rose stood in the dark, seeing the ghost of the bed and cabinet, the black abyss of the television screen. Closing her eyes, she breathed in slowly through her nose. The room didn't smell like the rest of Eamon's anymore. It now had that same slightly musky man smell that had made the hairs on her arms stand up that day at the council building—it was all around.

She flicked the light on. The room looked more normal lit up, but it made her feel exposed. The idea of Will coming in, busting her in this small space, the bed between them, made her shudder, but not out of fear. In fact, she almost wished he would.

Rose had been inside this room so many times, but Will's

things made the familiar space look different. She sat down on his unmade bed. The scent of his body was stronger there. On the nightstand was a hardback copy of *Birdsong* as well as a pair of black-framed reading glasses. She tried them on, staring at the rest of the room through the warping lenses. His suitcase was on top of the drawers next to the old television; three crumpled T-shirts lay on top of it. She saw the distorted edge of the case, a newspaper on top of it, and something poking out from inside. She could just see it, catching the light.

Blond hair. Shit.

Getting up, she put the glasses on top of her head and reached over to the suitcase. Her heart was in her mouth now. She felt sick. She wanted to run for it, to go get the cops, to get out of here. But she was frozen, staring at that centimeter of blond hair poking out of the case's open zipper. An image of a child stuffed inside in her head. She could call out; Frank would be here in an instant regardless of being pissed off. No. She took a breath, tried to steady herself. She was meant to be a journalist. Being a journalist meant investigating. Her hand flashed out in front of her and she flicked open the suitcase, stepping back away from it as she did.

She could have laughed. It was a teddy bear. Just a teddy bear. A big red bow around its neck and long soft yellow fur. Almost as quickly as it appeared, the smile slid off her face. The laugh evaporated. What was he doing with a toy? Was it his? Or was it a lure? This was way too weird. Next to the suitcase was the *Star*, still open to her article. Oh, God. It was starting to make sense. He wasn't grilling her about her sources because he was trying to put her down. He was trying to find out if they were onto him.

"Rose."

Shit. She jumped, her body lurching. Frank, not Will, was standing in the doorway, staring at her.

"What are you doing?"

"Nothing. Just cleaning. This is my job, remember?"

Usually she was a better liar. His eyes flicked up. Will's glasses were still on her head. She pulled them off.

"You're lying," he said. She didn't like his tone. It scared her. Her heart hammered loudly against her ribs.

She put the glasses back on the bedside table and went to step past him. Frank didn't move.

"I'm afraid I'm going to have to arrest you." His eyes were dark.

"What do you mean?" she yelped, then realized that he was joking. He smiled at her and the warmth came back into his face. She felt relieved and also slightly mortified.

"You shouldn't be snooping through your guest's things," he said, his face serious again. "That's not right."

"I know," she said, meaning it. He looked at her again, anger still in his face, but he took a step out of the doorway to let her pass.

Rose followed him, closing and locking the door. Looking up, she could see he was still staring at her, his face full of conflicting emotions.

"Look, I'm sorry if I made trouble for you."

"No, you're not," he said. She looked at him carefully, not sure if he was still just joking.

"I am!" she protested.

He waved a hand. "Rose, you drive me crazy, but you know I won't stay mad at you for too long." He smiled a little sadly. "Just don't go stirring up shit you can't control."

She watched his back as he left, her face reddening and her skin feeling prickly and sensitive from the panic.

Coming back to the bar, she saw Mia picking at the dry skin around her fingernails.

"Great lookout," she said.

"Huh? He's not back yet. I've been watching the door."

"Yeah, but Frank busted me."

Mia shrugged. "Did you find anything?"

Rose rubbed her arms. She still had goose bumps. She looked around to make sure no one was listening, then took a step forward and began to whisper.

Later on, when the last of the punters had finally left, Mia bleached the countertops, the smell stinging Rose's nostrils as she swept the floor. It was amazing how dirty it got every single day. Thick gray dust, soil and lots of loose strands of hair. Some of the cops must be balding at an alarming rate. By the end of the night there was always a scatter of moth carcasses near the door, attracted by the neon lights, or stuck to the bottom of shoes. Some of them still fluttered slightly as she swept them up. Usually, Rose would stare at them, the endless debate going on in her mind over whether they might live if she scooped them up and put them outside. It seemed horrible to just treat something living the same way as you treated a fluff ball or a piece of rubbish. Tonight though, her mind was whizzing. She was too distracted to feel depressed by the moths' pointless twitches. Rob was up to something, but she had no clue as to what it was, and no idea on how to figure it out. And Will. Maybe, just maybe, her article hadn't been an exaggeration at all. Maybe the dolls really were the work of someone with an unhealthy interest in kids. And as soon as she was done here she'd have to go home and write about it. The thought made her feel unsettled.

The front door opened and Will came through, the night air clinging to him. She could feel her insides lurching when he looked at her, like seeing a figure from a dream. He smiled at her.

"Sorry," he said and took a half leap over the little mountain of waste she'd made near the door.

She and Mia watched him go back to his room.

★ ★ ★

Rose didn't talk as Mia drove her home. There was too much to worry about; she could hardly even think straight. Mia pulled in outside Rose's house and turned off the ignition.

"Okay," she said, "spit it out."

"What?"

"You're being weird. Is it just Will that's worrying you, or is there more?"

She was right. Rose swallowed, not sure if she wanted to talk about it. She desperately hoped Rob was up to something dodgy, that he was fooling around with another woman or slacking off from work. It might mean her mother would divorce him, which was what Rose wanted more than anything. But looking at her house now, at the dark rooms of her sleeping family, she didn't know what to think. Rob was her siblings' father. As much as she hated him, he was always kind to them and she knew they loved him. She didn't want to mess that up for them.

"It's probably got nothing to do with anything," she said, "but didn't you think it was weird what Mr. Hane said about my stepdad?"

"I was wondering when you'd ask. I've been thinking about it too."

"It seemed like a slip. Like he really had seen Rob the night before. I went to the pub today and asked, and the guy was really weird about it." Rose looked at her.

"So, what? You think he's been planting the dolls? Pretending to be out of town as an alibi?"

This wasn't what she'd wanted Mia to say. The idea of Rob being involved with the dolls was too weird, too potentially disgusting, for her to even think about.

"It's not possible. Why would he give one to Laura?" Rose reasoned, "She's his own daughter."

"Maybe because he thinks that would make him even less of a suspect."

"This is fucked," Rose said.

Journalist Uncovers Own Stepfather Is Source of Town's Terror. It was a good headline, that was for sure. But if Rob really was involved, Rose didn't want to think of the implications. Already, the disgust was there in the back of her throat. The same sensation she experienced when watching someone puke.

"Well, there's an easy way to find out if he was working or not."

"How?"

Mia pulled out her phone. "It's Hudson's he works for, right? And they're twenty-four hour?"

"Yeah. Why?"

"I thought you were meant to be the journalist?"

Rose looked at Mia, who was smiling broadly, eyes dancing.

"Hello there. How are you?" Mia said into the phone, her friendliness dialed up to saccharine.

"Oh, that's great, darl. Now, I don't want to be a bother. I have a quick question for you—do you have a moment?"

Rose couldn't hear what the person was saying on the other end of the phone, only the deep tones of a man's voice.

"That's fantastic. Now, I had one of your drivers drop off a load a few days ago, and I just noticed the silly fellow left his hat behind. His name was Rob, I think. Rob James?"

She paused, listening. Rose couldn't believe she hadn't thought of doing this herself.

"Okay… No, that's okay. Thanks, darling! Bye-bye now."

Mia ended the call and looked at the phone in her hand.

"Well?" Rose asked.

"He said Rob was laid off six months ago."

PORCELAIN TERROR INTENSIFIES
AS MORE DOLLS DISCOVERED
by Rose Blakey

The mystery of the porcelain dolls continues to rock the quiet town of Colmstock. It has now been confirmed that four families have received these horrifying figurines, all nearly identical to their angel-faced young daughters.

Mr. and Mrs. Hane spoke to this reporter from their idyllic suburban home about the horror they have been experiencing during this bizarre case. "We thought it was strange," Mrs. Hane stated, her arm around her frightened six-year-old daughter, as if to shield her from the worst of human depravity. "These are our children!" her husband added.

The Hanes may be right to be worried. An inside source has revealed possible links to child abusers in the area. So far, local police have had no luck apprehending the perpetrator. The same source revealed they are yet to find a solid lead.

For the Hanes, who are currently living every parent's nightmare, their child will not be safe until this vile perpetrator is off the streets. As terrified mother Mrs. Hane stated, "It's enough to make you sick!"

13

Rose rubbed her eyes.

"Still hurting?" asked Mia.

"Yeah."

Her eyes were red rimmed and stinging from too long in front of the computer screen. She'd found the thing impossible to write. All she could think about was Rob, and everything she wrote made her feel even sicker about it. She knew the article didn't have to be long, but still, it had felt almost impossible to stretch the story any further. Plus, she hadn't wanted to focus on the police-incompetence angle like she had before. It didn't seem fair.

"What if they don't want to publish it?"

"They will. Here." Mia passed her the bag of sour worm lollies.

"These are so gross," Rose said, putting two in her mouth and wincing at the concentrated sourness on the back of her tongue.

"Yeah," Mia said, using her toe to skip the song that had just started playing.

They were in Mia's car, with the seats back as far as they would go, listening to one of Mia's favorite CDs.

"It was so crap—I already know they won't want it. There just wasn't anything new to say."

"Nothing new is kind of good though, right? It means no more families have gotten one."

"I guess."

Mia slumped back onto the headrest, recrossing her legs on the dashboard. "Do you really think Will might be involved? The teddy bear was probably for his niece or whatever. He did say he had family here."

"Maybe."

She knew Mia wasn't as convinced as she was that Will was up to something. It was a hard feeling to explain, but she was going to trust it. This was something she could figure out. Rob, on the other hand, could be up to anything right now.

Rose sucked at her bottom lip and tasted the rough, sweet sugar granules. They stared back out the windscreen. The car was parked across the road from Eamon's. They'd been waiting there for a few hours for Will to come out, planning to follow him. So far he hadn't made an appearance. Rose imagined him lying on his bed, reading his book probably. Resting her arms over her head, she exhaled slowly. They were probably going to be here awhile.

"We could just ask Mr. Hane what the deal is with Rob?" Mia said. "Maybe there's an innocent explanation."

"I already tried to get it out of him, remember? He's not going to tell us."

They sat in silence a few minutes longer.

"I think your car needs a wash," Rose said, eventually. The windscreen was grimy with dust and dirt. There were squashed bugs stuck on the sides where the windscreen wipers didn't reach.

"I know."

A plastic set of purple rosary beads were hung around the

rear-vision mirror. Rose watched Mia tap the cross with her toe, causing it to swing back and forth. The car was Mia's domain. It was where Mia seemed to feel the most comfortable. She had tampons in the glove compartment, cracked CD cases all over the carpeted floor and a Polaroid of the two of them taped onto the sun visor.

The sun started to sink. Will wasn't going anywhere.

"I'm sure if you told Mr. Hane how worried you are—"

"He won't tell me, Mia," Rose snapped. Then, "Sorry."

Truth was, she really was worried, no matter how much she told herself there was no reason the two things should be connected. That just because Rob had been fired didn't mean he had anything at all to do with the dolls. But still, the sick feeling in the back of her throat was growing.

Mia started the ignition. "This is dumb. If we are going to stake out anyone, it should be the Hanes."

"I guess it's worth a shot," Rose said. It seemed unlikely that Rob was just going to turn up at the Hanes' house, but she couldn't think of a better idea.

When they were almost at the Hanes' street, Rose caught sight of something out of the corner of her eye. A flash of orange.

"Shit," she said.

"What?"

"Turn around."

"Why?"

"Just do it!"

Mia swerved into a driveway and turned the car around, its joints creaking angrily.

"Go left. I think I just saw the Hanes' car go down that road."

"Are we following them?" Mia said, as she shot back down the street and turned the corner.

"Yeah!" Rose laughed; they were probably just going to the supermarket.

Mia caught up with the car when it stopped at the intersection. Through the back window they could see the back of Mr. Hane's head.

"He's by himself."

"This is exciting!" Mia said.

"I know. Is that depressing? We're young. We should have more excitement in our life than this!"

Mia shrugged, turning the music up a bit and following his red taillights. Rose was glad. She still felt sick, and she didn't want to talk about it anymore. Rob had been laid off. He was hiding it from her mum, letting her work in that factory while he did God knew what. Best-case scenario was that he had nothing at all to do with the dolls. But even then, with just her mother's wage, how would they survive? Streetlights flashed past and the other possibility forced its way back into her head. The one she and Mia had avoided mentioning. What if the dolls meant what she'd said they had meant in her article? If it was true, Rob might have been doing something to her siblings. Doing something to Laura, in her house. Even the idea of it was unbearable.

"Where on earth is he going?" Mia said over the music.

"Dunno."

"No, seriously." Mia turned the stereo down. "He's going out of town."

Rose looked around properly. Mia was right. He was leaving Colmstock.

"Maybe we should stop," Mia said.

"Aren't you curious though? It's Mr. Hane. It can't be that bad."

"You never know—what if he's one of those family-man serial killers you always hear about? I'm going to pull back a bit."

"Yeah, but don't lose him."

Mia slowed down, letting Mr. Hane get a strong lead. After driving for another five minutes, there were no more streetlights, so even from a distance they could see the red of his brake lights, and his headlights beaming left around the corner.

"Fuck," Rose said, "I know where he's going. Turn your headlights off."

"Why?" Mia said. "I'll hit a roo."

"He's going left—the only thing around there is Auster's."

Mia turned her headlights off and pulled the car onto the gravel side strip. They both knew that this wasn't good. Auster's Automotive Factory had been closed down for close to a decade. No one had a legitimate reason to go there at nighttime.

"I really want to know what he's doing." Rose was worried Mia was going to wimp out on her. She couldn't just leave it; she needed to find the truth.

"So do I," Mia said. They grinned nervously at each other.

"Okay," Rose said, whispering now, "why don't we drive up to the corner with the lights off, and then walk around the back way."

Mia started the ignition and began driving. "It's probably something innocent."

Rose let her believe it.

They didn't speak as Mia slowly directed the car up the road. The dark was impenetrable. Without headlights on it was like they were sliding through negative space. She couldn't see Mia's face. She could barely even see her own hands. Something bad was going on; Rose felt dizzy with it. She desperately wanted to tell Mia to turn back, but instead she crossed her arms tight to stop them from trembling in the black heat.

When they got to the corner Mia smoothly drove onto the dirt. Rose still winced at the crunch of the tires. They climbed carefully out of the car. Rose's knees felt soft. She looked at Mia over the car's roof but she couldn't see her eyes, just the line of the side of her face, the shadow of her hair. She didn't need to see her. She could feel fear coming off Mia in waves.

They didn't shut their doors, just in case the sound carried. The sky was vast and black all around them. In front of them, the steel car factory loomed, gray stone against the black. They tried to tread as lightly as they could as they approached it. Mia's hand grasped for hers and she held it tight, feeling its clammy warmth.

"Let's go in from the side," Rose whispered. Her voice sounded loud in the perfect silence. "There's more coverage."

They huddled down into a half run toward the side of the building. Then, very slowly, they crept quietly toward the front entrance. The factory wall was still hot from the day's sun. Rose could feel it radiating as she inched along next to it. Something stung at her arm and she almost yelped as she turned. It was Mia's other hand, her fingernails digging slightly into Rose's skin. There was light coming from somewhere; she could see Mia's eyes now. They were shiny and dark.

"Look," she mouthed, and Rose felt the word hot on her cheek.

To their left was the orange car. Rose inhaled sharply. Mr. Hane was sitting inside it. Fuck. That was where the light was coming from, the dim globe inside his car.

There was nothing between him and them. Despite the dark, he might have already seen their movement.

The click of his door opening echoed across the yard. Rose squeezed her lips together to stop any sound escaping. Mr. Hane took a step out, his sneakers grinding against the gravel. She could feel Mia's whole body tremble next to her. He slapped the car door closed behind him and strode past them, so close they could smell his aftershave. If he turned his head, even an inch, he'd see them.

A crack as he opened the heavy factory gate, and the whoosh of it closing behind him. He hadn't seen them, thank God. They looked at each other. Rose thought she might be sick.

"Hey, mate, you got it all?" Mr. Hane's voice came out of the silence inside the building.

They heard the rumble of a reply.

"So that's, what? Twenty kilos? Not bad!"

Rose squeezed Mia's hand tighter. They both knew exactly what that meant.

There was a window about a meter in front of Rose; pale gray light was drifting out of it.

She stepped forward, but Mia wouldn't let go of her hand. She turned back to shoot her a look, and then shook Mia's hand off. Colmstock's Drug Importation Exposed. It was too good a headline to pass up. She shuffled forward, her knees up to her ears, trying not to make a sound.

"And you didn't have any trouble?" Mr. Hane's voice.

The window was right above Rose's head now. Achingly slowly, she straightened up. Through the window, she saw Mr. Hane's bald head and a truck packed with lawn mowers, its trailer doors open, revealing stacks of delivery boxes. And she saw her stepfather. He was sitting in the back of the truck, swinging his legs in the same way Laura did.

"Show me," another voice said. Familiar. Sneering.

She craned her neck, searching for the source. There. Leaning against the wall right under her, the top of Jonesy's head.

"Okay, chill out, will you?" Rob went into the truck and pulled the front panel off the nearest lawn mower. Jonesy stepped forward to look inside.

Mr. Hane turned toward some tarpaulin, and Rose shot back down.

"Go!" she hissed at Mia.

They shuffled back down the wall, then leaped up and ran back to Mia's car.

14

Rose sat in front of her computer with the fan on high and Laura wedged between her knees. She was softly braiding the little girl's hair. The computer screen radiated heat onto her face, but the fan made her sweat feel cold.

Rose was alternating between Laura's hair and refreshing her email.

"Not too tight, Posey," Laura said.

She loosened her grip on Laura's hair slightly, trying to ignore the sound of Scott and Sophie squabbling from the other room. She'd yelled at them to stop it three times this morning already and still the noise was slowly rising up again. In some ways, she didn't blame them. Their bedroom was tiny, barely big enough for one kid, let alone two. This was one of the reasons her mum wanted her out. Rose refreshed her email again. Nothing.

"I forgive you," Laura said quietly.

"For what?"

"For getting my doll arrested."

Rose couldn't help smiling.

"Thanks," she said.

"When can I have her back? She didn't do anything wrong."

"I know," Rose said, deliberately ignoring the question. Laura was never getting that creepy thing back.

"So, why did the policeman take her?" Laura asked.

Rose wasn't sure how to answer. Laura was still so small, her shoulders impossibly narrow. She twisted another section of hair into the braid. She was going to make sure it looked perfect.

"He thought a bad man gave it to you," Rose said eventually.

"Why is he bad?"

"A bad guy like you see on TV." She wanted to explain it in a way Laura could understand.

"Was it a bad guy?"

Rose stopped braiding, four sections of hair held between her fingers. She thought of Will again. The way he'd pushed that she tell him what the police knew.

"Posey? Was it a bad guy?"

"I dunno," she said slowly.

"But when can I get her back?" Laura asked, turning her head. One of the bits of hair fell out from between Rose's fingers.

"Careful."

Rose picked up the pieces of hair she'd lost and continued the braid, thinking. What she'd seen last night had kept her up. If she wrote an article about it, the *Star* would have to publish it, surely. Maybe she could even try for the *Sage Review*. But if Rob went to jail, then her mother would have to support the kids on her own. Laura was already wearing hand-me-downs.

Mia wanted to tell the police, but had left the decision up to Rose. She obviously didn't want to be the one to ruin Rose's family either.

Rose's mobile rang and she jumped. Answering it, she held the phone between her shoulder and her ear. It was Mia.

"Hey," she said. "How'd you sleep?"

"Badly. Mr. Hane, a drug kingpin? I still can't get my head around it."

They both laughed. The fear from last night had lost some of its potency.

"Does that make Mrs. Hane a mafia wife?" Rose asked.

"I guess! Wonder if she's ever kneecapped anyone."

"Oh, God. Stop it!"

Mia laughed. "Heard back on the new article yet?"

Rose refreshed her email again. Nothing. "Not yet."

"So listen, okay." Mia's tone suggested she was going to say something that Rose didn't want to hear. "I know you don't like Frank."

"I don't!"

"I know," she continued, "but I quite like Baz."

Rose held the phone properly in her hand, gripping three sections of Laura's hair between her fingers on the other. "I know telling them is the right thing." She spoke seriously now. "And I don't want you to have to lie—"

"Oh, that's not what I meant," Mia said, cutting in. "That's still your call. It's just…"

Rose already had a feeling she knew what was coming.

"I really want to go out with Baz."

"Come on, Mia!"

"I've been flirting my butt off and he hasn't seemed to notice."

"That's because he's thick as fuck."

Mia didn't respond to that. "Frank mentioned that double date again and I really want to do it."

"No way! I don't want to give Frank the wrong idea."

"Why can't you just give him a chance? That's all he wants."

"Plus, I doubt he'll want to now, anyway. I bet he's still pretty angry with me."

Mia snorted, "I'd say you're still in with a shot."

"It'd be weird."

"Come on! I almost died for you last night."

"I know. I've got scars on my arm from your fingernails."

"Please! Pleasy, weasy, weasy…"

Rose could only just make out what Mia was saying. Sophie and Scott's argument was reaching a fever pitch. Her head was starting to pound.

"Pleasy, weasy with sugar on top," Mia continued. Rose groaned.

"Fine. I'll think about it! Okay?"

"Think about what?" Laura asked from between her knees.

"Best friend ever!" Mia squealed down the phone line.

"I know," Rose grumbled; she was already regretting it. Reaching out, she hit Refresh on her email. A new one appeared. From the *Star*.

"Gotta go," she said, hanging up and almost dropping the phone in her haste to open the email. For three torturous seconds she waited for the email to load.

"Muuuummm!" screamed Scott.

"Mummmmmmmm!" wailed Sophie.

Rose's face changed as she read the first few lines.

"'Not macabre enough,'" she read out aloud.

"What's that mean?" asked Laura.

"It means they said no," she said, not sure if she wanted to cry or hit something, but knowing that the pain in her stomach was as real as if someone had cut her. "They think I'm just rehashing what I already wrote."

"Who?"

The *Star* was basically a tabloid. If she couldn't even get a second article published there, what chance did she ever have of being a real journalist? She should just give up.

There was a knock on Rose's open door. It was her mum. The twins must have woken her up. She looked tired beyond tired and Rose already knew what she was about to say.

"Rob's back tomorrow."

Rose put her hands over Laura's ears. "Mum. I think Rob is doing something you don't know about... Something illegal."

She waited for her mother's shock; she'd been imagining it all night. She hated to admit it, but this had the potential to work out well for her. Her mother would kick Rob out, and she could stay here to pick up the pieces. She'd tell him that she wouldn't dob him in to the cops, as long as he kept paying generous child support.

Her mum's mouth tightened slightly, but apart from that her face didn't change. "You haven't packed."

Rose stared at her in disbelief, her hands falling from Laura's ears.

"Rose!" Her mother was now visibly upset. "You've had months to get this sorted. Don't you have anywhere lined up?"

"Didn't you hear what I just said?"

Her mother just looked at her, then down to Laura and walked away down the hall. Rose carefully picked up Laura's hand and put it onto the back of her head to hold the braid in place.

"I've just got to talk to Mum for one sec," she said. "Don't move or it'll fall out, okay?"

Laura nodded solemnly. Rose got up to follow her mother. She'd gone back to her room, which was next to Rose's. She pushed the door open. Her mum was sitting on the bed, her head down. Rose sat down next to her.

"He got laid off six months ago," Rose said quietly. "He's bringing drugs into town."

"That's not true," her mum said, not looking at her.

"It is."

Her mum looked up at her. Rose hadn't been so close to her mum in a long time. Most of their conversations these days happened through walls or across rooms. She looked old.

"I love Rob, Rose," she said. "He's the man of this house now, and we all have to respect that."

"Aren't you hearing me?"

"Posey!" they heard Laura call from the other room. "Are you coming back?"

Her mother looked away again. "We made a deal, Rose. You'd be out when he got home from work. Don't put me in the middle of this. You're an adult now, and you need to get your act together."

Rose stood. She was mute with anger.

Going back into her room, she resumed Laura's braid. She heard her mother sigh. The walls were paper-thin. She'd learned that when Rob and her mother had first started dating. Every night, she'd had to sleep with headphones in so she wouldn't have to hear her mother's simpering whimpers, Rob's grunts, flesh slapping against flesh. She'd thought it was the worst thing she could overhear from that room. It wasn't.

It was years ago now. She'd been in bed late one morning. Her shift at Eamon's had been busy, so she'd slept longer than usual. Her mother must have thought she'd gone out. Their low conversation filtered into her dream. Then she heard her name.

"And he was Rose's father?"

Her ears had pricked up.

"Yeah."

"Did you ever tell him?"

"About Rose?"

"Mmm."

She had held her breath.

"I did, yeah. When I first found out I was pregnant."

"And?"

"He gave me two hundred bucks to get rid of it."

Rose's breath came out, her head swirling.

"But you didn't do it."

"Yeah."

"You were so young. Why not?"

The sound of shifting weight, one of them rolling over.

"Two hundred isn't enough for an abortion."

They'd laughed, and Rose had wanted to die.

"Rose! Stop it!" Laura yelled from between her knees. "You're pulling too hard."

"Sorry," she said.

15

"Pluto, the dark knight, has entered your zone, bringing mysterious fortunes."

"What the hell does that mean?"

"Dunno," said Rose, peering at the astrology section of the *Star*. "'Fortunes' sounds great though."

Eamon's was quiet that night and not because the usual crowd wasn't there. The cops were there all right, but for once, they were talking quietly, heads together. The pain of the rejection had settled in Rose's stomach now. The feeling of disappointment had been a permanent fixture in Rose's psyche for so long that she'd become used to it. The short respite from the sense of hopelessness had been dreamlike—more exquisite than she had imagined.

She needed that feeling back. She had to know what the cops were talking about.

"Do you know what's happened?" she asked Mia.

"Nope. You should go find out."

Rose tried to walk very quietly over to the long table. But as soon as she was in earshot they stopped talking immediately. She picked up the empty glasses, peering over to see what they were looking at. Frank snapped closed a folder, but for a split second Rose saw what was inside—a photograph of a little blonde girl and an identical blonde doll.

"Don't stop on my account."

"Gotta keep a lid on things around you now," Frank said, smiling. She raised an eyebrow and took the stack of empty beer glasses back to the bar. When she got back, Mia was staring up at the photograph of the Eamons.

"What was it all about?" she asked, still looking at the picture.

"More dolls."

"Really?"

"Yeah."

Rose started stacking the glasses into the dishwasher while Mia continued staring at the picture.

"Mr. Eamon was sort of hot."

"Didn't he murder his wife?"

"I dunno. You know, I was reading this thing online about haunted places. It said walls and rooms remember things. Not just what happened in the past, but the future. They keep the trauma inside—it's like the walls exist outside of time. They carry the ghosts of all the trauma that has happened and will happen."

Rose tried very hard to look interested. She wanted Mia to trust herself a little more. She was always underconfident, putting everyone's needs and opinions before her own, and Rose hated that. But Mia knew her too well.

"You think it's stupid."

"No, no. It's just..." How could she put it? "I always think in a practical way, I suppose. If you're interested in tarot, that's cool. You can use it to make some cash. But all the hocus-pocus stuff... I mean, what's the point? Where's it going to get you?"

"Nowhere, I guess. I just think it's interesting."

Rose felt guilty already. "You're right. It is interesting."

"No, you're right."

Rose wished she hadn't said anything.

"Order up," Jean called, and Mia went to collect the black steaks that some idiot had been hungry or stupid enough to order.

She watched Mia deliver them to a table, and saw that tight-shouldered, defensive way that Mia walked when she was feeling hurt. Rose couldn't help feeling slightly infuriated. Mia was way too sensitive; it was frustrating. The way she spoke, it was like she couldn't see her way out of this town. Like somehow, she'd told bullshit ghost stories about Eamon's one too many times and now she thought they were true. Mia had absolutely no ambition; she was always so ready to accept things as they were even if she knew they weren't right. The bitchy part of Rose's brain told her that Mia was a bit pathetic.

Then Mia snapped back into focus. Her Mia. Who was smart and funny and so, so nice, and suddenly the guilt of thinking such a nasty thing overpowered her. Mia was upset, and it was Rose's fault for being so harsh.

There was one way she could make her feel better, she knew. The double date with Frank and Bazza. She looked over at Frank, and he raised an eyebrow back at her. He wasn't gagging for her anymore, which was great, but she knew he still fancied her. Mia had said she should just give him a chance. Maybe she was right. It could just be once-off. Mia would be happy and Frank would know she'd at least tried. She always felt like she had two options, joining the fossickers or working at the poultry factory. But really there was a third, and that was Frank. It would be giving up, but maybe it was time she did just that.

At closing time Frank was still at Eamon's. He was sitting up on a stool at the bar, not even trying to hide his staring.

The Father was sitting next to him, but the two had stopped speaking a while ago. Vaguely, he was aware that his mouth was open slightly and so he closed it. Sipping his beer, which he could barely taste anymore, he spun back and forth on the chair. Rose was cleaning the taps, really putting her shoulders into it. The crimson lights only made her look more perfect. His eyes traced her, taking her in. The curve of her legs, a spray of freckles above each knee. The faint pucker in her singlet over her ribs, where her bra was pushing against her flesh underneath. Her hair looked so soft, brushing against the bare skin on her shoulder. Her skin so perfect and unblemished against the black ink of her tattoo. Her lips were so supple. He wondered how they would feel around his cock.

"You're so pretty." His words sounded a bit funny, like he was hearing them on speaker rather than saying them out loud. "I don't know why you won't let me take you out."

Was it because of the paunch that had begun to form around his middle? He was almost certain it was. He should be going on runs or something; there was no way in hell she would go for him now that he was starting to look so damn middle-aged. He noticed Mia clear her throat in a strange way and shoot a look at Rose. He sipped more of his beer, spilling a little on his chin.

"You know, the tavern is closed on Tuesdays," Rose said to him.

"I know, I know. I have things to do, people to see." He wasn't going to let her think he was pathetic. Frank had friends. To be fair, most of them were on the force, but still.

"So you're busy Tuesday night?"

"So busy!"

She had no idea. He might have a date. Just because she didn't fancy him didn't mean no one else would.

"Pity."

"Huh?"

"Wrong answer," Father said from next to him.

He looked around at their faces. Why did he feel like they were all laughing at him? Something was going on but he couldn't figure out what it was. In fact, it was all starting to make him feel a little dizzy. He had an overwhelming urge to get off the stool and sit down on the floor, but then he really would look like a moron. Mia leaned against the bar, a huge smile on her face. She was pretty too.

"You, Rosie, me, Bazza. Pick us up here at eight."

"Really?"

Frank looked over at Rose, waiting for her to snap a rejection. But she just smiled at him. She was going to go out with him! On Tuesday night he was going to take Rose on a date.

"Woo-hoo!" Frank raised his glass in the air; a little bit of beer sopped out. Everything looked sparkly and magical. Rose was still smiling. Smiling because of him. Maybe she would let him kiss her. This was amazing.

The Father put his hand on Frank's arm and jingled his car keys.

"Okay, bedtime now, sweetheart."

"Who ya calling sweetheart?"

Mia and Rose watched as the Father led Frank out the door. He kept looking back and smiling at them both. When the door banged shut they couldn't help but laugh.

"You're the best."

"You owe me."

"I know."

Mia began lifting the stools up onto the bar. Rose went to get the mop.

"Hey, don't worry about giving me a lift tonight," she said

when she got back, the bucket steaming with the smell of detergent. "My mum said she'd pick me up later."

"Trying to make up for twenty-five years of bad parenting?"

"Yeah, something like that."

Jean locked up the tavern, the drop of the lock falling into place loud enough in the quiet night to be audible from the bushes. She made her way to her car, the only one left in the tavern's parking lot. She had almost reached the driver's-side door, car key wedged between her fingers, when she stopped. She'd heard the sound. The shifting of weight, the snap of a twig. She turned to the shadows of the bushes, like she saw a shape there, then got into her car, moving more quickly than before.

As Jean's headlights disappeared into the murky dark, the shape straightened from its hiding place. The streetlight illuminated Rose's face as she stepped forward toward the tavern. Her heart was still pounding. If Jean had caught her, she had no idea how she could explain hiding in the bushes like a creep.

Rose took a final look around before unlocking the tavern door. The tavern was like a second home, but being there when she wasn't meant to be, when it was all closed up and dark, made the place take on a sinister quality. She walked through quickly, her throat feeling tight again.

She crept down the corridor, trying not to make a noise as she slipped past Will's room. The light was off. Will must be asleep. She hadn't seen him at all tonight. If it wasn't for the Do Not Disturb sign, she might have thought he'd checked out. Without warning, a loud crack echoed down the hallway. Rose gasped, her hand over her mouth, but it was just the photograph that she had knocked down with the keg falling off its nail again. She didn't pick it up, but went straight into the room adjacent to Will's and closed the door.

Bending down, she pulled a bag out from under the bed. She had stashed it there at the beginning of her shift. From within, she took out her toothbrush. Going into the small adjoining bathroom, she brushed her teeth, staring at her own reflection, trying not to wonder how on earth it had come to this. Trying not to cry.

PART 3

It is not wanting to win that makes you a winner;
it is refusing to fail.

—Unknown

16

It was a pleasant, quiet morning until the woman started screaming. The street had been silent except for the sound of birds chirping in the sky and the distant rumbles of a lawn mower. Ms. Lucie Hoffman had opened her front door to collect the morning edition of the *Star*. Instead, she found a porcelain doll sitting on top of the paper on her doorstep, staring up at her. It had thick dark hair and glassy green eyes. That was when the screaming started. Her daughter, Nadine, ran toward her. She had no idea why her mother was screaming, but regardless, she started to sob. The noise was loud and her mum was upset, which was more than enough reason for tears.

The police arrived within the hour. Nadine never even had a chance to play with the doll. It was photographed in its place on the doorstep and then scooped up into a plastic evidence bag. Ms. Hoffman sat on the sofa with her daughter and elderly mother, answering questions from the police and accepting a hot cup of tea. She'd read Rose's article. Now she wished she hadn't. Sentences from it swam around and around in her head. She tried not to look at the doll as she answered the questions, wrapped in plastic like that and looking so much like her daughter. She was relieved when Frank took the thing with him as he left. She watched him out the window as he threw it into the trunk of his car.

Ms. Hoffman wasn't the only one watching Frank. Mia and Rose were ducking down in the front seats of Mia's car, stifling laughs. News moved quicker than the wind in Colmstock.

"You know, I called Lucie when she first got back," Rose said, her cheek pressed onto her knees, "but she never called me back."

Mia smiled from her cramped position. "I spoke to her at church once, but that's it since she's been back. This is going to be so weird."

They peered over the dashboard as Frank pulled out from the curb and accelerated away from them.

"Do you think he saw us?"

"Nah." Rose straightened up. "C'mon—let's go. Gotta get the tears while they're still fresh."

Slamming their doors shut, they approached the house. They both knew it well. They'd spent a lot of time there.

Rose knocked and, almost instantly, the door pulled open. "Hey."

"Hey, Lucie," Rose said. "Long time."

Lucie Hoffman shrugged. "I guess. You want to talk about the doll, right?"

Rose nodded and Lucie turned and walked in, leaving the door open for them. Mia hesitated, looking as awkward as Rose felt.

Rose stepped inside, and Mia followed. She went into the lounge room and sat on the sofa, noticing that it still smelled like cigarettes in here, like it always had. Lucie sat on one of the chairs, her head slumped forward. Looking down at the carpeted floor, Rose couldn't help but look for the wine stain. Almost ten years ago, when this was still Lucie's mum's house, she'd lain in the middle of this lounge room. Her mouth open, she'd tried to swallow, almost choking from laughing, as Lucie stood above her, pouring cheap boxed wine into her mouth. It had gone everywhere.

"Why is it that people always give you tea when something bad happens?" Lucie asked. "You could probably fry an egg on the footpath outside, it's so hot. The last thing I want to drink is tea."

Rose shrugged. "Dunno."

"How are you?" Mia asked. "I know not good today, but in general. What's been happening?"

"Nothing much," Lucie said. "You?"

"Um, nothing, I guess." She looked around, and Rose knew she was about to make this awkward. "I'm sorry I didn't, you know, try harder to get in touch when you got back."

Lucie didn't seem to care. "It's not like I made an effort either. It had been too long."

An awkward silence filled the room.

Rose decided to just dive straight into it. "How is Nadine dealing with everything this morning?"

"She's okay. Doesn't really understand."

"You read my article, right?"

Lucie nodded.

"Then you know that I'm trying to give a voice to the people of this town, to stop the police hiding information."

Lucie snorted, "Still as full of shit as ever."

"It's true!" Rose said, but she couldn't help but smile. She had forgotten how much she liked Lucie's dry way of telling things like they were.

"Yeah, okay. Sure."

"So how'd it go with the cops?"

"Fine. I think they were trying to find a connection between the girls or something."

"Did they find one?"

"Don't think so. Didn't tell me if they had."

"So, Nadine doesn't know the other girls?" Rose found this hard to believe. The town was small enough that you always knew the people around your age.

Lucie shrugged. "Nadine is friends with the Hanes' kid. Lily. They take her along with them to church sometimes when I can't be bothered."

"And the Rileys live just down the street—is she friends with them?"

Lucie just shrugged. "She hangs around with their daughter at school sometimes, and she used to love playing with Ben at church."

"Does she go around there?" Mia piped in.

"No," Lucie said.

"Why not?"

She didn't answer, but looked at Rose carefully. "Why don't you ask me the question you really want to know, Rose?"

"What's that?"

Lucie looked at her, raising her eyebrows just slightly.

"Okay, fine," Rose said. "Why'd you come back?"

"Rose!" Mia said, but Lucie waved her hand dismissively. "You don't have to be the peacekeeper anymore. I think we've grown out of that."

"Well, you guys would always argue!" Mia snapped. Rose and Lucie smiled at each other. In that moment, they really could have been sixteen again.

"You think leaving here will fix everything," Lucie began, looking at Rose only, "but trust me, it doesn't. The city can be a shitty place. I was working a job I hated, and everything just felt so pointless. No one gave a crap about me. One day, I wrenched my neck and fainted on the street. People just stepped over me. I was seeing this guy who didn't even like me that much, and I got pregnant."

"You always said you didn't want to have kids," Rose interrupted. That was one thing they had always agreed on.

"Yeah, well. I guess it just made me feel like I had a purpose again, like there was a reason I existed. So I came back here. I don't regret it."

"That's good," Mia said. "I'm glad things worked out."

Rose didn't say anything. It didn't make sense to her.

"It might have been years since I last spent time with you, but I know what you're thinking, Rose," Lucie said. "That's the thing about you—you always think you know better than everyone around you, but you don't. If you want to be a journalist you need to start listening."

Rose rolled her eyes. Lucie was just saying that because she had given up.

She tried to get more out of Lucie, but it was pointless. Lucie didn't have anything interesting to say. So Rose shut her notebook and said they had to get going. On their way out, Nadine appeared at the top of the stairs.

"'Bye, 'bye!" she called, waving at them and grinning.

"'Bye!" Mia waved back, then cooed "So cute!" when the door closed behind them.

"Total waste of time," said Rose.

"You think? I thought it was great to see her. I'm glad she's happy."

"Yeah. I guess. Did you think it was weird that she didn't want to let her kid play at the Rileys' house?"

"Not really," Mia said. "After all that's happened she probably just wants to give them space."

"Maybe."

"Did she get to you?" Mia said, getting into the car and then leaning across the seats to unlock the passenger-side door.

"No!" she said, getting in, then, "You know where we have to go next, right?"

"Oh, God. Don't say the Rileys." Mia started the ignition, and the radio blared. She turned the volume down as she pulled out from the curb. "It'll be way too intense."

"Exactly. Mr. Riley was so mad with Frank. He'll definitely have some things he wants to say on the record."

"Yeah, but it'll be so horrible. That poor family lost every-thing, and now they have to deal with all this crap."

"Almost feels like someone is targeting them," Rose said, already thinking hard, already trying to find a reason why.

"Maybe," Mia said, stopping at the lights, even though there was no other traffic on the road, "or maybe they just have the worst luck ever."

"I want to find out."

Mia didn't say anything. But her mouth was closed tightly. Rose knew that meant she disapproved.

"What do you want to do now?" Mia asked, changing the subject.

"I'm going to go look at rentals at the council building," she told her.

"How much longer have you got at home?"

"At least a week or so, I'd say," she lied.

"Do you want me to come?" Mia looked worried.

"Nah, that's okay. I'm fine, really. I'll see you at work."

She said goodbye to Mia and hopped out of the car in front of the council building. Depressing as it was, she was fairly sure she wouldn't get caught sleeping at the tavern as long as she was careful at night and kept away during the day. It had been a strange experience. This morning, she had jerked awake, not knowing where the hell she was. It had taken a full two seconds for the familiarity of the room to hit her. The cracked nightstand, the broken lamp, the fan whirling slowly above her head. The memories had come slithering back to her. The rejection, her mother, agreeing to go out with Frank. What a mess.

As she walked she checked her email. Nothing. She hadn't had any bites from any of the jobs she'd applied to in the city. It wasn't really how she wanted to do it. Her dream was always that she'd go to the city because she'd got a journalist job there, but right now she'd take anything she could get as long as it meant she could move. When she got to the city, it would be nothing like it was for Lucie. She didn't need to get knocked up to have a purpose.

She was sure if she could just find a new angle on the dolls that the *Star* might give her another chance. Lucie hadn't given her anything to go with; the interview with her had been as pointless as the one with the Hanes. She needed more. Something big. If she solved it, if she was the one who found out who was behind it, that'd definitely do it. They'd probably give her a job on the spot if she could do that. Luckily, she was pretty sure now that she did know who was behind it. Will. There was something about him, something weird that she couldn't put her finger on. Somehow, every time she was with him, she felt angry. There must be a reason for that. Maybe it was her journalistic instinct kicking in.

When she got to the council building she went straight up the stairs. She didn't even pause to enjoy the air-conditioning. Everything with Rob had distracted her from what she knew: that Will was involved.

Luckily, there was still no one at the records office. It was so silent in there that she could hear the faint hum of the air-con, though the circulation of air wasn't strong enough to blow out the smell of decomposing paper. Sidling through the narrow gap on the side of the desk, she went over to where Will had been standing. There was a wall of filing cabinets.

Closing her eyes, she tried to remember which one he had been in front of, which drawer had been open. It had been the third cabinet, she remembered, the second drawer down. She could see him now, that patronizing expression as he looked up at her. She went straight over and pulled the drawer open with a metallic squeal.

Inside, filed alphabetically, were school enrollment records. Rose pulled a sheet of paper out. Listed on it was the name of a child, and underneath were her parents' names and their address. In the drawer were over a hundred sheets, each with the information of a child who had enrolled in the primary school. She had him.

Marching in through the back of the tavern, she knocked on Will's door. Standing there, arms crossed, she couldn't wait to confront him. Her phone was in her pocket, recording. He just had to say something incriminating. Then she could print it. She'd take it to Frank as well, of course, but it would have been her who had the scoop.

There was no answer. She knocked again. Nothing. But she heard the sound of someone moving around at the bar. He must be in there. Walking toward the sound, she began to worry that this wasn't her greatest idea. Confronting someone about possible criminal activity, especially the sort she was accusing him of, probably wasn't something she should do when there was no one else around.

Looking around the corner, she heard something smash. She jumped backward. There was another smashing sound, a loud tinny jangle. The second time, she recognized it.

"Hi," she said, walking into the kitchen, relieved.

"You're here early," Jean said, throwing another handful of cutlery into the dishwasher.

"Am I?" she asked, looking around.

There he was, sitting alone at a table, reading his book.

"Guess I'll just sit down until my shift starts," she said.

Jean followed her gaze to Will, then smiled. "Suit yourself."

Rose walked toward Will. Now Jean was here, she didn't have to be so careful. She turned before she reached him to check her phone. It was still recording.

"Hi," she said and sat down at his table. He looked up at her quizzically. He had his reading glasses on and was drinking a glass of red wine.

"Where did Jean find that?" she asked, indicating the wine.

"The bottle did look a bit dusty," he said, then went back to reading. He was ignoring her, actually ignoring her.

"No one here orders wine," she said.

He didn't even look up.

"So where's your family?" she asked, leaning forward.

That got his attention. Will folded the corner of his page and set the book down in front of him. She noticed how long his fingers were. Piano player's hands. He leaned back in his chair and smiled.

"You always have the strangest questions for me."

"Mia said you were here visiting family, but I haven't seen you with any," she pushed on.

"Well, if Mia said it, it must be true."

"Is it true?"

"That I'm here to see family? Yes."

"Then why are you being so elusive about it?"

"Because it isn't any of your business."

This was not getting her anywhere. She'd have to warm up to it, let him get comfortable.

"How about you tell me what you do for work? You know what I do."

He shook his head incredulously. "Why do you care?"

She shrugged one shoulder, just an inch, and smiled. "Maybe I'm just interested."

Flirting. She should have thought about it earlier. He took her in, unsure.

"I'm a graphic designer," he said.

"Really?" She'd never met anyone with a job like that.

He nodded. "Yes, really."

"God, why do you have to be so patronizing!" she said, before she could stop herself. But, surprisingly, he laughed.

"I'm not patronizing you, Rose. You're just asking me dumb questions."

"Fine! I have a question for you. Why are you looking up kids' school records?"

The smile disappeared from his face.

"Don't have a smart-ass comeback for that, do you."

"No," he said, "I don't. But I'm still not sure why you care what I'm doing."

"I don't care what you're doing, unless it's hurting people."

"What?" he said, really taken aback now. "How am I hurting people?"

She stared at him, really looked into his eyes, her heart in her mouth. She said, "I know exactly what you're up to. I just want your side of the story."

His eyes darted away. She had him. He stood, took the wine off the table. "If that's true," he said, "then you should know it's absolutely none of your business. You need to back off."

He leaned down, so his face was close to hers, and for an instant, crazily, she thought he might be about to kiss her.

"Understand? Stay out of it."

Then he was gone. Leaving her sitting alone in the bar, her heart hammering, until the front door opened, and Mia appeared.

"You're early!" she said.

17

The next day, when three o'clock swung around, Rose was waiting by the school gates. She always liked these seconds just before the bell rang—where the school yard was silent, the play equipment empty except for a lost hat and forgotten lunch box, and you could smell the dried-out grass on the oval. She leaned against the wire gate, letting the edges imprint patterns on her forearm.

The bell rang, and instantly, everything changed. There were yells and shouts as the tiny people exploded from the building. It was crazy to think that she'd gone to this school once. She had been one of those tiny people. She spotted Laura before Laura saw her. Her sister was walking with a group of other little girls, all swinging their backpacks and giggling. Then Laura looked up and caught sight of her. There was nothing like seeing her little face light up, to have her run toward Rose and charge her with a hug that almost pushed her off her feet, to make Rose forget whatever was making her feel like shit.

"I was thinking maybe we'd go to the library?" she said

when she caught her balance. Laura grinned up at her, her chin pressing into Rose's stomach a little too hard.

"Just us? Or do Scott and Sophie have to come too?"

Rose looked around and saw the two of them already on their way home, mucking around and not even noticing Laura wasn't behind them.

"Just us!"

Near where Scott and Sophie were walking, she noticed someone who shouldn't have been there. He stood out. A man in a sea of mothers. It took half a second before she recognized him; she was slowed by the improbability of him being there at all. Will. When she'd sneaked out of the tavern she was sure he had still been in his room, but there he was, standing next to the footpath as the kids barged their way past him. He was looking around, at the kids and their mothers, intently. He didn't appear to even see Rose, but she couldn't help but wonder if he'd followed her.

Journalist Stalked by Graphic Designer. It didn't sound right. He wasn't here for her. She didn't think he was a predator; he couldn't be. But why else would he leave the dolls? And, more important, how could she prove it?

Laura was jerking her hand. "Come on, come on," she was saying, trying to pull Rose toward Union Street.

Rose had felt guilty about being so tactless with Will. Now she only wished she had pushed harder.

"Rose!" yelled Laura, and he looked up. Locked eyes with her. He nodded to her, not embarrassed or caught out, just nodded at her and looked away.

As they strolled toward the library, Laura kept looking up and smiling at her. They held hands and walked slowly, Laura talking in a loop about some kid at school, Rose barely listening because she was thinking about Will.

"Boo!"

Something jumped out at her and Laura, and they both gasped. It was one of those goddamn paper-plate kids.

"Go away! You're so annoying!" Laura yelled.

They ran away fast, giggling. The one who had yelled out at them looked back, and Rose saw his mask. This one had been colored in blue, with big orange eyebrows above the circular eye holes. Creepy. The kid looked about ten.

"I hate it when they do that," Laura said, grumpily, before continuing her story. Rose hoped neither Scott nor Sophie would start playing with the paper-plate kids. She didn't care what Mia thought; they really were weird looking.

As they walked past the burned-down courthouse on Union Street, Laura stopped talking abruptly. Rose didn't blame her. The place was an eyesore and creepy as hell.

"That's where Benny died," Laura told her.

"I know," she said. "Does it still make you sad?"

Laura nodded.

Even though Ben was thirteen, he used to play with all the younger kids after church. They had run around the churchyard, giggling madly, getting their good clothes dirty. He had given Laura a piggyback and she had told him she would marry him. When he died, Rose hadn't known how to explain it to Laura. No one had. Poor Father had got stuck with the task. That day in church was horrible. All the little kids were crying. There was a big photograph of Ben at the front, a child-sized coffin with only ashes inside.

She squeezed Laura's hand. "He's happy now—he's playing in heaven."

"I wish he'd come back and play with me as well."

"Hey, Laura," she said and squatted down next to her. "Last one to the library is a rotten egg!"

She bounced up and started running; Laura ran after her, squealing. She slowed down and let Laura overtake her.

"When did you get so fast?" she said, pretending to puff, as they got to the library entranceway.

"You're just a big old slow coach!" Laura told her, taking her hand again and leading her into the hush of the library.

Everything in the library was paneled in pine. They didn't have air-conditioning, just a set of ceiling fans pushing around the hot air, but Rose's skin already felt the relief of being out of the sun. Even though it wasn't a beautiful place, there was something about the library that she loved. There was so much knowledge, everywhere. Displays of new books were near the entrance, their pages white and their corners crisp and unbent. The place smelled of lemony air freshener, but behind that it still had the faint pong of sweaty bodies. Laura headed straight for the children's section, which was piled high with red-and-blue beanbags. Most of them were taken, with mothers reading quietly to their kids, most of them younger than Laura. Rose couldn't help but notice that some of the mothers were younger than Rose herself. She vaguely recognized their faces from the years below her in high school.

In the corner was Mrs. Hane. She sat with Lily on her lap, reading a picture book in silence. Rose hadn't thought it would be possible for that woman to shut up, even in the library. Laura was running around, collecting books.

"I'll be back in a sec," Rose told her quietly, hoping Mrs. Hane wouldn't notice her there.

Her fingers brushed across the spines of the books in the fiction sections, each one of them containing so many stories, so many ideas, that she probably would never read. Then she reached the Fs and slid the title she wanted off the shelf. *Birdsong*. The book Will had been reading. She wanted to read the same words that he was, see the same story that was playing out in his head.

After that, she went straight for the psychology section. It was upstairs, in the small mezzanine of the library. The sun streamed in through the window, lighting up the spines of the thick books. There wasn't much there, unfortunately, only half the length of one shelf. She was hoping there might be something about criminals, something that might help her understand why Will was doing what he was doing and what he might do next. Luckily, one of the few books bore the title *The Criminology of Major Cases: from Al Capone to the Zodiac.* That was probably the closest she would get.

Rose put the books under her arm and took them back to the children's section. She sat down next to Laura, who had luckily chosen the beanbag farthest from Mrs. Hane and her daughter. Laura put her head on Rose's shoulder, a copy of *Possum Magic* in her hands. Rose opened the criminology book to page one and began to read.

When Rose woke in the tavern motel room the next morning, she felt sick. She looked over at the time. It was past midday. Fuck. She shouldn't be here now. She jumped out from between the thin sheets, took her notebook off the bedside table and pushed it under the pillow, kicked her bag under the bed and started smoothing down the covers.

She ran out of the room, smack into Will.

"Sorry!" she yelped. "I was just cleaning that room."

He looked at her and then into the room. He wasn't buying it. He was going to ask her if she'd been sleeping here. It would be so humiliating. *Don't ask. Please don't.*

"I'd kill for a coffee—do you guys have any?" he asked.

She laughed, a nervous false laugh. "I'll see what I can find."

Walking toward the bar, he followed one step behind her.

He knew she was onto him—what the hell was she doing here alone with him? It felt safe enough when there was a locked door between them, but now she felt incredibly vulnerable. He was probably a psycho.

"I should go," she said, as they reached the bar.

"What about my coffee?"

Her eyes flicked between him and the front door.

"I'm sorry, Rose," he said. "I shouldn't have snapped at you the other day. I was being an arsehole."

"You were," she said.

"Sorry." He smiled. His face was softer than she'd ever seen it. She looked at him slowly, trying to decide if he meant it. As long as she didn't let him get between her and the door, she'd be okay.

She went to the fridge, letting the cold air inside wake her up a little, then took two cans from the shelf. She clunked one can of Coke in front of Will, then hesitated, not sure if she was meant to be the waitress or not right now. If she sat with him, she'd still be closer to the door than to him. Though she'd be close enough that if he lunged at her, she wouldn't stand a chance.

"Sit," he said.

She sat. Instead of looking him in the eye, she watched the condensation drip down the side of the can on the table.

"You know, I heard noises last night," he said. "It sounded like footsteps. Like someone was coming in and out."

She opened her mouth to retort, but noticed the corners of his lips twitching.

"Rats," she said. "Big ones."

"They must be really huge," he said.

"They are."

Rose laughed, and then out of nowhere, she felt her chin wobble. Things had got so fucked up, so quickly. She didn't even know what she was doing anymore. But no, not now. She couldn't cry in front of him! What was she doing? She put a hand over her face.

"I won't tell your boss," he said.

Her face heated up; this was so humiliating. She took a swig of her Coke as an excuse to break eye contact. Gulping down the cold syrupy liquid.

He leaned over the table and she froze, but he was moving too slowly for it to be an attack. He softly put a warm hand on the side of her face. His eyes were so close to hers.

"It's going to be okay," he said.

Then he stood up, took his Coke and went back toward his room. Rose watched him go, still feeling his touch on her cheek. She stared down at the wet ring left by his can on the table. She dipped her finger in it and slid a line through the empty circle.

18

On Tuesday, Frank couldn't wait for his date with Rose. It had been a horrible day at work and he shouldn't be taking the night off, but there was no way he was going to stand up Rose.

"What are you doing in there, Francis?"

"Nothing."

"Nothing has taken you half an hour! You know I have a weak bladder."

"Sorry, Ma."

Frank was inches from the bathroom mirror, so close his nose was almost touching the glass. His fingertips were slick with gel as he tried to navigate his hairline. Thanks to his Italian heritage, his hair was still thick and dark. He was far from bald, but still, he could see at least a centimeter more of his forehead than he used to.

He stood up on the toilet seat to get a look at himself from head to toe in the small mirror. Not bad. When he sucked in his gut, he looked even better, but there was nothing to be done about that. His stomach was already fizzing with nerves.

"Frankie?"

He sighed, squirted on a little more cologne and then

opened the bathroom door. His mother clapped a hand over her mouth dramatically.

"*Cuore mio!* Who is the special girl? Is it the barmaid?"

Frank couldn't help but grin. He let his mother, who was even shorter than him, wrap her arms around him, enjoying her old-lady smell. Her steel-wool hair scraped against his cheek.

"You look brilliant."

"Thanks, Ma."

"Remember, don't bring up the case, okay, mate?" Frank said to Bazza as they drove toward Eamon's.

"Yeah, course," Bazza said, hardly listening.

If Baz ruined this, he'd kill him. The dolls case was the one thing he didn't want to talk about. Before, it might have been okay. But now Rose was getting articles published in that rag, he had to watch his mouth. That last article had not been helpful to him. The calls to the station had doubled the day it came out. Now that it was newsworthy, the parents of those little girls felt like every goddamn paranoid theory was worth his time. The squad was searching the records of every single person who hadn't been born in Colmstock, just to be sure there were no creeps who'd slipped in while they hadn't been watching. The constant phone calls were making the process much slower than it should have been. It was doubling his workload. As long as they steered clear of the topic, tonight should go fine. The problem was, something happened to Frank when he was around Rose. If she asked him questions, it would be hard for him to resist answering her. Hard to resist telling her things that would make her look at him that same way she had at her house. Like he could be her protector.

He pulled into the tavern parking lot and reached down to unclip his seat belt. Baz didn't move.

"Coming?" Frank asked him.

"Yeah," he said, still not moving. "I'm a bit nervous, mate."

Frank leaned back in the seat. "It's me that should be nervous."

"Not really," Bazza said. "I mean, it was Rose that asked you out. Mia probably only agreed to it so Rose didn't have to come alone."

Frank patted Bazza's shoulder. "Suck it up," he said. "If she doesn't like you already, just win her over."

He got out of the car and walked up toward Eamon's, allowing himself a look at the station. Through the window, he could see the activity going on inside and felt another pang of guilt for not being in there himself. The dolls case had stepped up a notch. The psycho had sent them a note last night, and it had proved their worst fears about his intentions. They had a real sicko on their hands, and Frank had to find him before he made good on what he'd promised in his letter.

Frank and Bazza sat on the stools at Eamon's. They faced outward, toward Mia, who was sitting on the edge of one of the tables. The rest of the seats were still upside down on the tabletop. Frank took another look at his watch.

"Don't worry, Frank. She's always late," Mia said.

"I didn't say I was worried," Frank barked. His heart was already starting to slip. He would not be able to take it if Rose stood him up.

"You did in the car on the way here."

"Shut up, Baz."

Mia's laugh tinkered around the bar. Their voices didn't reach all the way to the bathroom of room two, where Rose was blow-drying her hair.

All day, she'd been feeling a strange combination of dread and excitement. This was going to be so awkward. Then again, there was a strange curiosity inside her that she was trying hard not to think about. It was like having a chance to take a peek at another life. The life that everyone in town seemed to expect of her. To marry Frank, to stay in town. To have a family and never leave. She shivered—sometimes she was sure she'd rather die.

But other times, when the battle was just too hard, she couldn't help but think about how much easier that would be. To give up. To live a quiet, easy life of regret and keep her dreams as dreams.

Tonight, since she was pretty sure Frank and Bazza would pay, it would just be nice to have a proper dinner.

All day, she had lain on her bed reading Will's book *Birdsong*. She wanted to understand him, know if it was possible for him to leave those dolls. There might be a clue in there. Like maybe it was some kind of weird social experiment he was doing, or a strange art project. He was from the city, after all. The book didn't help, but she was surprised at how romantic it was. She imagined him reading about the longing the character felt for the woman he loved but couldn't have.

She had made an effort for tonight. Being homeless had made her want to look good, look polished, perhaps to prove to herself that this was not the kind of person she was. She had put on a nice-looking dress and even some lipstick. Now she was using the dodgy old blow-dryer that was attached to the bathroom wall to style her hair in loose waves. She bit back a swear word as the blow-dryer zapped her. *Stupid thing!* Rose returned it back to its cradle on the wall and ran her fingers through her hair. It was good enough.

Rose circled around the back. As she stepped up toward the front door, she could hear Mia's voice. "You might want to wash off some of that cologne."

"Huh?" she heard Frank say.

She took a breath and opened the door to the tavern.

"Hi." She smiled at them.

"Hi!" Frank jumped down off the stool, took a step toward her, then froze. Oh, God. This was going to be worse than she'd thought. She'd never seen him with so much gel in his hair; it was actually reflecting the blues and reds of the beer signs.

Mia looked between them. "Shall we go?"

"Yeah."

They all piled into Frank's car, he and Bazza in their normal seats and Rose and Mia in the back. Rose was already regretting this. It was so awkward. The way Frank had looked at her, like she was beautiful. It made her wish she had never got dressed up; that she'd never agreed to any of this in the first place. She turned to Mia, who smiled weakly at her. Obviously, Mia knew what she was thinking.

She tried to forget where she was. Instead, she thought about all the cons and killers who had sat where she was sitting now, their hands handcuffed behind them. All of them with stories that she would have loved to have known. She stared out the window as they passed the bus station. There was a bus waiting there, one that was going to the city. Soon, she would be on that bus.

They paused at the corner of the parking lot of Milly's Café, a large squat white restaurant that sold burgers and chips that were actually pretty good. The sound of the indicator filled the car, click-clock, click-clock, click-clock. It sounded strange. Mia turned to look at Rose.

"Stop it," Frank muttered, and the indicator noise stopped abruptly.

They turned into the parking lot.

"I'll park close. Don't want you dolls walking too far in those heels," he said.

Rose wanted to roll her eyes; she wasn't even wearing heels. "We're fine."

"There's one!" Mia said, pointing to a spot right next to the entrance. As Frank pulled in, the strange indicator noise started up again. Rose leaned forward in her seat and could see Baz clicking his tongue.

"It's you!"

Mia burst out laughing; Bazza started giggling.

Frank gave her an apologetic look and she smiled tightly in return.

Rose dipped her last bite of hamburger into the ketchup and stuffed it into her mouth. She hadn't eaten anything that day apart from the bag of chips she'd pinched from the tavern. Chewing, she savored the salty sweetness of it before she swallowed. It was the first proper meal she'd had in a while, and it made her stomach feel stretched. Although, given the opportunity, she wouldn't have turned down another course. Their plates were all empty now except for a single fry in the basket in the middle of the table that everyone was too polite to take.

"Last fry! Do you want it, Baz?" Mia said, smiling.

"No. You have it."

He wanted it. Rose could see it written all over his face.

Mia could too, it seemed. "Open up," she said. He obliged her and she threw the chip into his mouth. Disgusting. Why was Mia playing the wide-eyed idiot for this guy? Throughout their meal she had moved closer and closer to him. Now she was basically in his lap, laughing every time he made some dumb-as-fuck joke.

Frank cleared his throat and looked at her. Unlike the other two, they were sitting as far apart as possible in the small booth. Or rather, Rose was sitting as far from him as possible.

"So how long have we got you before you blow this town?" he asked Rose.

"I think it'll be a while yet."

"That's good." He beamed. "If Steve's plan goes ahead, and the shale mine opens back up, then things might be different around here."

"How likely do you think that is though?" Mia asked.

"It's possible," Frank said. "It's all about the crude oil prices. If they keep rising then it could happen. They reopened one in Brazil last year. The surveyor is coming next month, so we'll see."

"That would be so amazing," Mia said, then, looking at her, "I don't think it's enough to keep Rosie in town though."

Rose shrugged. "Journalism is hard to crack into. Just because they published one thing I wrote doesn't really mean anything."

"I dunno. I hate to say it, but you're a great writer," he said, and she beamed at him, hoping he really meant it, that he wasn't just using it to try to get in her pants.

"They are getting her to write another one," Mia said proudly. "They think she's great too."

Rose wanted to change the subject; she hadn't told Mia about the latest rejection. It was something she was trying her hardest not to think about.

"Yeah, maybe. Any new developments?" she asked.

"Off the record?" Frank said with a wink.

"Of course."

"Nothing new to report, I'm afraid."

Bazza looked at him, confused. "What about the note?"

"Baz!" yelled Frank.

"What note?" asked Mia, as Baz apologized.

Frank's eyes ping-ponged between them. He looked a little overwhelmed.

"Why don't we go for a walk?" suggested Rose.

She slid out of the booth and walked toward the front door.

The air felt hot and thick compared to the air-conditioning inside. The sun had all but set, leaving the sky a steely pink color.

"Those two seem to be getting on. Thought we should give them a minute," she said to Frank as he kept pace beside her.

He stuffed his hands into his pockets. "Look, I know you want to get out of here and be some big-shot city journo, but—"

Rose stopped in her tracks and stared him down, annoyed.

"Don't forget my sister got one of those dolls."

He dropped his eyes from hers. "I know. I'm sorry."

"Good," she said.

"I wouldn't worry—I think it's just a hoax. But still, I can't talk about—"

"Did I ask?" she said and kept walking. He smiled at her and she wondered how she'd look to him right now, the pink sky broad around them. She was going to find out more about the investigation, and she was sure if she asked the right questions, he'd tell her. But first she just walked with him toward the horizon, enjoying the silence.

19

"I always put my foot in it," Bazza said, staring at the dirty dishes on the table in a sulk.

"Do you think he's mad?" Mia asked.

"Yeah. He's always getting mad. Especially around her. For some reason, when I know I have to be careful I always end up blurting out the wrong thing."

The guy was so cute. He was big, probably twice her size, but Mia felt a strange wave of protectiveness over him.

"Don't worry—I do that too." It was true. Often, when she got home late from work, she wouldn't be able to sleep, worrying that she'd offended someone or said something wrong. She began brushing at the crumbs on the table, pinching the stray bits of salt between her fingers and putting them onto the plate. She noticed him watching her, and stopped it. She was so used to cleaning up. If it wasn't at Eamon's then it would be at home. The idea of leaving a mess for someone else felt foreign.

But she wasn't on this date to clean. So she brushed the salt on the plastic of the booth and very lightly touched his arm. Usually, Baz wore T-shirts. But tonight, he'd worn a pale blue button-up shirt, rolled up to just past the elbows. His forearms were brown and strong. Mia ran her finger over his cuff. He looked up at her and smiled. They'd been mucking around this whole time, overplaying the date thing. She'd fed him and flirted outrageously. But now the moment felt real. It felt charged.

"Why'd you ever agree to go out with an oaf like me?" he said, still smiling. But he meant it, she could tell.

Mia let her hand slip down over his starchy shirt. She let her fingers lightly touch the side of his elbow. His skin was rough, but so warm. She leaned toward him and kissed him softly on the corner of his mouth, his lips delicate against hers, her chest pounding.

"Wow," he whispered.

He put his big hands on either side of her face, cupping her cheeks, and brought her to him again, kissing her so softly it was almost unbearable. Then he beamed, actually beamed, like there was light coming out of him. He looked so exposed, so vulnerable, she almost had to turn away.

"I've wanted this for so long."

He meant her. He wanted her. No one had ever wanted her before. She leaned over, kissed him again, let her lips part slightly this time, feel the wetness of his mouth on hers. His hand left her face, glided down her arm. The soft muscle of his tongue went into her mouth, brushing gently against hers.

"Break it up," said Frank roughly.

Baz's body snapped away from hers. She looked around, hand instinctively going to her lips and brushing away the traces of his saliva, still warm. Rose grinned at her and slid into the booth, followed by Frank. He was smiling too. Maybe she and Baz hadn't been the only ones to have a moment.

A waitress came over. "Any more drinks, Frank?"

Frank looked around at them. Mia shrugged. It wasn't like the date was going to get any better.

"Just the bill, thanks, Molly," he said.

Underneath the table, Baz took her hand. His fingers laced between her own, making her heart beat faster again.

"You're Rose Blakey, right?" the waitress asked.

Rose looked surprised. "Yes?"

The waitress just smiled at her and walked away.

"Famous already," Frank said, a hint of annoyance under the teasing tone.

Rose nudged her as they walked toward the car. "How'd you go?" she whispered.

"Awesome," Mia said. "And you?"

Rose just shrugged, her eyes focused on something in the distance. Trust Rose, evasive as always. Mia clicked open the car door, smiling at Baz over the roof.

"What's that?" Rose said.

"What?" Mia followed her eyeline. All she could see were the sprawling white brick houses, ugly fences, the road sparkling in the low evening sun.

"That." Rose pointed, and Mia saw it. A whisper of gray snaking from behind a terra-cotta roof.

"Fuck," said Frank, who'd seen it now too. "Get in."

They jumped in the car, the four doors snapping closed. No time to even put their seat belts on as Frank reversed, then sped around a corner, jolting them toward each other, banging shoulders.

"Might be just burned toast, someone with their window open," Mia said.

"No," Frank muttered, "it's him. The bastard's at it again."

The car sped around another corner. Mia's elbow hit the armrest at an awkward angle and she rubbed at it. She didn't want to be part of this. Whoever it was, she didn't want to know. She looked to Rose, who had the window open and was craning her neck to look out, eyes bright and focused. Probably already writing an article in her head. But Mia wished they could just go back to the restaurant.

Too late now. The smoke was thicker already, and as they got closer Mia could smell it. Sharp and toxic, burning her throat. She wrapped her fingers around her rose quartz. The brakes squealed and the hand brake crunched and Frank was out of the car, running, Rose and Bazza hot on his heels.

Mia's hand shook as she opened the door. She didn't want to go, not a bit, not at all. But she didn't want to be left alone either. She ran after them, toward the gray smoke down the side of the house, hoping everyone was okay, thinking of poor Ben Riley. The smoke festered down her throat.

It was a bin. A green plastic recycling bin, already half melted. Splitting at the sides and collapsing into itself. Rose was coughing, viscous and hacking, bent over at the waist. She'd got too close, as always. Baz was running to the garden hose, turning the tap. Holding the orange nozzle tight in his hand and spraying it into the bin, which began smoldering straightaway. Frank was banging on the back door of the house.

"Anyone in there?"

And beside Mia was a sound, breaking sticks, a voice hissing, "Shut up!"

She turned into the spindly bushes. A white face stared back at her. A white moon with dark crater eyes. She screamed, jumping back, hand to mouth.

"Mia!" Baz dropped the hose and ran to her as the face pulled back into the bush.

"He's in there!" she squealed. Frank was beside her, peering into the leaves, listening.

"We've got you," he panted.

Then the crunch of sticks, farther up now, toward the back

fence. Two kids jumped out, no older than eleven. Their paper plates bobbed over their faces as they ran, high-jumped onto the fence and scrambled over it. One turned back, straddling the palings with his little Bambi legs, stuck his middle finger up and jumped down the other side.

20

"I can walk you in?" Frank asked, already unclipping his seat belt.

"It's okay!" Rose said, snapping open her car door. "Thanks! See you guys later."

Bazza smiled, and Mia said "'Bye" quietly, her head on his shoulder. They'd had to hang around the scene for an hour and now they were all exhausted.

Rose hopped out of the car and walked toward the house, then turned and waved so he'd drive away. Turning back to the door, she put her hand into her bag, as though fishing for keys.

Frank's car turned the corner, and she retreated back down the path, hoping her mother hadn't heard anything. Standing out the front, she surveyed her house. How humiliating that she was saving face by pretending she still lived here. It looked like such a trash heap. The paint was peeling off the bricks, the grass had grown long and dry, and there were old broken bits of furniture and an old dog kennel down the side of the house that Rob had promised to take care of. Their dog had died six years ago. Still, this was preferable by multitudes to admitting she was squatting at the tavern.

The sky was gray now, but the air was still heavy. Dusk was when mosquitoes were out in full force; already she felt the tiny prickle on her arm. She swatted it, and her own blood smeared across her skin. The bricks of each house she walked past were exhaling the heat from the day. She quickened her pace. It wasn't safe to walk the streets at this time, and wearing a dress made her feel like a target. As she reached the corner she almost tripped; she hadn't been looking where she was going and she hadn't noticed the corner of a rolled-up newspaper sticking out of the dead grass of a house. She pushed it off the footpath with her foot, noticing that this house was in worse shape than hers. The grass was almost knee length, pushing out onto the path to the front door, which was littered with copies of the paper, still rolled and unopened. Rose considered taking one—this person obviously wasn't reading them—but in the gloom she couldn't see which were the most recent. She kept moving.

Before they'd got in the car, Frank had taken her aside. He'd asked her not to write about the fire, or the paper-plate kids they'd seen at the scene.

"They might not even be connected," she'd told him.

"Exactly," he'd said. Neither of them were convincing. They both knew that, one way or another, they were definitely connected. If the kids hadn't lit the fire themselves, they'd definitely seen who did. She considered asking Frank if he'd tell her when he found out the answer to that, but he'd probably say no. It didn't matter anyway. She had a better story.

Approaching the tavern, she felt relieved to be back. The date had gone fairly well, all things considered, but she knew for sure now that it would never happen with Frank. It would be a good way out, the easiest way, but she would never be in love with him. Being in a relationship that one-sided would be cruel. It felt wrong.

Rose took the back stairs and unlocked the main door. It was nice not to have to worry too much about being quiet now. She wasn't afraid of Will anymore either. Maybe she should be, but she wasn't. Walking down the hallway, she looked down at the slit under his door. The light was on. He was still awake. She imagined what he was doing. Lying on the bed, shoes off, reading glasses on, his eyes flicking across each line of his book, the world inside it filling up his head. Or maybe brushing the hair of a porcelain doll. She sniggered as she put her key in the lock.

"What's funny?"

She jumped. He was leaning against his door frame in a white singlet.

"What?"

"You were laughing."

"No, I wasn't. Must have been the ghost."

He smiled at her, the whispers of lines around his eyes crinkling deeper. "Where've you been?"

She raised her eyebrows. "On a date."

"Really?"

"Yep."

"With that fat cop who's always staring at you?"

"He's not fat!" she said.

He shrugged. "If you say so."

She let her door swing open but didn't go in. Instead, she leaned against the wall next to it.

"What have you been doing?"

"Nothing. Just reading."

They smiled at each other.

"So did he have anything to say about those dolls?" he asked, and the moment was broken.

She stared at him. "Why do you care?"

He put up his hands, exasperated. "I'm just asking."

"You seem pretty interested." She stepped toward him.

He shook his head. "You're the one that's writing about them. I'm guessing that's why you went out with the guy. Hoping for the inside story?"

"No!"

"Yeah, okay," he said. His hand went to his doorknob. Before she knew what she was doing, Rose's own hand shot out, hitting the wood with a thunk, stopping him from closing the door.

Will looked from her hand to her. "What are you doing?"

"What are *you* doing?"

"I thought you said you already knew?"

"I do." She swallowed. "I just want to know why."

He pulled at the door, but she locked her elbow. He'd have to push her out of the way if he wanted to close it.

"This is really none of your business," he said, his voice raised. She could feel the heat trapped in his room, smell his sweat.

"It is my business," she said.

"How? You think you're important because you're a cheap hack now rather than just a waitress?"

"Fuck off!" she said, getting in his face. "You gave one to my sister, so yeah, I think it is my business, you piece of shit."

"What?" he spit. "You're not even making sense."

"I won't tell the cops it's you," she lied. "I just need to know why. Why do you cut their hair so that they look like the kids?"

He looked at her, eyes narrowed. Then he did the last thing she thought he would do. He laughed, the crinkles around his eyes reappearing.

"What?" she said.

"You think I'm leaving those dolls?"

She looked at him carefully. Was this a trick?

"I'm not." There was a chuckle in his voice. "I'm really not."

She took a step closer to him, trying to see in his eyes if he was lying.

"Rose. I'm not leaving those dolls."

His eyes were clear. He was close enough that if she leaned forward, she could kiss him. So, without thinking about it, she did. She took her hand from his door and clasped the back of his neck, pulling him toward her. His mouth was on hers. He tasted hot and sweet. His fingers reached around her waist and he pulled her to him, pressed her against his chest, so that he fell against the door frame. Something warm and wonderful fizzled down from her belly. He breathed in heavily through his nose. Then he pulled his head to the side.

"I shouldn't," he said, his face still so close to hers, his arms still around her. She stepped back, and his hand fell away.

"Why?"

"Sorry," he said, not looking at her. Then, "I'm really not leaving those dolls."

He pulled the door closed.

She stood in the hallway alone. Her lips still hot and tasting of him. Her insides twisted. What an idiot. Why the hell had she kissed him? He didn't want her. He was trying to be nice to her and she'd literally thrown herself onto him.

The door to her room was still hanging open. She slammed it shut behind her as she went in. She'd start writing her new article tonight. She had the note, and with that they'd have to publish her.

21

First thing the next day, Frank told the teachers he wanted to interview the kids about the dolls. The principal agreed hastily, letting Frank use her office for the *little chats*, as he'd called them, which took all day. The publicity Rose had generated had come good for something. People were scared now. Frank could work with scared people; it meant more trust in him, less questions.

The kids weren't scared though, and that surprised Frank. He'd expected the little shits to be pissing their school shorts. A real cop questioning them one-on-one. Telling them that if they lied, they'd be in real, serious trouble. He barely got them to blink. A few got slightly pale, but that was it. He'd spoken to six kids already, put a real lean on them. Nothing. Now he had the Hanes' kid in front of him. Denny. He wasn't even looking at Frank, just picking at the scab on his knee.

"Are you worried for your sister? Getting one of those dolls?" he asked. Denny shrugged. Kid couldn't care less.

"Look, I'll level with you, man-to-man. If you tell me about the fires I won't tell your parents, promise."

Denny was still more interested in the scab. He'd got his

fingernail under it and was slowly levering the dark red mound from his skin.

This wasn't working. If he was going to get anywhere with these kids he needed to start thinking like them. He tried to remember his own time as a kid at this school. When it was all about rumors, and who was mates with who, and what girl wanted to hold your hand on the playground.

"I know it was you—Sam told me."

That got Denny's attention.

"Which Sam? Sam Hodgkins or Sam Long?"

Frank had only picked the name Sam because it was so common.

"He said it was all your idea."

"Nah!" yelled Denny.

"That's what he said."

"As if! I'm not even in."

"Why not?"

"It only counts if the police get called! Mine went out after five minutes. Ask anyone!"

The confusion showed on Frank's face; he saw Denny read it.

"What do you mean 'in'?"

Denny just shrugged and went back to his scab.

What he'd just said sounded like some sort of gang initiation. It was the kind of thing you heard about happening in big cities. Troubled teens in turf wars over drugs and violence. But this was a tiny town and this boy wasn't even twelve years old yet.

"You have to light a fire to be part of the group?" he asked and got no answer. "Do you mean the kids who wear those stupid masks are like a gang?"

Denny just sniggered, staring down at his knee. It was laughable, stupid, ridiculous. But Frank had noticed it, seen it with his own eyes. That swagger those kids had, that careless, self-assured way of walking that didn't sit right on their narrow shoulders. These kids had done it. They'd lit all those fires, burned down the courthouse, killed Ben Riley, and what the hell was Frank going to be able to do about it?

Denny's scab tore from his skin, dribbling a watery line of pus.

Frank left his car at the primary school and walked back to the station. It was rare for him to do this. But today, he needed some air. There was a lot to digest.

Right now, he was the only one who knew what the hell was going on, and he was happy with that. Once he filled the rest of the squad in, everyone would have an opinion. Before that, he needed to get his head around all this.

Instead, he kept thinking about his own childhood in the town. It wasn't something he thought about often, but whenever he did it made him smile. Even as a kid, he'd loved this place. Loved the smell of it, loved the pavement under his feet, the constant heat in the air and sweat on his brow. Colmstock was the only thing he loved more than Rose.

He had no idea what he was going to do to fix this, to fix what felt so broken it was incomprehensible. But he had to fix it, somehow. Because this was his home, his world, and it meant more to him than anything.

At Eamon's that night they were all drinking, hard. Frank, Bazza, Jonesy and Steve. Lucky Father was there; he'd probably be playing cabbie tonight for all of them.

"God, they're always doing that these days," Mia said, staring at the small group of wretched-looking men. "This place is no fun anymore."

"Was it ever fun?" Rose asked.

"Yeah! Friday nights here could be great! Don't you remember?"

Rose did, vaguely. When she'd first started working here, before it had got so depressing, when it still felt temporary.

The place had been full on a Friday. People would play darts, do shots at the bar. Rose would sometimes join them. But now that she'd become such an epic fuckup, there didn't seem to be any reason to celebrate anything, least of all a Friday.

Rose had sent another article in to the *Star* last night; she'd sneaked into Jean's office to type it up and email it. It was still early, but having had no response, the low feeling of rejection had already settled on her shoulders.

She didn't want to stay at the tavern anymore. Not with that arsehole across the hall. Plus, she was bound to get caught eventually.

Wannabe Journalist Discovered Squatting, Becomes Homeless and Jobless. No one would want to read about that. The panic had soured in her stomach now. She no longer worried about the future, about how the hell she was going to get through the rest of her life. Now she only worried about how she was going to get through the day.

Mia was beaming at her, talking quickly and quietly about Bazza. Again. Rose tried to tune her out. She was sick of hearing about it. Licking her finger, she dug into the corner of the empty chip packet, trying to get the crumbs, letting Mia blabber on. As long as she only stole one packet a day, Jean probably wouldn't notice.

Finally, she'd had enough.

"The guy's a dipshit, Mia. Why do you fancy him so much?"

Mia's face went cold. "He's not."

"Why on earth would you want to settle down with someone like him? You'll be stuck here forever."

Mia shrugged tight shoulders.

"We're better than this place," Rose said, although sometimes she worried that Mia wasn't. Some of the shit Mia said sometimes, it was like she forgot that they were different. It was like she was just like every other idiot in this backward town.

"Not everyone is as smart as you," Mia said, voice stiff, eyes downcast.

"What do you mean? You think we aren't better than all this." Rose waved her hand around. At Eamon's, at Bazza.

"You're saying *we*, but you're just talking about yourself," Mia said, not looking at her.

"What do you mean?"

"I'm sick of hearing how stupid everyone is apart from you. You think you're better than everyone."

"And you're saying I shouldn't think that? That I'm not as good as the fucktards who come in here?" Rose's voice was hushed but she wanted to yell. Mia couldn't even look at her when she insulted her. But then Mia did look up, and her face was stony.

"Why are you whispering?" she asked, then, her voice raised, "If you really think that, say it. Say it loud enough for everyone to hear."

A few heads turned to look at them.

"Mia—"

"Thought so." Mia brushed past her and went into the kitchen. Rose scrunched up her chip packet and threw it into the bin. Of course, it missed and dropped down into the alcove behind it. Fuck.

She jolted the bin out of the way. No one had done it in years, and there were thick dust bunnies and bits of rubbish on the ground. Everything around her was always squalid and rank.

Clattering out the dustpan and brush, she squatted down. How could Mia be all right with this? All right with making the minimum wage cleaning out the crap behind rubbish bins on your hands and knees?

The balls of filth and dust were in clumps; she swept at them angrily. One of them flicked up into her face. It was a rat. Another fucking dead rat. She scooped it up with the dustpan, put it into the bin and walked back toward her room. They weren't meant to leave the bar unattended but who cared? The place was full of cops anyway.

She opened the door to her room, not even checking to make sure no one saw her, and slammed it behind her. Sitting on the floor in front of the bed, she put her head on her knees and took some deep breaths. Getting angry wasn't going to do shit. She'd put absolutely everything into her last article. If that wasn't good enough, maybe nothing would be.

She pulled her phone out, hoping and praying that somehow the *Star* had called her and she hadn't felt the buzz. Nothing. She refreshed her email. A new one appeared. Sent ten minutes ago from the *Star*. She knew that address. It was the one she'd got a rejection from last week. Fuck. She didn't want to open it. Fuck. She pressed down on the email. Scanning it, looking for the *unfortunately*, instead she saw the word *enthralled*. Her heart lifted and she took a deep breath and read it properly, from the beginning.

When Rose came back to the bar she was grinning. Mia was there with her back to her. She put her arms around Mia, rested her chin on her shoulder.

"Sorry. I'm a bitch. I know."

Mia didn't say anything. She was stiff.

"If you like Baz, that's all that matters. I just want you to be happy."

"He makes me happy."

"Good."

Rose let her go and grabbed a bottle of Bundy.

"Jean's doing the books," she said. "I miss Fridays too."

Mia didn't look at her.

"Enough with the somber bloody mood." The men looked up at Rose as she lined up some shot glasses. "Whatever's going on will still be there tomorrow."

Frank pushed his chair back, smiling at her in the new way. There was a confidence in his eyes now, a look of ownership. She would have to talk to him, and soon. Her new article would be run in the Sunday paper again. The *Star* seemed to believe that people liked light reading about potential pedophiles after church.

"Frank?" she said, rum hovering over the shot glass.

"All right. Why not."

She began filling up the line of glasses, knowing the others would agree if Frank did. The smell of the Bundy was strong when she got to the last glass. Steve Cunningham came to the bar for his straightaway. Like she had a few times before, she itched to ask him about how his family was dealing with the doll. But not with Frank right there.

"Shall I put apple juice in yours, Father?"

He smiled his wide, whiskered smile. "I'll stick with Coke."

Rose noticed Mia still wasn't looking very happy. She was picking at the gross dry skin around her fingernails, squeezing at a droplet of fresh red blood. Usually, Rose would nudge her and tell her to stop. But it didn't feel like that would go over well right now.

"Here." She slid the shot to Mia. "We can play darts later too if you want."

"Please, girls," Frank said, "I don't have time to deal with manslaughter right now."

Steve and Baz chortled a laugh; Rose raised an eyebrow. She did the shot, flinging her head back and letting the liquor burn down her throat, then went over to the board and pulled a dart out.

"I was just kidding."

"No, you weren't." She took three steps back, feeling all the eyes on her. She'd had seven years of practice, but still her heart pounded. She'd look so dumb if she missed. But somehow she knew she wouldn't. It was the success; it was like a drug. Making her feel confident, untouchable. It made her feel like she could do anything, like finally, it was all possible.

Leveling the dart above her shoulder, she flung it back and threw it evenly. It hit the board with a pop. Not quite in the center, but not far off.

"What were you saying?"

Before he could eat his words, Frank's cell phone rang. He answered it quickly and listened to the voice on the other end.

"Really?" His voice was surprised and—Rose was sure of it—his eyes flicked over to Steve Cunningham. "Right, okay. On my way."

Frank slipped his phone back in his pocket. He took his shot glass and swallowed the liquid in one easy gulp.

"Thanks." He sucked the liquor from his bottom lip and turned to go.

"Hang on one sec," she said. This wasn't going to be easy. His smile slumped, like he knew from the expression on her face what was coming. She came out from behind the bar and put a hand on his arm, guiding him away from the others.

"Thanks so much for yesterday," she began. "I had a great time."

He looked at his shoes, then back up to her. "I really have to go."

"I know, but—"

He turned and began walking away. "We'll talk later."

"I always break them."

CHILLING NOTE INTENSIFIES
PORCELAIN TERROR
by Rose Blakey

The police force of Colmstock was horrified to receive an anonymous note on Tuesday evening.

Unsigned and undated, the note is believed to have
been written by the unknown perpetrator who has
left a series of porcelain dolls on doorsteps, terror-
izing local families.

*I am not sick. I just like the little dolls. I always break
them. I see them and I want to collect them. I want to line
them up, so perfect and untouched. I want them to be perfect but I can't help it.*
—D.C.

The parents of the young girls who have received
dolls are duly concerned over the safety of their
families, some believing the police are not doing
enough to protect them. "It's enough to make you
sick," Jillian Hane, whose angel-faced six-year-
old daughter, Lily Hane, received a doll, stated.
"These are our children!"

There have been no arrests and no suspects in this
beguiling case. "They can't find a connection,"
said Lucie Hoffman, mother of another victim.
The Colmstock police have declined to comment
on any progress in apprehending this threat to the
most precious members of the local community.

22

Mia hadn't been able to sleep.

She'd put the television on, like she sometimes did, to replace the thoughts invading her brain with infomercials for blenders. Fighting with Rose was rare, and the few times it had happened Mia was always the first to apologize. She just couldn't bear the idea of Rose being angry with her.

It was church today, so she had to be up early. Her father couldn't come with her to church anymore. Before, he'd been able to make the journey from the car to the inside of the church with his cane. He no longer could. Or perhaps he just didn't want to.

"Rose was being a bit of a bitch last night," she told him, as she lifted a heaped spoon of mush into his mouth. "I don't know if maybe she's jealous of me and Baz or something."

He was sitting at the table with a tea towel around his neck. She was so used to the way he looked now, the way half of his face almost collapsed inward. This was her father. When she looked at the old photographs on the wall, it was the strong, good-looking man who appeared strange to her.

"She always talks to me like I'm some idiot pushover."

He put a hand on her arm. He couldn't speak anymore, but it didn't matter. She knew what he would say if he could.

"I know, don't talk myself down," she said. "I'm just getting so sick of her thinking she's above everyone, you know? I mean, we are all trying our hardest. What makes her so much better?"

She gave him another spoonful. "She thinks Baz is an idiot, but if things work out between me and him it'd make such a big difference for us, Baba. Things could be so much better."

He dropped his hand.

"Plus, he's gorgeous! Anyway, Rose is getting out of here. She is going to have this great big-city life, so can't she just let me enjoy the things I have? She keeps going on and on about us going together, but you know she's never actually asked me if that's what I want."

Mia got up to put the food back in the fridge and the spoon in the sink. One way or another, Rose was going to be leaving soon enough. Mia had to start thinking about how her life was going to work once she was gone. She checked her reflection in the glass door of the mirror, slipped some loose strands of hair behind her ears and turned back to her father.

"Do you need to go to the bathroom before I go?" she asked. He shook his head.

"Are you sure?"

He didn't look at her. Last week he'd said he hadn't, and when she'd come home from work she'd found him lying on the floor near the bathroom door, the back of his pants soiled.

She wiped his chin with the tea towel and smiled at him. She turned back to the television and switched it on to the sports channel.

"I'll come back straight after, okay? Rose can figure out her own way home," she said, then kissed him on the cheek and went out the door.

It was too early for church. She knew that. Mia was driving the opposite way, toward Rose's house. When she reached the lake, she took a sharp turn left.

She pulled into the dirt clearing. She left her car there and walked toward the metal fence. There was a gap around the side, where someone had pulled the wire away from the iron post. It was the same one she and Rose had used to slide through when they were kids. She could still fit, just.

Suicides were a dime a dozen around here, especially with young men. She didn't know why. Dave wasn't the first boy in their class to do it, and he hadn't been the last.

When she got to the mouth of the mine, she stopped. She squatted down in front of the black hole and closed her eyes. The air inside it was colder; if she concentrated she could feel cool whispers of a breeze on her cheeks.

There would have been a few seconds after he jumped where he was suspended, weightless, in the dark. She wondered, as she often did when she came here, if Dave had thought of her in those moments. If he had thought about the wedding that wouldn't happen, the faces of the children they'd never have. She wondered, if she were to jump now, if she'd think of Rose.

She hoped that she wouldn't. She hoped that in the seconds of nothingness before the final oblivion, she would appreciate the lightness. She would be able to know what it felt like not to have the heaviness that now seemed to be with her always. Even if just for an instant, she would know how it felt to be weightless.

Turning, she headed back toward her car. She didn't want to be late for church.

23

Now that she was no longer living at home, Rose didn't have to go to church. After all, she hadn't believed in God for a long time now. Somehow, it seemed beside the point. It would just feel wrong to sleep in on a Sunday, to not be there with everyone else.

The humidity was high today. Sweat prickled between her shoulder blades as she hurried down the road. She noticed the old woman she'd avoided outside the council building waiting by the pedestrian crossing. She was looking distressed as the cars zoomed past her. Part of Rose wanted to keep walking, but by the looks of things, the woman was never going to get to church if Rose didn't intervene.

"Do you need a hand?"

Instantly, the old woman took her arm with an iron grip. Why was it that these frail old ladies were so strong? She looked up at Rose; her eyes had a sheen behind the glasses like she might cry. Rose hoped she wouldn't.

"They just keep driving past. They aren't stopping," she said, staring up at Rose.

"They won't stop until you are actually on the road," she told her.

"Pardon?"

Rose held the woman's arm, and they took a step onto the road together. The cars stopped. Some inching forward impatiently as they began walking across. The woman's walking stick was made of a deep red wood, and it clunked against the road with each step they took.

"They always used to just stop if someone was waiting," the woman said. Rose wondered how long ago that had been. It definitely had never happened in her lifetime.

"I guess times have changed."

"Pardon?"

Rose raised her voice. "Times have changed!"

"No, no," the woman said, gripping her arm even tighter. "It's hearts. People's hearts have changed."

Rose noticed the tense knot of people outside the front of the church. Many of them were holding newspapers. Rose's breath caught. They were reading the *Star*. She dropped the old woman's arm.

"Thank you, darling," she said as Rose hurried toward the crowd.

The two women Rose had met with Mrs. Hane last Sunday stood at the edge of the crowd; as she got closer she could hear their conversation.

"I think I might faint."

"No!"

"Yes."

Rose snatched the paper from the woman's hands.

"How rude!" she clucked, but Rose ignored her. It was her article, on the cover. That was better than she could ever have hoped. Giddiness overtook her. It really was happening.

The cover. That meant something. Things would change. She needed to find Mia.

"You!"

Mrs. Cunningham marched toward her, pulling her husband behind her.

"You need to tell me, right now, what your game is!" Mrs. Cunningham was blustering and angry, almost stepping on Rose's toe as she got closer. Rose folded the paper carefully under her arm.

"My game?"

"Yes," she said, cheeks pink. "We don't need the whole state knowing about this. It's our problem, and we'll deal with it."

Steve smiled apologetically at Rose over his wife's head.

"Don't you have any respect for my husband? For Frank?"

"Hang on. That's not fair," said the woman whose paper Rose had snatched. "We have a right to know what's going on. The police should have made this public as soon as they got it. They are our children! We should know if there is a threat like this being made."

People around her nodded and Mrs. Cunningham plastered on a smile.

"Oh, don't worry, Fiona. I agree," she said to the woman, "but this girl is stirring up a storm. This is our town and we'll deal with these things our way."

"But if she hadn't written the article, we never would have even known to be worried. I would have let my—" the woman swallowed "—my poor, poor baby walk home from school on her own."

"No one would want to kidnap her, trust me," Mrs. Cunningham said, then turned back to Rose. "What I want to know is how on earth you got a copy of what that letter said."

Rose didn't like this woman. She'd always been a bitch.

"I can't reveal my sources."

"That's bullshit. You don't need to tell me, anyway. We all know how little sluts like you get what they want."

Just as Rose opened her mouth to retort, the crowd began to murmur.

"Oh, no. Have they seen it?"

"Surely they would have known."

People had twisted their gazes away, peering over heads to look at something on the other side of the crowd. Mrs. Cunningham turned to see, as did Rose. The Rileys had arrived, bringing along the heavy hush that seemed to follow them wherever they went. They were dressed for church, Mr. Riley in black trousers, Mrs. Riley in a knee-length dress the same blue as her eyes, their daughter, Carly, wearing a blouse buttoned right up to her chin. Rose tried to remember what they had been like before the fire. She'd been going to their grocery store her whole life. She remembered Ben. His big smile if he was behind the counter, stacking silver coins into towers. She tried to remember Mr. and Mrs. Riley's faces as they had looked then, but she couldn't. The idea of those mouths being bent into smiles seemed impossible.

Mr. Riley had a copy of the *Star* in his hands. Both he and his wife were reading her words on the front, their eyes flicking down the page. Rose knew the moment their eyes took in the note. Mrs. Riley looked away from the paper and into the crowd. There was fear all over her face, as though someone was about to leap out of the group and attack her. After pulling her daughter onto her hip, the two of them turned and walked back the way they'd come without saying a word.

The chatter of the crowd began to rise back to normal. Mrs. Cunningham turned back to Rose, shook her head then stalked off, Steve mouthing "Sorry" as he hurried behind her.

"That poor family," Rose heard the woman behind her say. "This is the last thing they need."

"What did she mean that no one would want to kidnap my daughter?"

"On top of everything they have already been through. What's the world coming to?"

"My daughter is gorgeous."

"I'm going to give Frank a piece of my mind," said the other.

"I think you'll have to line up."

Rose followed their gaze toward the parking lot. Mr. Hane was talking to Frank and Baz. He was almost unrecognizable from the man that she and Mia had spoken to a week ago. His face was red and twisted with anger as he got right up into Frank's face. The idea that he could be dangerous didn't seem so ludicrous now. Rose wished she could hear what he was saying, but they were too far away. Behind him, Mrs. Hane held Lily tightly in her arms. Next to her, Denny stared right back into Rose's eyes, his finger in his nose.

Rose turned her back; she didn't want Frank to catch her watching. She wished she'd had the chance to talk to him about all this last night. Mia was standing up near the doorway of the church, speaking to one of Bazza's brothers. Rose began to approach, but then Mia's eyes slid toward her and then looked away. Rose stopped. Mia must still be angry. This was stupid. She had so much to do; she didn't have time to hang around listening to one of Father's boring sermons. She left the churchyard, walking in the direction the Rileys had gone.

It took her about twenty minutes to get to their house. By the time she reached their door, she had sweated so much that her hair was sticking to her neck and her top was damp. She wanted to look professional, but there was no way she'd cool off out here. The air was heavy with humidity. Fanning her face with her hand, she knocked.

Mrs. Riley answered the door. Rose expected her to be surprised to see her, but her face stayed as vacant as before.

"Hi, I'm Rose. I wrote the article you read this morning. I was wondering if I could come in and we could talk about it?"

Mrs. Riley took her in, face emotionless. Then she turned. "It's the journalist," she said to someone in the other room. "She wants to come in."

"If it's an okay time?" Rose added to the side of Mrs. Riley's face.

"Okay," she heard a man's voice say, and Mrs. Riley stood aside.

"Thanks," she said, feeling the relief on her skin of being out of the sun.

Mr. Riley was sitting in the living room on the sofa, still in his church clothes. He stood and reached out to shake Rose's hand. His palm was cool against her clammy one. Embarrassed, she took her hand back and wiped it on her shorts.

"Take a seat," he said, and Rose took a small armchair near the door.

"Would you like a cold drink?" Mrs. Riley asked, her voice still so quiet that Rose had to strain to hear her.

"A water would be great, if that's okay?"

Mrs. Riley nodded and walked out of the room.

Rose hadn't been sure what to imagine. How the everyday domesticities of tragedy would appear. The house was similar in layout to the Hanes'. A small living room to one side of the front door, kitchen to the other. She presumed the bedrooms were farther down the hallway. She wondered if Ben's room was still the way it had been left.

Everything in the living room was clean and simple. The only real decoration was three framed photographs on the mantel. All three were of their daughter. Rose looked away; staring at them felt like intruding. It seemed strange that there were no photographs of Ben, but then, how was she to know what was strange in this situation. This couple had had to stand back while their son burned; how could she ever judge anything they did as strange. Mr. Riley was looking at his knees in front of him on the sofa. She was imposing. She shouldn't be here.

"I'm sorry if my article upset you this morning," she said to Mr. Riley.

He nodded. "It's okay."

"Frank didn't tell you about the note?"

"No," he said, and she saw anger flicker across his eyes. She took out her notebook.

"Is it okay if I quote you in my next article?"

"I'd prefer if you didn't," he said, plainly.

"Oh." She hurriedly put the notebook back into her bag. "No, that's fine. Sorry, I shouldn't have assumed." She felt like such a dickhead.

Not knowing what to say, she just smiled at Mr. Riley. He had the vestiges of good looks, a straight nose and startling blue eyes. But his skin looked weathered from too much sun. The end of his nose was pink, and thick creases were cut into his forehead.

"Here you go."

Rose almost jumped out of her skin; she hadn't even noticed Mrs. Riley had come back in the room. She was holding out a glass of water, cubes of ice bobbing inside, drips of condensation sliding down the side of the glass.

"Thank you." Rose took it from her and gulped half of it down, enjoying the cold running down her throat and into her veins.

Mrs. Riley sat down next to her husband. She was very thin. The woman was probably only about six or seven years older than Rose herself, but you'd be forgiven for thinking she was in her forties. When she sat down, her dress rode up a bit. Her knees looked oversize and knobbly because of the absence of any body fat around them. Rose looked up, catching her eye and coloring. What was she doing staring at this poor woman's legs?

"I'm sorry to intrude," Rose said, cutting into the viscid silence. "I just wanted to check if you were okay, really. I didn't know my article would be the first you'd see of that note."

Mr. Riley nodded.

"I really don't think you need to worry," Rose said. God, she wished Mia was here. "I mean, Frank's not worried, and he would know. It doesn't necessarily mean something."

She took another swig of water, swallowing loudly. She felt so big, so messy and obnoxious in this house. She wanted to get this over with and get out of here. "I was just wondering if you guys thought—" How could she word this? "If you thought that there was any connection between what's happened. The fire, I mean, and now this. The doll."

"I think you should leave," Mr. Riley said.

"What? I'm so sorry—I didn't mean to offend you."

"You have," he said.

Mrs. Riley walked past Rose, not even looking at her, and went to open the front door. Feeling beyond awful now, she stood.

"I'm really sorry." She couldn't look either of them in the eye as she went back out into the blistering heat.

24

"Is this Rose Blakey?" the man on the other end of the phone asked.

Rose was sitting on top of one of the kegs in the storage room, the phone pressed hard against her ear. She'd ducked out from setting up the bar when the unknown number lit up her cell.

"This is Damien Freeman, deputy editor of the *Sage Review*."

Rose opened her mouth and a strange croaking sound came out. She'd never made that noise before.

"I saw your article before it went to press yesterday. It's been garnering quite a reaction around the office. We're all talking about it."

"Thanks" was all Rose could muster.

"Rich down at the *Star* gave me your details. I hope you don't mind me calling?"

"Down at the *Star*?" Rose repeated, so taken aback that she didn't even know what she was saying.

"Yes. They're on the floor beneath us. We're both Bailey."

The edge of the keg dug into her thigh, but she couldn't even feel it. For a moment the name meant nothing to her.

Then it clicked. Jonathan Bailey, the media mogul. She'd heard his name many times and knew he owned newspapers, television stations and radio, but the idea that the *Sage Review* and the *Star* could be part of the same company seemed absurd. She swallowed, forcing herself to focus.

"Thanks for calling. It's really great to hear from you."

"It's great for me to talk to you."

"Thank you," she said, hardly believing what she was hearing.

"Have you written for any other publications? Anywhere a bit more—" he paused "—intellectual than the *Star*?"

"Not really."

"Okay, that's fine. Now, Rose, we really feel like this story has huge potential. We think it could be something more suited to *Sage*."

"Really?" It was happening. Her dream was coming true.

"What we do in cases like this is send a senior journalist down to write a feature. Of course, we'll pay you for bringing the story to our attention."

The drop of her stomach was agonizing.

"I've written for a few blogs and stuff," she lied.

"Good. That's great." He was fobbing her off. "Now, I think Chris might be available to come next week. It'd be great if you could show him around, give him any recommendations of places to stay."

The only place to stay in Colmstock was Eamon's. If this guy came, he'd not only be taking her story, but he'd be taking her bed too.

"Okay," she said, because what else could she say?

At the bar, Mia was making out with Bazza. Their lips eased and swelled against each other, the hint of tongue appearing and disappearing. They stopped abruptly when they sensed Rose's presence.

"Don't let me interrupt."

The look on Baz's face made her stomach drop even further. It was real hatred, like he just might hit her. But he didn't. He turned and walked back to the table of cops. Jonesy was staring at Rose; an identical look of loathing was on his face. Even Father was looking at her with disappointment, although Steve Cunningham was closely inspecting his beer glass. Probably feeling embarrassed that his wife had called her a slut that morning. Frank hadn't turned. His hunched back was to her, again. She had a feeling it wouldn't be so easy to get his forgiveness this time.

"What's going on?" she said quietly to Mia, who was wiping her mouth with the back of her hand. They had barely spoken while they packed up last night. Rose was annoyed at her for ignoring her in church, but she also hoped Mia wasn't still mad; she had enough to deal with.

"They're pissed about the article. Frank is in big trouble."

She'd known this was coming, but it still hurt. "I never said he was the one that told me what the note said!"

"You didn't need to. It's obvious."

"I don't want him to be in trouble."

"Too late now." Mia still sounded cold. Rose didn't push her. She was sure she'd apologize later once she had cooled down.

Swallowing her guilt about Frank, Rose grabbed a pile of napkins and some loose cutlery and started rolling. Jean wasn't there tonight. Sundays were always quiet. They had to make sure everything was perfect when she got in tomorrow.

She looked up as Will walked in and took his usual seat. They locked eyes and Rose felt the knots inside her loosen a little. Then she turned back to her cutlery and tried, desperately, to figure out a plan.

★ ★ ★

Across the room, the men spoke in lowered voices.

"What a bitch," Jonesy said.

"She's not a bitch," Frank protested.

"She's a fucking cow."

"We have more important things to worry about right now," Frank said, giving Jonesy a look.

Jonesy turned to the Father. "You didn't get any interesting confessions today, did you?"

"No," the Father replied solemnly, "but you know that I couldn't tell you if I had."

"D.C., I keep thinking about it," Steve said. "Initials would be too obvious, right?"

"Who knows," said Baz. "Could mean anything."

"What's your middle name?" Jonesy asked Steve. "It's not David, is it? Or Daniel?"

"Afraid not."

They paused, collectively taking deep drinks from their pints.

"So what do you think, Steve? Is it a local?" Frank asked.

"I don't think so—no one in Colmstock would do this," Steve said, looking straight over at Will.

"We think it's a local," Bazza muttered, causing both the Father and Steve to look up, surprised.

"What makes you think that?"

"What would drive someone to do something like this, Father?" Jonesy was talking to the Father, but it was Steve who he was fixing with a steady gaze.

"I don't know," the Father replied.

Jonesy persisted. "But if you had to guess."

They were silent as Rose cleared the glasses from their table. Pointedly, none of them looked up at her.

When she walked out of earshot, the Father said, "I suppose it would be someone who was losing control."

"Losing control of what?" Jonesy asked.

"I'm not sure. They are sending you notes and haven't done anything yet. They're hesitating."

"What do you think, Steve?" Baz asked. Steve hadn't really been listening. It was his fourth beer.

"I don't know. I just know the vise is on my balls right now. The wife is pissed and everyone wants answers and I've got none."

Jonesy watched him, taking a deep drink of his beer, then looked back to the Father. "So why send it? They want us to know they're serious?"

"They want you to know what kind of person they are," the Father said slowly.

"Someone with urges?" Frank asked, his eyes not leaving Steve's face.

"Filthy ones," added Baz.

"Maybe."

Jonesy sucked the liquid from his top lip. "But how could you find out who had filthy urges?"

Frank smiled. "Technology is amazing these days."

"Really amazing," added Baz.

"You can find anything you want."

They were all looking at Steve now. "I don't think I know what you boys are talking about. Do you have a lead or something?"

"You could say that," Jonesy said, leaning forward now.

"Well, go on, then." Steve was chuckling, although in truth he was getting a little exasperated. It was like they were talking in riddles.

"We've had the rookies going through the records of every adult in town who wasn't born here. Slow process, but we've found out some things we didn't know," Frank said.

"Like the school principal got thirteen speeding tickets, lost her license three times."

"Really?" asked Steve, although the smile had left his face. He was staring intently at Frank's hands. As though the thick hair on each of his fingers was somehow fascinating.

"That's right. Don't know if I would want that woman to be in charge of my kids," Frank said.

"Good thing you don't have any," Jonesy told him.

"Not now, but one day. All those speeding tickets, it shows bad judgment."

"And recklessness," the Father added.

"What do you think, Steve? Your daughters are at that school."

Steve shrugged. "You know, I think I've had enough. My wife wants me coming home a bit earlier."

"Really?" said Frank. He was smiling, but it didn't look right. It was a broad, toothy smile, but his eyes were dark.

"That's not all," Baz said.

"Before she bought this place, Jean claimed to be a victim of a crime," Jonesy said. "But she dropped the charges half-way through the trial."

"Didn't think she was the kind of woman to lie, but there you go," Frank added. "We learned a lot about the people of this town."

"We learned loads," Bazza said.

"You think you know everything about everyone in a town like this. But you don't. Not everyone was born here—you forget that," came Jonesy's hard, even voice.

"Where were you born again, Steven? London?" Frank said, still smiling.

"Nottingham."

"Oh, yes—that's right. It was in a Nottingham toilet that you were arrested, wasn't it?"

Steve didn't reply. He looked toward the Father, eyes pleading.

The priest did not look back. "I should be going," the Father said, rising from the table.

"I'll get a lift from you," Steve said, beginning to stand. Frank's hand was on his arm in an instant.

"You haven't even finished your beer."

"I really do need to get home," he said feebly, but the door had already swung closed. The Father was gone.

"So," Frank continued. "Now that the good Father is on his way, can you tell me what is it about public toilets attracts sick fucks like you, Steve?"

"Do you get off on getting your dick sucked by strangers?" Jonesy asked in his low drawling voice.

Steve was looking between them.

"I dunno," Frank said. "They say a mouth is a mouth, but the idea of getting beard burn on my balls doesn't do it for me."

"Or is it because you can get kids on their own there?" Jonesy asked.

Steve's voice was high and pitchy. "Kids? Hang on there!"

Jonesy pushed back his chair with a squeak. "I'm going for a smoke."

"I'll join you." Baz also stood up.

"You guys have the wrong end of the stick."

"Come on," said Frank. "Don't want to talk about this sort of thing in front of the ladies, do we?"

Bazza grabbed Steve by the shoulder, a little too hard, and the men walked out toward the back corridor.

Rose watched them go, feeling the shift in the air. Something was wrong. She'd noticed Baz's grip on Steve's arm, the paleness of his face.

"Are they arresting him?" she asked Mia.

"Baz said he's a pervert."

A muffled yell echoed down the corridor. Will stood so quickly that his chair fell onto the floor.

"What's happening?" he asked. It was only the three of them in the tavern now.

"I guess they're teaching him a lesson," Mia said, apprehensively.

"Are you kidding?"

Another yell. Rose ran. Down the corridor and out to the back entrance.

Steve was on the ground next to the bin. Bazza, Jonesy and Frank were all kicking him, their boots cracking into his ribs. He was trying to crawl, trying to get back inside.

"Cut it out!" Rose yelled.

She grabbed Frank and tried to pull him off. His shoulders were hot and wet with sweat. But he was stronger than she thought. She couldn't even move him.

Steve was almost at the steps, but Rose knew that would do him no good. If Jean was here she could fix this, but Rose didn't know what to do. Will and Mia appeared in the hallway.

"Stop!" Will yelled, taking in the scene. As they got closer, Mia saw Steve on the ground. She put her hands over her eyes.

"Oh, God," she murmured.

"We'll decide when we'll stop." Frank's chest was heaving.

Will walked toward him, his fists clenched. "No, this stops right now."

Bazza muscled forward, standing between Will and Frank. "Or what? You're going to call the cops?"

Mia came over and put a hand on Bazza's chest. "We're going now, Baz. Right now."

She grabbed his arm and started trying to pull the hulking man away.

"Go," Frank said, not breaking eye contact with Will. "It's under control."

"Come on," she said quietly and Bazza let himself be dragged away.

While the others watched them go, Rose looked down at Steve. He was still crawling. His clothes were ripped and he was making quiet groaning sounds. She was going to have to take him to a hospital.

"Can you get up?" she said quietly, feeling queasy at how defenseless he was. He turned over and stared up at her, his eyes rolling around in their sockets. She imagined this was what a cow looked like before it was slaughtered.

"Oh, God. Fuck!" She bent down onto the ground next to him. Jonesy stepped closer to them.

"Will you help me carry him?" she called to Will, not wanting to leave Steve here in the dirt. Something whizzed in front of her face.

Jonesy's boot.

It smashed down onto Steve's face. His nose crunched. His teeth shattered. Blood sprayed over Rose and she screamed.

Jonesy laughed, scraping the blood off his heel on the edge of the step.

"Enough," Will said, his eyes hard on Frank.

Frank took a step forward, so he was right in Will's face. Jonesy's hand went to his gun.

"Get the hell out of here!" Rose yelled.

Frank turned to her, his eyes softening. "He's a pervert, Rose."

"I don't bloody care. Get out. Now!"

Reluctantly, Frank took a step away from Will. "Come on."

The two of them, Jonesy swaggering a little, walked back toward the car park, leaving Rose and Will alone with the unconscious man.

25

They carried Steve between them. They couldn't just leave him on the hard dirt ground. Will held him under the arms, and Rose held his ankles. As they turned the corner into room two, his head clunked against the door frame. They dropped him carefully down on the bed.

Rose tried not to look at him. What had once been a clean-shaven, neat-looking face now more closely resembled raw meat. He writhed, making a horrible throaty sound, then coughed, blood and teeth splattering onto the quilt.

"I'll call the ambulance," Will said, leaving the room. Rose went to the bathroom and got a towel. She put it under the tap and waited for the water to turn warm. She looked at herself in the mirror. Her face was white. Splatters of red dripped down from her chin, cheek and neck. The anger that surged through her before was now completely gone. Now she felt shaky, and her head pounded. She splashed herself with water, rubbing at the blood roughly, trying to hold it together.

When the towel was damp with warm water, she came back into the room and sat down next to Steve. Carefully, she started wiping away the blood. His nose was bending at an impossible angle. His jaw must have been broken. It was hanging open crookedly. As she tentatively wiped at it, she saw that the sides of his mouth were split. His teeth were completely shattered.

Blood bubbled out from his mouth. He was trying to talk.

"Shhh," she said.

Another bubble came out, popping in the ripped corner of his mouth. He was almost crying, trying to get the words out through his delirium. She swallowed. She could hear Will from the other room.

"At Eamon's Tavern Hotel on Union Street. No, I don't know what the street number is."

"Seventy-two!" she called, desperate for him to come back in.

Steve's lips were moving again, making her wince. She leaned in closer.

"What is it?" she said, just wanting him to stop trying to speak.

"She knows. It's...not kids... How could they ever...?"

Rose wasn't sure what he meant, but she was sure he wasn't any kind of child molester.

"I know," she said, barely able to look at him. "Just try to rest."

She kept wiping his face, hoping it was soothing somehow. There was nothing else she could do. Will came back in and sat next to her. He put a hand on her knee. She kept softly wiping the man's face, watching his features swell and bruise, until, faintly, she could hear the ambulance's sirens.

The paramedics took Steve away, leaving Rose and Will standing in the corridor. They stood in silence.

"Good night," she said eventually, going into her room and closing the door.

Rose sat up on the bed, looking at the bloodstain on the sheet. She could still see his face, still hear the sound of Jonesy's boot. The crunch it had made on Steve's nose.

She closed her eyes and put her hands over her ears, but it was still there. It was almost two in the morning; she should try to sleep. All the adrenaline had leaked out of her, and now her limbs felt heavy and her head throbbed. Kicking the bloody sheet off the bed, she lay down and closed her eyes. The room swung around, like she was drunk, so she sat up again, her back against the wall.

Sometime later, there was a soft knock on her door.

"Rose?" Will's voice.

She stood, her legs feeling wobbly, and went to the door, opening it. He looked so young all of a sudden.

"Were you asleep?"

She shook her head.

"You can come into my room if you want," he said, "if you don't want to be in here with—" His eyes looked at the bloodied sheet on the carpet. "If you don't want to be alone."

She looked at him, not knowing what to say.

"I don't want to be alone," he said. Then, "Just to sleep. I won't try anything."

"Okay."

Her shoulder brushed across his chest as she passed him to cross the corridor into his room. He followed, pulling the door shut behind them.

Will stood next to her as she sat down on the bed. Then he walked around the other side and got down onto it. He pulled the sheet over him, lifting it on her side. She climbed underneath it and lay on her back. They weren't touching, but being encased in his sheets, surrounded by his warm smell, was soothing. Her head didn't spin now.

"I've never seen anything like that before," he said, staring at the ceiling.

She closed her eyes. "Me neither."

★ ★ ★

Unexpectedly, sleep came quickly. Will's smell was like a sedative. But the dreams were horrible. She was running, Frank and Jonesy behind her. They knew. They were going to kill her. She ran, saying sorry, screaming, waking up as Frank was on top of her, pinning her down. Jonesy lifted his boot above her eyes, its mud-encrusted sole inches from her face, and then it came whooshing down.

She woke up panting like she was winded, her body slimy with sweat.

"It's okay." A voice came from next to her. She turned around, scared again. Will was next to her, looking at her with concern.

"Sorry," she said.

"Don't be. If I could have slept I would have had nightmares too."

She felt like she had only been asleep five minutes, but the room was filled with a pale gray light. It must be early morning. She put a hand over her eyes and tried to steady her breathing.

"I'm here for my kid," he said.

"What?"

"You keep asking me why I'm here," he said. "I'm here to find my child."

She took her hand away, looked at him. He was staring up at the ceiling, the gray light tracing his profile.

"Ages ago, when I was still a young, arrogant jerk-off, I was dating this girl. Bess," he went on. "She didn't really talk about it, but I think she'd had a bad relationship before me. We went out for just a few weeks. I think I liked the idea that I was saving her, you know, showing her how she should be treated or some bullshit like that."

Rose was going to tell him that he didn't have to tell her, but he just kept on talking.

"It was pretty casual, so when she stopped calling me back I didn't think too much about it. Then, months ago, I got this letter. It was from Bess. She said she'd had a kid. My kid. Honestly—" he looked at Rose then "—I swear I had absolutely no idea."

Rose wanted to reach out and touch him, show him that it was okay, that she wasn't judging him, but she didn't.

"Anyway. It was bizarre. Who writes a letter? An email maybe, or a phone call, but it was a letter. She said she was in trouble, and so was our child. She said she knew I was a good guy, and I'd do the right thing. She said she needed me to take the kid, to be ready, and she'd write me again to say where and when."

"She didn't write again?"

"No. I waited a month, longer maybe, and nothing. Something must have happened to her. That's why I came. I gave up my job, everything. But I can't find her."

"How did you know she was here?"

"There was no reply address or anything, but the stamp had a postcode. The letter came from Colmstock."

"Do you have a picture of Bess?"

He shook his head.

"And that's why you were looking at the files? That's why you've got that bear?"

He looked at her. "How do you know about the bear?"

She tried to think of a lie, but he smiled for the first time, rolling onto his back and shaking his head. "You're terrible," he said.

"So that's why." She took a breath. This felt so awkward, saying this when they were in bed together. "Why you didn't want to kiss me. Because you want to make a family."

"No," he said, still smiling, looking at her from only the corner of his eye. "It's because I know you're trouble, and that's the last thing I need right now."

"I'm not!" she said. "In fact, I was just going to say I'll help you. This town is a small place, and I doubt there are many mums named Bess. We can figure it out. Don't suppose you can remember the last name?"

"Yes, of course!" he said. "I'm not that bad. Last name was Gerhardsson. But I've looked. No Bess Gerhardsson."

She tried to think about it, remember if she ever had heard that name before, but her head was still swimming.

"So you'll help me?"

"I thought you wanted me to stay out of it?"

"You seemed like you wanted to know too much, like you were hoping to write some horrible sob story for your paper about it."

"I wouldn't do that!" she said, genuinely offended. "I'm definitely not going to help you now."

"Come on," he said, a grin in his voice. "I can tell you're dying to meddle."

"I'm not!" she said. "Screw you."

He rolled onto his side. "Please."

"Nope," she said, the warmth of his skin radiating onto her.

He reached out and touched the tattoo on her arm, tracing the pattern that reached up to her shoulder.

Her insides quivered, but she tried not to show it. Shifting even closer, he ran a finger over her eyebrow. His face was serious, like he was committing the lines of her to memory.

She wanted to touch him. Wanted to so badly it was like her body was aching. She managed a smile. "I thought you said you weren't going to try anything."

"Please help me find them," he said, his finger now tracing her jawline.

"Okay," she said, the word riding on one breath.

His eyes were dark in this light, his face beautiful. She leaned forward, kissed his mouth so softly, so slowly, that it made her whole body prickle with goose bumps through her sweat.

"This is such bad timing," he said, pulling back. "Why couldn't I have met you earlier? Or later?"

"Are you saying you like me?" she said, and she was grinning. "Even though I'm trouble?"

He looked back at her. "You're okay, I guess."

Will pulled her into a hug, and she rested her head on his chest. She could hear his heart beating hard; as they breathed softly together it began to slow. Within a minute, she'd fallen back to sleep.

26

Rose's phone rang; she could hear it through the wall. Her limbs were wrapped around Will's, her head still on his chest. He groaned, eyes blinking. The light in his room had turned bright; it must have been midmorning. Rubbing her face with her hands, her cheek sweaty from where it had been pressed against him, she rolled off and got up. By the time she'd crossed the corridor to her room, the ringing had ceased.

She opened the door. It stank of wet, rusted metal. Steve's blood on the bedspread had changed color. It was now a dark burgundy. The splatter thick and congealed. She sat down on the bed and fished for her phone among the sheets.

Whatever way she looked at it, what happened to Steve last night had all been started by her. By what she had written.

It had been Mia on the phone. Rose was glad she had called. She wanted things to go back to normal again. They shouldn't be fighting; there was no point to it.

"Hello?"

"Hey. Did you sleep?"

"Not really. Did you get home okay?"

Rose eyed the bloodstain. "Yeah. How'd you go with Bazza? Was he pissed you made him leave?"

"Nah, he was fine."

There was a pause. Usually Rose didn't have to do the work in their conversations.

"I can't believe they did that," she said. "I wonder what'll happen to them."

Rose could hear the sound of fabric shifting against fabric. Mia must be sitting up or rolling over. "I don't know. Nothing probably."

"What?" Rose asked. "You think they'll get away with bashing up an innocent man?"

"I told you—Bazza said he's a perv. He's got a record."

Rose couldn't believe she was hearing this. "That doesn't mean he deserves to get his face smashed in!" She swallowed, trying to push her tone back to neutral. "You should have seen him, Mia. Even when he heals, there's no way his face will ever look the same."

Mia didn't say anything. Rose couldn't understand how someone so warmhearted could be so callous.

"Listen, I think we should go and talk to his wife—"

"You just want an interview for your article!"

"No!"

"Yes! Come on—be honest."

Rose hesitated a second too long.

"It's not fair to bother her today. Leave the poor woman alone."

Rose almost bit back, but she knew she'd say something she'd regret.

"I gotta go." Mia sounded so tired.

"Okay, fine."

"'Bye."

"'Bye."

Rose hung up, looking down at the blood-splattered sheet crumpled on the floor. She pulled it together into a bundle, the bloody mess in the center, and threw it in the bathroom sink. The longer she left it, the more likely it would be to stain.

She went to the kitchen, slid on rubber gloves and picked up bottles of detergent and bleach then came back to her room. She turned the hot tap on full blast. Squeezing the detergent in front of her, she watched the yellow soap run down from the bottle like honey. She hadn't thought for a second that Mia wouldn't be with her on this. Mia had always been the one to understand her, and she felt like she understood Mia too. But maybe she didn't.

Trying to breathe only through her mouth so she didn't have to smell it, she scrubbed at the bloodstain, watching as the hardened globules separated from the cotton. The frothy water was quickly turning pink. She tipped in some powdered bleach and tried to rub it into the material. She pushed the stain section back under the water with the heels of her hands, the tops of the rubber gloves going under the surface. She almost yelled out as they filled with scalding hot, pink water. When she pulled them off, there was an off-white chunk of tooth stuck to her wrist.

Hands shaking, she flicked it off into the water and washed her hands. Without even thinking, she'd been cleaning up Frank and Jonesy's mess, letting it all run down the drain. She turned the taps off and left the bathroom, hands still shaking. She wouldn't be part of pretending it didn't happen, that it didn't matter.

This was fucked. She was going to make it right. Rubbing her hands hard with a towel, she headed down the corridor. She kept to the shadows behind the bar. It was early, but still, people were walking down Union Street and she didn't want anyone to see her here. Quietly, she sneaked into the small alcove Jean used as an office. Plunking the brick of a phone book down with a bang, she opened it up to *C*. Her finger swept the pages, until she got to *Cunningham, S, D*. Her rage didn't let her hesitate. She picked up the landline phone and keyed in the number. As it rang, she sat down on the floor, her back leaning against the side of one of the fridges.

"Yes?"

"Hi, can I speak to Mrs. Cunningham, please?"

"Speaking."

Rose hadn't recognized her voice. Usually she sounded so affected with her fake English accent. There was no pretense now.

"Listen. I was there last night when Steve…" She wasn't sure how to finish that. "It was me who called the ambulance. It was the cops that did it. Frank, Jonesy, Bazza—"

"I know."

That was a relief. "Okay, good."

"My husband is not gay. We have an…arrangement and—"

"No, that's not what I mean. It's just…if you want to do something. I don't know. Press charges. I'm happy to come and talk to you about what happened."

"That won't be happening. Who is this?"

"It's Rose. Blakey." She bit her lip, the word *slut* ringing in her ears.

"No comment."

The line went dead.

Rose's hand dropped to her lap, the phone still clenched in it. Those fucking arseholes were going to get away with it. The anger pushed her guilt away instantly. This wasn't her fault. It was theirs. They had kicked a man when he was already down, not even stopping to hear him out. Maybe they didn't care.

She sat in the shadow, staring around the bar. It was drenched in golden sunlight, reflecting off the bottles of liquor. Their glass glowed green and brown, throwing the colors onto the backboard behind them.

It wasn't she who had to take responsibility for all this. It was them. Never, ever had she hated this town so much. This place where small-mindedness was celebrated and people never questioned anything. Somehow, she had to show them. Show the people of Colmstock that they couldn't trust the cops and show the *Sage* that they needed her. That she wasn't some uneducated idiot who couldn't string enough words together to write an article about her own town.

Standing, she turned on Jean's old desktop PC. It whirred slowly. The thing was about twenty years old, huge with a small screen. Not that her computer at home was that much better.

Waiting impatiently for the computer to load, she tried to remember if the *Sage* deputy had mentioned this Chris guy's last name to her on the phone yesterday. She didn't think he had. She would find it, eventually. Then she would read every article he'd written and make sure whatever she wrote was a million times better. Finally the computer loaded, the green screen lighting up the alcove. As she looked at the mess of icons on the desktop, an idea snaked its way into Rose's mind. An idea so deliciously reckless it made her legs break out in goose bumps.

Instead of opening the internet, she slowly moved the mouse over and double clicked on the Cameron Security icon instead. Jean was really safety conscious. She'd always be on at them about double-checking they'd locked all the doors on the nights they were left alone to close up. She never actually checked the video-camera footage, but Rose knew that Jean felt better that it was there in case they ever got robbed.

With one camera out the front of the tavern and one out

the back, the security system was motion activated and only kept footage for a fortnight before saving over the top of it. Rose smiled wickedly as she opened the folder for the rear camera. The first footage, startlingly, was of her. A digital green-and-black image of herself was pulling a full rubbish bag carelessly down the outside stairs. She watched herself yank the bag over her shoulder and throw it into the Dumpster. It was so strange to watch herself this way. She looked so much smaller than she felt, her shoulders looked so narrow, as she stood there staring at nothing. Rose wondered what she had been thinking about as the digital version of herself slapped her hands together and went back inside. The screen went black for a second, then snapped back to life. Now it was Jonesy who sauntered down the stairs. He slid a cigarette between his lips, then cupped his hand around his lighter. Taking a drag, he began scratching his back with his other hand. Gross. Rose began fast-forwarding the footage. Jonesy moved in double speed, the cigarette going in and out of his mouth quickly. Out of nowhere, he started moving in a strange way, like he was dancing. She quickly hit Play. Jonesy was rubbing his back on the bricks, turning slightly as he did it, scraping his arm on the wall. She peered closer, trying to figure out what the hell he was doing. But he stubbed out his cigarette and went back inside.

She fast-forwarded through more of the footage, which mostly featured herself, Jean and sometimes Mia taking out bags of rubbish and another strange back-scratching dance from Jonesy. Then Frank appeared on the screen. She hit Play and swallowed apprehensively. Jonesy followed him, then Bazza, his arm tight around Steve's shoulders. If she hadn't known what was coming next, it would have almost looked like a friendly embrace. Rose watched as the men spoke. Steve's head jerking back and forth between them, obviously trying to dissuade them from doing what Rose knew was inevitable. Bazza took his arm from around Steve, and she could see his body poised to run. But Bazza abruptly gripped his forearms from behind. Rose felt sick inside as she watched Jonesy and Frank take it in turns to punch him. Their enjoyment was unmistakable. There was no audio, but still she could hear their laughs and jeers in her head. And Steve's yells.

He was down on the ground now. Rose could almost feel the boots in her own stomach. Then there she was. Grabbing Frank's shoulders, trying to pull him off. She stopped the video there. She'd been there for the live performance last night; she didn't want to see it again. Quick as she could, she emailed the file to herself. No way they'd get away with it now.

Journalist Blows the Whistle on Police Brutality. She liked the sound of that.

"So you're sure, these three men are police? And the man who was beaten is a civilian?" Damien, the *Sage Review* deputy editor, asked, when she finally got ahold of him.

"Yes, definitely."

"From what you've described, it sounds like it has potential. Can you email me the file now?"

Rose was sitting on the very edge of the bed. She had to play this conversation very, very carefully.

"I'm very invested in this case," she said, trying to keep her voice quiet. She didn't want Will to hear this conversation.

"Yes, I'm getting that impression."

"All my sources trust me and I know this town better than anyone. If there is another note, I'll know about it straightaway. Your reporter will just scare people off." She swallowed.

The line was silent. Every part of Rose wanted to keep talking, to babble on like Mia did when she was nervous. But she had an edge now, and saying any more would make her lose it.

Eventually, he let out a low whistle. "Sounds like Chris has missed the boat on this one. Send me the footage, and you can write us an article. I want it by the end of the week. Make sure it's good."

Rose forced the excitement out of her voice; she had something they wanted now. "And if it is good?"

"If there's a strong reaction to the footage, and the article is proper journalism, not like that lurid bullshit you wrote for the *Star*—" he paused to think and Rose wished she could push the cogs in his brain, make him say what she so desperately wanted him to say "—then we'll see."

When she hung up, the screen of her phone was clammy with sweat.

27

Mia's father sat in a bath of milky water. Mia was perched on the side, her fingers underneath the running tap, which was steadily warming. Her father loved bath times. He had been sitting there for twenty minutes already. His fingers and toes were wrinkled and pink, but he had not wanted to get out and who was she to deny him?

"Warm enough, Baba?"

He attempted a smile. Mia turned off the tap and kissed him on the top of the head.

She had left Baz in the kitchen but now he was gone, although the fridge door had been left open. She closed it, noticing another six-pack of beers was missing. Baz had come over for the first time last week, a few days after their date. She could feel that he'd been sure he was going to get lucky. But really, she wanted him to meet her father. You could never be sure how people would react to her father. Some people couldn't look straight at him, or other people stared. If Baz were one of those people, then there would be no point in her spending time with him. Or if her father didn't like him, then she would call it all off too. It had gone well though. Baz had brought over his own beer and when he saw her father was there he didn't even look disappointed. It might have been because her father used to be a cop too, although they'd only been on the force together about a year. Baz had cracked open two beers and sat down next to her father to watch the game, chatting to him throughout even though her father was unable to answer. It was like he didn't even notice that he was different.

She was liking the guy more and more but that was just making her scared. It was possible it wasn't reciprocated. She was getting too old to have her heart broken. Plus, she was starting to envision a life with him, which was always a bad idea. It was just that she knew how much better things would be if she was with him. There'd be so much less for her to worry about. Sure, it would mean yet another person to clean up after but she was used to that. The only thing she had going for her now was that she hadn't slept with him yet. Too many times, guys had lost interest the second their faces screwed up in orgasm. There was too much pressure, too much riding on it, for her to be able to just let go. Every time they kissed all she could think about was how long to let it go on, how much was too much. The last thing in the world she wanted was to look desperate, even though that was exactly what she was.

She found Bazza in her father's room, standing by his bed, looking at the framed picture that her father insisted was kept on his bedside. Baz's jacket was off and he had his black leather holster on top of his shirt. The beer was on the table and she came over to put a coaster underneath it.

"Your mum?" he asked, looking around at her.

"Yeah." She shrugged. "Baba likes to look at it as he falls asleep."

Baz replaced the picture on the table, next to his beer. She wondered if it was because he sensed that her mother was not a topic she liked to talk about. He turned to Mia and for a moment she thought maybe he was going to give her a hug. His arms wrapped around her and she tried to let herself relax into him but then his lips found hers. He pushed into her mouth hard, using his tongue to open her lips, his stubble rasping on her cheek. He kissed down her neck, his hand in her hair.

"Have you ever done it in your dad's room?" he whispered into her neck.

"I told you—I'm a virgin," she said, letting her voice go all simpering.

He took a step back and looked at her. Then he pulled her dress off from over her head and threw it onto the carpet. He took her in, her simple white underwear, her soft stomach, her breasts pushing against the cups of her bra as she breathed. His palms rubbed all over her body, touching her like she was something he didn't just want, but something he needed. Something he would ingest if it were possible. Her skin started to respond to his touch. Closing her eyes, she thought of Rose. How she might react to Bazza's hands on her, whether she would lie down on the bed, spread herself open and let him do what he wanted, or if she would be the one to take control. A tiny moan escaped her. Every part of her wanted to reach down into his pants, to feel the hot pulsating flesh under her hand. Instead, she swatted him away. She couldn't let herself get carried away.

"Stop it."

She flopped down onto the bed. If she really wanted him to stop, she should probably put her dress back on, but she wanted him to want her. Knowing she was desired, knowing someone desperately wanted to make love to her, turned her on more than sex itself.

"I swear, my balls are actually going blue."

Mia laughed. He was so cute. He sat down on the foot of the bed and began pawing at her again. She turned and pulled his gun out of his holster.

"Hands off," she said, a wicked smile on her face.

Baz grinned and put his arms in the air. Mia pointed the gun at him.

"Bang," she said, pretending to shoot.

"You shouldn't play with that," he said.

The gun felt heavy in her hand. But still, it was amazing to think it could take a life. That you'd just need to squeeze your finger to kill someone.

"Have you ever shot someone?"

"Yeah."

That surprised her. "Killed someone?"

"Nah."

She was glad of that. His hands would feel different on her body if they'd killed. Turning the gun over in her hand, she wondered what it would be like to be the cause of someone else's death. To end a life.

"I wonder what it would be like," she said out loud.

"To kill someone?"

"Mmm."

His warm hands ran up the flesh of her legs, him barely looking at her as he said "Frank has."

"Really?"

"Yep."

"How horrible."

It didn't seem possible that Frank could have killed someone and still seem so normal. Still just be that short, sweet guy who sat in the corner and got too drunk at closing. But then she thought of the way he'd panted, standing over Steve's body. That look in his eyes, like somehow, he was enjoying it. But still, killing someone was different. If someone had taken a life it should color them. It should be something that everyone could see, a stain.

Mia carefully pushed the gun back into Bazza's holster. She didn't want the thing in her hands anymore. She knew that if she were to kill someone, she'd have to stop living. It wouldn't matter what they had done.

"Frank kind of scared me last night," she admitted. "I've never seen him like that before."

"He was just doing what he thought was right," Baz said.

Mia shrugged. "I know. But Rose said they really messed him up after we left."

"Yeah." He brushed a hand over his face. "To be honest, I think it went too far. It got out of hand."

Mia kissed him on the cheek. She knew he was different, not like other guys. She sat up and pulled back on her dress, despite Baz's painful groans of objection. Right now, those blue balls were working in her favor.

She smiled at Baz over her shoulder. "Back in a sec."

Going to the bathroom, she knocked on the door.

"Time to get out," she called, before opening it.

It took a moment for her eyes to make sense of what she was seeing.

The hair dryer was floating in the bath. Her father was straining with effort, leaning forward, his walking stick at a right angle in the air. He was trying to flick on the power switch. His tear-streaked face was determined.

"Don't!"

She rushed forward and pulled the hair-dryer cord out, fished it out of the bath and put it on the wet tiles. She wrapped her arms around her father. His bare skin was so hot against her arms. Her dress was drenched from the water and his sweat. He was crying quietly, shaking in her arms. She wanted to cry too. If she'd just taken thirty seconds longer she might have found him jerking, steam rising. Mia swallowed.

"I'm going to make things better for us," she told him quietly, "I promise."

28

Bazza and Mia kissed passionately in a corner. Frank ignored them. He had been trying to get Rose's attention all evening. He hadn't slept a wink last night. Rose's face screaming in his, Steve's blood dripping off the tip of her nose, kept appearing on the backs of his eyelids.

He didn't feel remorse over what they'd done to that homo, no. But Rose was pure. She was innocent and he hated thinking that she had seen the side of his personality that thoroughly enjoyed cracking the ribs of people who tried to destroy his town.

He approached her as she leaned over a table, wiping it down. The angle of her neck was so perfect, every part of him wanted to touch it.

"Rose? I'm sorry."

She ignored him, just moved on to the next table and continued wiping.

"You shouldn't have had to see that," he said to the back of her head.

She didn't even turn around when she spoke. "He didn't do it, did he?"

"Does it matter?" he asked. The way he saw it, Steve had been a kiddie fiddler waiting to happen. People were always going on about prevention, and that was exactly what he had done by putting that pervert in the hospital.

Frank stared at Rose's back, wishing there was something he could say. Something that would bring them back to the moment they had shared outside the café less than a week ago.

A stray hair clung to her shoulder, glinting in the light. He plucked it tenderly.

"I've got to know. Was it Baz?" he asked.

"What?"

"Baz told Mia what was written in the note and she told you, right?"

Rose turned to Frank and looked at him like he was dirt. "Does it matter?"

"I guess not."

She turned back to the table. He would have to give her time to calm down. She would come around eventually.

He'd had the shittiest of days. He'd been trying to sort out this crap with the fires, but it was way outside his know-how. Worst of all was the house call he'd had to make to the Rileys. He'd promised the wife he'd find the pyro. Now it looked like it was just some stupid dare among a bunch of kids. He'd already told Mr. Riley that, said the case had been passed on to child services, that rehabilitation was better than punishment, but the man had insisted he was wrong and who was Frank to argue? If he was going to argue with anyone, it wouldn't be that guy anyway. Frank could see how tight his fist had been clenched on the table, how white his knuckles. Worst of all, they still didn't have any rock-solid evidence. All he had was the loose lips of that little shit Denny, and he wasn't saying another word.

"Come on, Baz," he said, taking out his car keys and jingling them as he headed for the door.

Bazza extracted himself from Mia, following Frank like the obedient dog he was.

Jean was barely out the door when Rose came around the back, straight to Will's room. She'd been thinking about him all day. It was terrible; there were so many other things she should be focusing on, but her head kept coming back around to him. She'd been to the shop and, red faced, bought a packet of condoms. It had been a long time since she'd had sex—years. She'd been so determined not to put any roots down in Colmstock that she hadn't done a lot of dating. Plus, none of the guys in town had ever been very appealing. But this was different. She couldn't focus on anything else but him all day, couldn't think straight.

She rapped a knuckle on his door.

"Hi," she said, when he opened it.

"Can I help you?" he asked, face formal.

She couldn't believe it. Was he really going to do this? Was he going to act like nothing had happened between them last night? Then he broke into a smile, grabbed her arm and pulled her into his room.

"What time do you call this? I've been waiting for you all day," he said, closing the door. Then his mouth was on hers, his hands were in her hair. They made it to the bed, and her legs wrapped around his waist. His body pressed her into the mattress, all his weight on her, and he was heavy but she wanted more. She wanted to be even closer to him, to put her hands through his skin.

She reached down to undo the top button of his jeans.

He closed his eyes, his forehead pressing against hers. "You really are a go-getter, aren't you?"

"Apparently I'm trouble."

She slipped her hand under the tight line of his underwear, feeling the searing hot flesh underneath. She bit his earlobe, tightened her teeth slightly. Underneath her hands, she could feel a tremble going through his body.

He pulled her shorts off and then stood to remove his own clothes. Rose ripped the condom packet she'd had in her pocket open, took out the little white circle. He sat down on the bed and she swung on top of him, one knee on either side of his hips, and rolled the condom on.

"Hi," she said, nervous all of a sudden, her face so close to his, so close she could see the tiny flecks of different shades of brown in his eyes.

He grinned, pulled her face to his and kissed her again, one hand tangled in her hair, the other stroking down her spine. She pushed him inside her slowly, then sat down hard, the impact of his body against hers making her want to scream with relief. They moved together, and she pulled off her singlet and bra, wanting to feel his warm flesh against hers. He gripped her waist.

"I've got to slow down," he whispered.

"No." She grabbed the skin of his lower back, pushed him deeper, so deep it almost hurt. She didn't care if it was over too soon. They had all night.

Rose woke with a start. It was time. The ceiling fan revolved above her head. She watched as the reflection from the streetlight slid around on its shiny plastic surface. After another ten minutes of listening to Will's breathing, making sure he was truly asleep, Rose carefully got out of the bed. She sat on the edge, waiting, making sure her movement didn't wake him. She dressed in the dark, slid her feet into the shoes waiting at the side of the bed and slung her bag over her shoulder.

As she walked through the tavern, she picked up the pink rubber gloves from next to the sink. She stood still on the footpath. It was almost four in the morning now and the street was totally empty. The only movement came from inside the police station. The white fluorescents were on in there. There were a few cops inside, the poor souls on night duty. They worked, hunchbacked on computers, or just stared into their cups of coffee in the break room.

Within an hour, the place would be blazing with action. Now it was the slow pace of any other uneventful night. Just the occasional callouts to domestic disputes—although if you had seen one woman lying through her bruises you'd seen them all. There would be a car crash, as reliable as clockwork, but if you'd seen one head smashed into a steering wheel you'd seen them all.

If the blinds of the incident room had been open, Rose would have seen the board mocked up with the photographs of five young girls and five identical dolls. The first note taped up in the center, scrawling handwriting on a piece of blue lined paper.

Rose reached a pink rubber hand into her bag, very carefully withdrawing a plastic sleeve. From within the sleeve, she removed a piece of blue-lined paper, covered in scrawl. A sibling to the one taped up on the board inside the incident room, though this one had taken her even longer to write. Carefully, so carefully, she folded it in half.

PART 4

Liars prosper.

—Unknown

29

"Posey!"

Laura ran toward her from the school gates.

"Want to go to the library?"

"Yeah!" Laura said, taking her hand.

"How was your day?"

"It was okay, but they canceled our excursion to go to the museum." Laura kicked at a rock.

"Why?"

"Dunno. Cos they're dum-dums."

Rose laughed. "But what was the reason they gave you?"

"Umm…" The little girl thought hard. "They said they needed more supervision because of recently events."

"Recent events?"

"Yeah! But really it's because they're dum-dums. Tara said she was happy because she gets bus sick and because it's three hours she would definitely get sick."

"Did you want to go?"

Rose hoped she'd say no. She hadn't thought about her articles this way. She knew they affected the cops, but she hated them now anyway. She hoped Frank popped a blood vessel trying to decode her note. But she'd never in a million years thought it would affect the school.

"Yeah," said Laura, "but mostly because I wanted to see Tara puke."

"Ewww!" Rose said, jokingly.

"I bet it would have gone everywhere! It would have been so gross!"

The kids section of the library was empty. This was rare; usually after school was one of the busiest times. Today, Laura had the whole place to herself. Rose laughed as Laura rolled around on the carpet, whispering, "It's all for me!"

"Laura," Rose said, reaching out to touch her, "are there any kids in your class with the last name Gerhardsson?"

"Girl or boy?"

"Either," she said.

"Nah. There's Stephanie G., but her G is Godden."

Rose knew it wasn't going to be that easy, but it was worth a try.

"Okay, well, I'll be back in a sec," she told Laura. "Pick a book and I'll read it to you."

"Really?" Laura's eyes lit up and she jumped to her feet and rushed to the shelves.

Rose went up to the mezzanine. She flicked through the books, trying to find any other mention of the Zodiac Killer. It was such a great story.

Writing like a deranged psychopath had been harder than she'd thought. What she'd written in the note had seemed laughable, it was so over-the-top, so ridiculous. She couldn't believe everyone thought it was for real. Still, if she was going to write another one, it had to be even more intense. She had to up the ante, somehow, if the story was going to be considered interesting enough for *Sage*.

So far, her articles had been short and simple. But the *Sage Review* was a real, proper newspaper. Her article couldn't be salacious. She had to make the story sound plausible. When she'd called the deputy editor and said she had got her hands on another note, he'd asked if this one showed signs of intent. The way he'd asked, she knew the answer he was looking for. She was hoping to get a bit of inspiration from the Zodiac, but there didn't seem to be anything.

Enjoying the quietness of the library, she leaned her head on the window. Ideas swam through her head. Creepy words and imagery that the public would eat up. Why was it that people loved such fucked-up stuff?

The glass was hot against her head, but felt soothing. Her shoulders relaxed, her muscles loosened. She hadn't even realized how tight she'd been holding herself. This was going to work. Everything would be fine. No one would ever find out, and even if they did, what was the worst that could happen? It was only pen and paper. Frank might yell at her but she could deal with that. She'd get a job, she'd help Will find his kid, then she'd move to the city. Maybe he would come back too after he'd worked everything out here. Mia would forgive her soon. It was all going to be fine. Slowly, when her forehead felt smooth and her muscles slack, she opened her eyes, looking down onto the charred debris of the courthouse.

Her brow furrowed again. There was something down there that was out of place. She craned her neck, trying to get a better look. There was rubbish, silver and bright against the tones of black, in the gap between the courthouse and what was left of the storage shed. The rubbish looked like chip packets. And next to them, what looked like a dirty white T-shirt. It shouldn't surprise her that some homeless person was desperate enough to move in for shelter but she was. It was so dangerous in there. Surely sleeping with the fossickers would be preferable; they protected their own. Her muscles tensed again.

Laura would probably trash the children's section if she left her much longer, so she hopped back down the stairs. Rose couldn't help but laugh when she saw what Laura had done. The beanbags were all stacked in a corner, creating a sort of cubby house, four on the bottom and one on top as a roof.

Rose got down on her knees. "Knock, knock."

"Who is it?" Laura called.

"The boogeyman."

"Is not," Laura said.

Rose squeezed inside the little cavern. Laura was sitting next to a pile of books. The light looked orange in there, shining through the gaps between the red beanbags.

"You have to read all of them," said Laura, pointing to the pile.

"Okay," Rose said; she wanted to make up for the canceled excursion, even if it was just that Laura missed out on seeing some poor girl puke. She picked up the first book, *Fitcher's Bird*, and began to read.

When she finished, they bundled up Laura's books and went to the counter.

"You've got your library card?" Rose asked her.

"Yes." Laura put her backpack onto the floor and began shuffling through it, pushing aside her exercise books and a lunch box. Rose wondered what Laura's lunch was like now that she wasn't at home to make it. The bread of her sandwiches was probably torn and holey. Laura held the library card up to her, smiling widely as though she had genuinely been worried that her schoolbag might have eaten it.

Rose handed her the two picture books back. "Now give these to the lady behind the counter."

She was trying to encourage Laura to do these things for herself now that she was getting a bit older. Growing up in that house, the kid was going to have to learn to be self-sufficient fast.

The two of them stood side by side in front of the counter. The librarian was scanning books; the mechanical process of the way her hands moved without really looking at them reminded Rose of drying dishes in the tavern. She waited with Laura, knowing how annoying it was to be constantly interrupted while you were trying to finish a menial task, but when the stack of books was done the woman started on another.

"Hi," she said, thinking that perhaps the librarian just hadn't noticed them. The woman considered them, her face hard, and then went back to the books. Laura looked up at Rose, unsure, her library card still in her outstretched hand.

"Can my sister please borrow these books?" Rose asked and then jumped as the woman banged the pile down, came over and ripped the card out of Laura's hand. The librarian put the two picture books through quickly, not even looking at them.

"Why was she in a bad mood with us?" Laura asked as they walked back out into the heat.

"I don't know," Rose answered, and she didn't. She didn't even know that woman. She took her phone out from her bag; it had been on Silent in the library. There were two missed calls from Mia and one from the *Sage Review*. She checked her voice mail. There was one hang-up, one from Mia telling her to call her and one from Damien.

"Hi, Rose, the video is live. We're getting a great response already. Give me a call."

Laura was pulling at her hand, and she felt unexpectedly unsteady. She'd wanted to make an impact, but right now, she wasn't sure if she was ready to deal with the fallout. Maybe no one would see it.

"Are you walking me home?" Laura asked, almost making her overbalance.

"Okay," she said; she could use the computer in her old room to see what Damien had meant by *a great response*. She took Laura's hand and began walking quickly. Laura trotted along next to her, talking more about Tara and vomit, but Rose wasn't listening. She knew she should be excited about the video, but she wasn't. Really, she felt a little sick with apprehension.

"Rose!" Laura said, stopping suddenly.

"What?"

"You're going too fast! My legs aren't as big as yours!"

She was just about to bend down to apologize when the car going past them honked loudly, making them both jump.

"Bitch!" someone yelled, and then they sped away, tires squeaking.

Laura looked up at her, chin wobbling.

"How about a piggyback?" Rose said.

Laura's face lit up. "Okay!"

Rose bent down, looking around edgily. It probably had nothing to do with the video; she was just being paranoid. But still, she didn't want any trouble coming her way with her little sister around.

"Not on the neck, remember?" Rose coughed.

Laura was climbing onto her back and using her neck as a handhold.

"Sorry!" Laura held her shoulders instead. Carefully, Rose stood, the backpack adding to the little girl's weight so she felt like a turtle.

"Ready?"

"Yeah!"

Rose started running toward home, Laura squealing "Giddyup, horsey!"

By the time they arrived, Rose was sweaty and out of breath but happy to be able to lock the door behind them. Laura wriggled off her and went into her room to change out of her school uniform. Rose went straight to her old room. It looked almost exactly the way she'd left it, except for a few of Sophie's toys scattered on the floor. She wished that she could turn the fan on and curl up in the bed. But it wasn't hers anymore. She sat down in front of the computer.

Rose only had to scroll midway down the front page of the *Sage Review* site to see it. The video she'd nicked from Jean's security camera. Underneath was the headline Hero Journalist Breaks Up Police Beating. Rose's mouth actually gaped. She thought the police would be the focus, not her. She didn't play the video, which already had thirteen thousand views, but scrolled down to the comments. People were angry. But not at Frank and Jonesy. At her.

"Should I be asking for your autograph?"

Rose spun on her chair. Rob was leaning in the doorway behind her.

"Or should I be asking why the hero journalist still hasn't cleaned all her stuff out?"

Rose resisted the urge to swear at him. If he knew what she was covering up for him, he'd be a lot nicer to her right now. The last time she'd seen him, he'd been smuggling meth.

"That's why I'm here."

He stood, surveying her. Then his eyes flicked to the screen behind her. "Making sure it got your best angle?"

She was surprised; Rob wasn't the kind of guy to read the newspaper, especially online. "You've already watched it?"

"Everyone has seen it, Rose. My mother can't use a computer and even she has watched it."

"Really?" she asked; nothing had ever moved so quickly in Colmstock. "What are they all saying? Are they shocked?"

She'd done it; she'd actually made a difference. No one could deny the barbarity of Colmstock's police now.

"They're shocked at how disloyal you are—they think you're trying to make a mockery of honorable men."

"Honorable?"

"Yes, honorable. I know you think you know everything about everyone, but you don't."

She leaned back in her chair, just looked at him.

"You need to back off the things you don't understand."

"What do you mean?" she asked, her voice threatening to rise.

"I mean exactly what I'm saying. Be careful."

"Daddy?" Laura called from the kitchen.

"Coming, sweetheart," he said, then turned back to her. "I'm serious, Rose. People do dumb things when they're desperate. Or angry. Watch your back."

By the time she got to Eamon's the view count of the video had doubled. She'd thought Rob was being his usual idiot self, but the majority of the comments were similar to what he'd said. And the few comments that weren't in defense of the police were mainly discussing the size and shape of her arse. There were a few expressions of shock about the attack, but they were the minority, and Rose got the impression that they came from people who didn't live anywhere near Colmstock.

As she approached the back door of Eamon's it was like she was walking onto the set from the video. The place had taken on an unreal quality. Her phone rang. It was Damien again. She sat down on the step to answer it.

"Have you seen the reaction?"

"Yes," she said. "I can't believe it!"

"It's incredible. Better than I'd hoped, and you've got a platform now too, which is great."

"A platform? They're all just calling me a bitch or saying they want to fuck me."

"Don't read the comments," he said, "but be happy you've started a discourse."

"A discourse?" she scoffed.

If he noticed her tone, he didn't react. "I want that article first thing tomorrow."

She already had the article written up in her notebook, so that wouldn't be a problem. But as she walked toward the kitchen she felt slightly sick. The comments were so aggressive, so full of hate. They went around and around in her head. Another article would make everyone even more angry with her.

"Hi," she said to Jean, as she put her bag down in the kitchen. Jean turned to her, and she could tell that she'd seen it too.

"Everyone's angry with me," Rose said. She put a hand over her face, and her throat constricted and a choked sob came out of her. Jean took Rose's other hand and held it between her two palms.

"I'm not."

"Really?" Rose asked. "You're probably the only one."

Tears were dribbling out of her eyes now. She tried to brush them away.

"I know you were trying to do the right thing," Jean said warmly, "but you've got to understand that this is a man's world. There's nothing we can do to change that. The best we can do is try to live in it without getting hurt."

"But it's so unfair. Steve didn't deserve to be bashed, and I don't deserve to have everyone saying such horrible things."

Jean's eyes turned pitying. "Rose, you're an adult. You won't survive if you keep being that naive."

They both turned as Mia walked into the kitchen. Seeing Rose's wet cheeks, Mia grabbed her into a hug and Rose hugged her back tightly as Jean went back to prepping the kitchen.

"Those bastards," Mia whispered.

Finally, Mia was seeing the cops for what they were. Rose hoped this included Bazza. Maybe all this was worth it just to have Mia back on her side. Embarrassed, Rose pulled back and went to the sink. She ran cold water onto her hands and splashed it onto her hot, blotchy face. The worst thing would be for Frank to arrive and see she'd been crying.

"I tried to tell Baz it wasn't you, but he wouldn't believe me."

Rose looked up at her, not understanding.

"I can't believe they hacked our security system. I knew stuff like that happened, but not here."

Rose opened her mouth to respond, but before she could, Jean cut in, "It's my fault—I didn't put a password on it."

"It's no one's fault but theirs." Mia grabbed a tea towel. Rose followed her toward the bar, but Jean softly touched her elbow.

"Just leave it. You won't be able to make her understand."

Rose nodded. Jean was right. She couldn't deal with anyone else being angry with her.

As the bar started filling up, Mia was extra nice to her. She did most of the serving and let Rose stick to the back. Washing dishes and making runs to the storeroom.

"Did Bazza mention if Frank and Jonesy are in trouble?" she asked Mia quietly, when their punters were sat down with their pints.

"Nah, not really. He said they might have to do some sort of disciplinary action for show, but really it just takes the pressure off a bit. Everyone in town knows how seriously they are taking those notes now."

Rose couldn't believe it. She stood still, watching one of the moths bash itself between the red beer sign and the window. She could almost hear the soft thud. She'd be cleaning its carcass off the floor when she swept tonight.

"Not working tonight, hero?" It was Jonesy. He, Bazza and the Father were sitting at their usual table. She'd been avoiding even looking in their direction.

"Leave her alone," Mia said. "It's not her fault."

"Never said it was. I just want my beer poured by Rose. Don't see why you should be doing all the work."

Rose grabbed a pint glass, staring Jonesy right in the eye as she filled it. He put his money on the bar and returned to his seat. Arsehole wanted her to bring it to him. Stuffing the money in the register, no tip, she picked up his pint and walked to their table. She was determined to conceal how much it was all getting to her.

"Here." She went to put it in front of him, but his foot whipped out from under the table, kicking her ankle. She gasped as she half fell forward, saving herself with her hand, but the icy liquid covered her shoes as it splashed onto the floor.

She stared around the table. Jonesy and Bazza stared at her. The Father averted his eyes, but said nothing.

"Didn't know you were so clumsy," Jonesy said.

"Didn't know you were such a fucking prick," she snapped. "Oh, wait—I did know that."

She turned to get a rag.

"I'd still like my beer," he called after her.

She grabbed a dirty tea towel, expecting Mia to offer to help. But she didn't. Mia didn't meet her eyes.

As if waiting for the exact right moment, Will walked in. Great. All she needed was this guy, who finally liked her as much as she liked him, seeing her humiliated. Her ankle throbbed where Jonesy had kicked it, but she resisted bending down to rub it. She repoured the beer and stared at Jonesy as she put it on the table, daring him to try it again. He didn't.

Her face burned as she squatted down to clean the spill as quickly as she could. Trying to hide her blush, she kept her head down, noticing their ankles. That was the point, she supposed. For her to be at their feet. But it was Jonesy's ankle that got her attention. His pants were hiked up slightly because he was sitting, and there was a gap between his sock and the cuff. His hairy skin was blotchy with a pinkish, scaly rash. Psoriasis. That was why he was scratching himself every time he went outside for a cigarette.

Something cold and wet dribbled down her back. She looked up.

"Sorry," Jonesy said, and she heard people laughing. Just as she was about to stand, more liquid dripped down her back. He was leaned over her, tipping the contents of his pint onto her head.

"Fuck off!" she yelled, and looking around, she saw people were laughing, smiling behind covered mouths, even Mia. Will stood up, looking confused. No. No way was she going to let these guys have a punch-up over her honor. That was just what they wanted. It was like Jean had said, that it was a man's world. Fuck that. Walking swiftly to the sink, Rose grabbed the moisturizer Mia used on her hands. She put it down on the table in front of Jonesy.

"Here. This might help with the itchiness."

Everyone stopped laughing, looking at him in confusion. He opened his mouth to say something else, but she leaned closer.

"My stepdad says hi."

Jonesy looked at her, and she looked back, refusing to drop her gaze. Then he held up his hands.

"Just having a laugh. Don't get your knickers in a knot."

"Right." She walked back up to the bar.

"Are you okay?" Mia asked.

"As if you care," she said, not even able to look at her.

She asked to use Jean's computer on her break, where she typed up her article and emailed it to the *Sage Review*. There was nothing like anger to bring back her determination.

SECOND ANONYMOUS LETTER
THREATENS DAUGHTERS
OF COLMSTOCK
by Rose Blakey

The police department of Colmstock has discovered an anonymous letter delivered directly to their station. This is the second letter they have received, but the first to directly threaten the town's children. The unknown assailant, who has named himself "The Doll Collector', has rocked this small community over the last fortnight. The situation began with five families discovering porcelain dolls left anonymously on their doorsteps. The dolls each bore an uncanny resemblance to the primary-school-aged daughters of the families. The case escalated when the first note was received; now a second note has been exposed by an anonymous source.

I am not sick. I just like to play with dollies but they don't like to play with me. Pretty hair, pretty faces. When I'm done they won't be pretty anymore. I think I'll break one soon.
—*The Doll Collector*

Despite the explicitness of intent in this letter, the police are still yet to make an arrest. Senior Sergeant Frank Ghirardello, the head of the investigation, refuses to comment on the case. However, a mother of one of the victims, Lucie Hoffman, states that the police have informed her that they still cannot find any connection between the girls. The people of Colmstock are afraid the local enforcement is ill-equipped to handle the seriousness of this case. A video, which can be watched on this paper's website, depicts Senior Sergeant Ghirardello, along with two other Colmstock police officers, beating a man outside a local bar. The man, whose identity has not been released, has been cleared of all involvement in the Doll Collector case.

30

When Rose checked her phone at the end of her shift, she had seven voice mails. They were all the same: heavy breathing, words like *bitch* eventually whispered into the phone.

She was uneasy waiting for Jean's car to pull out of the tavern's car park. No one but Will knew she was sleeping at the tavern, but still, crouching next to the police station didn't feel as safe as it once had. Above her, a bushy-tailed possum jumped from the tavern roof onto the power lines, and the sound almost made Rose have a heart attack. When Jean's taillights finally disappeared from view, she straightened and crossed the car park, around to the side of the building.

As she walked toward the stairs, she took out her keys. She held the longest one between two of her fingers, gripped it tight. The sound of heavy footsteps. She turned, already knowing who was behind her. Jonesy. They looked at each other, neither speaking. This wasn't a game anymore. There was no audience for either of them to prove themselves to. If she yelled out, Will might hear her. But Jonesy wouldn't hurt her. He just wanted to intimidate her.

"What did he tell you?" he said.

She looked between him and the stairs. If she ran she might make it, but she didn't want him to know that she was scared of him. If he knew that, he would have won.

"Who?" she said, although she knew exactly who he meant.

"Rob."

"Nothing," she said, stepping backward without being able to stop herself. "I was only kidding."

Three steps and he was right in her face, pushing her into the wall, and she cried out in surprise at the pain of the brick scraping into the bare flesh of her shoulder. His forearm pressed across her chest so she couldn't move, and he whispered into her ear.

"Just remember what I did to Steve. He's on the council and I fucked him up. You're a little slut with a death wish. No one will even blink if something happens to you."

The back door swung open.

"Hey!"

Jonesy released her and was gone. She fell forward, her hands on her thighs.

"Rose?" Will pounded down the stairs. "Who was that? Are you okay?"

There was too much going on in Rose's head for her to speak. She couldn't breathe.

"Come on," Will said. He grabbed her hand and led her to the stairs.

Her knees were wobbly. She slipped on the bottom stair. Her head felt light and cold; it spun. If they beat the shit out of Steve for nothing, what the hell would they do to her?

Police Reap Bloody Revenge on Local Journalist.

"Sit down," Will said. He pulled her onto the stair. Her vision was starting to swim. His face was out of focus.

She put her head forward, her throat clenching, sure she was going to be sick. Her body was heavy but she wanted to run, to get away. He was right. If they found that it was her who wrote the notes, they'd do more than just bash her.

Body of Local Journalist Discovered, No Leads. Oh, God.

"Are you all right?"

She needed to be alone. Somewhere safe. But there was nowhere. She couldn't breathe. She was going to pass out.

"Rose?"

Will's hand rubbed her back but she could barely feel it.

"Just focus on breathing," he said.

What the fuck was she going to do? Her skin was prickling. Cold and hot and shivery all at once. Her fingers were going numb. She couldn't feel her feet. Her heart was beating too fast, way too fast. Clattering between her ribs and her spine.

"Rose. Just breathe."

Will got off the step and bent down in front of her; she tried to focus on his eyes, looking into hers with concern. He put a hand against her chest.

"Follow," he said and breathed in slowly, and Rose followed. Then out, letting it whoosh from her mouth.

"Again."

Will's hand was an anchor. Pulling her back from the panic. Letting her feel her fingers again as she wrapped them around Will's wrist. She breathed again. Then started to laugh. A weak, scared giggle.

"Sorry," she said.

"Don't say sorry. You scared me. Who was that? Are you hurt?"

"Jonesy. I'm fine," she said. Rose was trying to focus on breathing, but her mind was still so scattered it was hard to talk.

"That piece of shit," Will said and began to stand.

"Don't," she said.

He took a deep breath, this one more for himself, she suspected, and reached out to take her hand. He held it tight as she walked up the stairs into the tavern. She hadn't slept in her room since Steve's attack, and she was glad she didn't have to tonight. Smelling his blood was the last thing she needed right now. She made a mental note to herself to wash the sheet properly tomorrow. It was still in the sink in her room; she hadn't been able to stomach finishing cleaning it.

Will pulled her singlet off her and put her down on her stomach on the mattress.

"It's just a scrape," he said. She heard him go into the bathroom and wet a towel. He dabbed it onto her back; she winced.

"What was going on with you guys tonight?" Will asked.

Slowly, she told him the story. About what she and Mia had seen at the factory. About how she'd taken the security video and given it to Damien.

"Do you think I did something stupid?" she asked.

He lay down on top of her, putting his cheek between her shoulder blades.

"Yes," he said, his breath stinging the scrape on her back, "but I also think it was brave."

"Thank you."

She tried to breathe deeply, but in the silence her mind started racing again.

"Tell me something," she said.

"What?"

"Anything. Something that's got nothing to do with any of this. Tell me about your family."

"My family?" He laughed, a light, easy sound. "What do you want to know?"

"Anything," she said, still smelling Jonesy's rank breath in her face.

"Okay, well, my mum is amazing. Her mother was indigenous and so my mum is really passionate about land rights.

She's a lawyer. She's one of those people who is the sweetest person you'll ever meet at home, but at work people are terrified of her."

Rose smiled. That was the kind of person she'd like to be. "And your dad?"

"My dad was brought up in Brunei. He moved here when he was a teenager. He doesn't work anymore. He just cooks and goes on long walks with our dogs and calls me every day."

"They sound nice."

She was feeling a little stronger again, more herself. He put his arms around her waist then pulled her onto her side.

"Feeling a bit better?"

"Yeah."

"Do you need a Band-Aid?" he asked.

"No, it's fine."

"Good. I know how much they make you cry."

"Shut up!" she said, elbowing him in the ribs, but unable to stop herself from laughing.

The first thing Rose did when she woke up the next morning was go into the hallway to call the *Sage Review*. She got the receptionist, her affected voice telling her that Mr. Freeman was in a meeting. The woman told her to wait and some awful piano music began to play. Rose wondered how big the office was. In her imagination it was huge, white and sparkly. Windows that went from ceiling to floor. Ten stories up at the very least. But now maybe she'd never see it. She had decided she was going to ask the editor to pull the article before it went to press tomorrow.

The piano music went on and on. She opened the door to the back and leaned against the wall, feeling the muggy air from outside, which was already starting to heat up. Looking down to the spot where Jonesy had pushed her into the wall, she remembered what Lucie had told her. About fainting in the street and everyone stepping over her. Lucie must have thought things were different in her hometown, but she was wrong. Colmstock was probably worse. You knew the person lying weak on the street, but you stepped over them anyway, maybe even gave them a kick.

Lucie. She hadn't thought about her since they'd left her door.

The piano music clicked off, and the receptionist came back on the line saying Damien was going to be tied up for at least a few hours.

"But tomorrow's paper hasn't gone to press yet, has it?" she asked, charging back toward Will's room. It hadn't. She quickly thanked the receptionist, asked her to tell Damien to call her then opened Will's door.

"Will!"

He opened his eyes with a start. "What?"

"Wake up." She sat down on the bed, crossed her legs in front of her. "Do you think that maybe Bess wasn't her real name?"

Will blinked, rubbed a hand over his face.

"I don't know why she'd make it up," he said.

"But it's possible, right? It's just…this old friend of mine went to the city for a while and came back with a kid. Her name's Lucie. That's why I didn't think of it."

He sat up, propped his elbows on his knees. "Do you think it could be her?"

"I have no idea, but it's possible," she said. "Only one way to find out!"

It was odd to walk down the street next to Will. He looked so different from everyone they passed and didn't seem to fit with the ugly houses and decaying fences around them.

His eyes were dark again, and he hadn't said much since they began. His hand was constantly swiping at his face.

"How do you deal with the flies here?" he said. "It's non-stop."

She shrugged. "You stop noticing it after a while."

"I can't imagine you growing up here."

She grinned at him. That was a big compliment, in her opinion.

"Have you met them?" He swallowed. "Lucie's kid?"

"Yes, only briefly. She's a girl. Her name's Nadine."

"Nadine," he repeated, his face drenched in emotion.

"She's gorgeous," Rose told him.

He reached over and took her hand in his.

"It's this one," Rose said, as they reached Lucie's house.

Will looked up at it. "I don't think I've ever been this nervous," he said, then laughed a panicky high laugh.

"Come on," Rose said to him. She tugged his hand, and together they walked down the path. Rose knocked, praying that Lucie would be home.

There was a shuffle inside. Footsteps. Then the door swung open and Lucie stood in the doorway, looking surprised.

"Didn't expect you to come back," she said to Rose. Then she looked at Will. Rose waited to see recognition appear in her eyes. It didn't.

"Who's your friend?" she said.

Rose turned to Will. The disappointment on his face was crushing.

31

I think I'll break one soon.

Frank must have read the words at least a hundred times. The note was taped up on the wall next to the first one on the board. The paper, the handwriting, it was all identical. It was definitely from the same person.

Frank sat in a chair, staring up at the scrawling letters. Feeling as though, somehow, he'd figure it all out just by looking at them. Like it was some sort of jigsaw puzzle. But it wasn't. He knew that. It was just some sick fuck with terrible handwriting and a thing for little kids. Some freak who wanted to taunt him.

Everyone bustled around the station. The phones were constantly ringing. Parents of the girls wanting someone to yell at, nosy idiots calling to blame their neighbors, lonely oldies who just wanted to voice their concern and people wanting to pat them on the back for their performance in Rose's bloody video. It was constant, and he thanked the Lord that he wasn't the one who had to answer the damn things. When he got home he could still hear the phone quietly ringing in his ears.

His head was pounding. Having a night off the sauce was meant to make him feel great, but it didn't. He felt like complete shit, worse than a hangover. Still, he was in strife with the chief, and turning up with even a hint of liquor on his breath could have been the end of him. He'd been reprimanded twice this week. The first was because of Rose. The girl was causing him nothing but trouble and she didn't even give a shit. Everyone seemed certain he'd spilled the beans on the notes, no matter how much he denied it. The thing was that he couldn't prove it. Especially now that she was so angry with him. There was no way for him to find out for sure where the leak had sprung from, although he was fairly certain he had guessed right with Bazza.

Where was Baz, anyway? He was meant to be here, with Frank, staring at the damn notes and trying to come up with a new lead. The guy was no bloody help.

The second time Frank had been reprimanded was yesterday, which was Rose's fault too, now that he thought about it. When he'd got home from Eamon's he'd felt like absolute shit. The way she'd looked at him when he'd tried to apologize, it still made him shiver with embarrassment and shame.

Maybe Jonesy was right. Maybe she was a bitch.

When he'd woken up that morning he had a heap of missed calls. He'd drunk himself to sleep, anything to stop the writhing humiliation and rejection in his belly, and been too far gone for even the shrill ring of his cell phone to wake him. When he'd hurried into the station, still stinking of his nightcaps, the chief had brought him straight into his office and served him his balls for breakfast. The note had arrived at four in the morning and every other cop in town had been at the station from five. This was Frank's case, and he hadn't got there until eight. That made him look bad. Rose thought she was fucking with him even more with that security footage she'd given to the papers. Turned out it was the first good thing that had happened since that first bloody doll appeared. Now at least people knew he'd do whatever it took to get the sick fucks off the street. That wasn't why she'd done it. He wasn't stupid enough to think that. The girl who he'd broadcast his affection for despised him, and she wanted the world to know it.

Last night, he'd had to sleep without any help even though the shame and humiliation of the day were fucking tenfold.

He stared up at the board of notes and photographs. The dolls' glass eyes stared benignly back. If he could find the connection between the families, he was sure he could crack it. They vaguely knew one another, sure, but so did everyone else in this town. They were all so different—Rose's sister with her absent parents, Carly Riley's arsehole dad, Lily Hane's weirdo brother. They were all strange enough, but then there was Nadine Hoffman. Her mother and grandma seemed to be doing a decent enough job raising her. He'd pressed her about the kid's father, but she'd maintained he didn't even know he had a daughter. Whoever the guy was, Frank couldn't rule him out. The Hoffmans knew the Hanes, but not the rest of them, and Carly was homeschooled, so that ruled out a teacher. The phones started ringing again and Frank threw his head back in frustration.

"Where've you been?" he asked, when Bazza finally ambled his way into the station.

"Hospital." Baz pulled off his jacket and swung himself onto a chair, leaning back and staring up at the board.

"Who's in the hospital?"

Bazza didn't even look at him.

"Don't tell me you went to see the faggot."

"So what if I did? Thought he might have some info."

"Bullshit. Mia put you up to this, didn't she?"

Baz just shrugged.

"Don't let her get on your back already—you haven't even had a ride yet."

"She's saving herself."

Frank wanted to groan, but didn't. Mia was nowhere near a virgin; anyone could have told him that. Jonesy said Mia had sucked him off outside the tavern without even being asked. But the truth was, he liked the two of them together. Baz seemed happy. In fact, he seemed fucking joyous. He came into the station every morning with the biggest grin on his dumb face, and he wasn't even getting laid. Mia was a good egg. Looking after her father the way she did, never giving you a hard word at the tavern no matter how far off your chops you were. She was good for Bazza, and if he wanted to believe he was going to bust her cherry, Frank wasn't going to ruin that for him.

"How's he doing?"

"He'll be okay." Baz kept it vague, and Frank was happy about that too. It wasn't something he really wanted to think about right now. He had enough on his plate.

"Frank?" one of the uniforms called, a phone pressed against his chest.

"Yeah?"

"Mr. Riley."

Great. The guy was skinny as a beanpole but he scared the shit out of Frank. He had the sort of eyes that told you he'd kill you without even blinking if he could get away with it. Frank had been over to their place a bunch of times for domestics. He had a feeling that was why the kid was always hanging out behind the courthouse in the first place. If Mrs. Riley was tending the grocery store, she'd send him there to play rather than having him be home alone with her husband. Frank didn't blame her, although she was probably blaming herself for it now. Poor woman.

"I'm out following a lead," he said.

The uniform looked at him, unimpressed. He knew why. If Mr. Riley wanted to talk to Frank he was going to give the guy hell until he did. Mr. Riley wasn't the best family man in town, but still. He'd had the worst time of it, his business literally going up in smoke, his kid dying. Now there was all this business with the dolls. It would have destroyed most men. Somehow, it had done the opposite to Mr. Riley. Made him even more determined. Maybe Frank should be trying to take a page out of his book. The crap he'd been through made Frank's week look like a walk in the park. There was still time to fix all this.

He turned away from the uniform toward Bazza and sat up as straight as he could.

"We've got to get this guy," he said. "'I think I'll break one soon'… That's intent right there."

"Makes me sick," Baz said.

"We'll get him."

Things were going to be all right. He was going to cut down on the booze, he decided. Refocus. He'd sort things with Rose too. The girl had gone out with him and he'd been a gentleman. You couldn't just go on a date with a man and then treat him like dirt. No. She wasn't going to blow him off. He would win her over. She owed him a second chance.

32

"We'll figure it out," Rose told Will. "Seriously, we'll keep looking until we find her."

He was sitting on the side of the bed, as she pulled on her work clothes.

"I know," he said. "I just shouldn't have gotten my hopes up. It didn't even make sense that she would change her name. I'm starting to think maybe she's not here at all. What if she just sent the letter from here? Or what if the thing she was scared of already happened?"

Rose took his head in her hands. "We'll find her." She leaned to kiss him. "Okay?"

"I hope so."

Rose listened at the door to make sure no one was coming, then went out into the corridor. She paused, leaning on the wall with her eyes closed and listening to the sounds of Mia setting up for the night. The crinkle of plastic as she put a new black liner into the bin. The wet sucking-thunks of her clipping the beer taps back into place. The clinks of glass as she unpacked the dishwasher. The quiet whir as she turned

the stereo on and then the beginning of a harmonica playing over piano.

Sitting on the back step, she breathed in the smell of hot
rubbish and pulled out her phone to call *Sage* again. Damien
hadn't returned her call, and she didn't want to leave it too
late. The receptionist answered, telling her again in her snooty
voice that the editor would call as soon as he had the chance.

The fear that had overwhelmed her earlier had subsided,
leaving just sweaty detachment in its wake. She was so close,
and now she was going to blow it. Again, her life would be all
about rejection letters and Eamon's. It would be even worse
now that the whole town hated her. Part of her felt like she'd
rather die.

Frank watched Rose and Mia work. They weren't speaking
to each other, mostly just dancing around each other as they
did various tasks. Maybe they'd had a falling-out.

He knew he shouldn't be here right now. There were only
three places he should be: the station, out on the streets looking for the freak or at home catching some z's. But he'd been
working hard; he deserved just one drink to take the edge off.
One beer was okay, normal. If he couldn't have a beer with
his mates after a hard day then he really did have a problem.

He watched Rose work, then saw her look up and smile.
A smile he'd never seen on her face before. Sensual and open.
Will, who'd just sat down at a table, was smiling back. They
were looking at each other like they shared some fucking secret.

Frank pounded back his beer, not even tasting it. This
wasn't how it was meant to go. He'd taken her out, put his
best shirt on, paid for her burger. Now she was meant to be
waiting for his call. She was meant to be gagging for a second
date, where he'd take her out to some nice restaurant, ask her

back for a coffee and then fuck her brains out. That was how this went. She couldn't just go out with him and then act as if it never happened. You couldn't go on a date with someone one day, then humiliate and betray them the next. No. That just wasn't how it worked.

He went up to the bar, slamming his empty glass down. She took it from him without even looking up. Mia began pouring him another.

"So how about a second date?" he said to her back, unable to hide the aggression in his voice.

She turned and scoffed. Actually scoffed, "Not likely."

Bitch. She really was a fucking bitch.

"Just give her some time, Frank," Mia said softly.

"Yeah, sure."

He took his beer back to his seat, knowing they'd be exchanging a look behind his back right now. Laughing at him. He would drink this beer quick and get the hell out of here. He should be home, not hanging out in this shit hole. There was still half a bottle of bourbon on his nightstand, so there was no point even being here.

For the first five minutes after Rose heard the voice mail, she told no one. Jean flicked the lock on the front door, and finally, the cops were gone. Rose tried to think while she washed glasses. Mia was collecting them from the tables, bringing stacked towers to the sink. Rose had on the pink rubber gloves. Her hands moved like a factory worker. Emptying dregs into the sink, three pushes into the detergent and then into the glass washer. There was a pint glass in each of her hands at every moment, but she never, ever had dropped one. Mia was singing along softly to "Dancing in the Dark"; Jean was keying sums into a calculator. For Rose, the words on her voice mail were spinning around and around in her head.

"Hi, it's Damien from *Sage*. Sorry it's taken me a while to get back to you. The video is still trending and I just had a chance to read your new article. It's great. That note… Wow."

And then the last thing he said, the thing that she was sure she must have imagined: "Once all that crazy doll shit wraps up in Colmstock, we want you here. You're not really qualified, but I've pulled some strings and we'd like to offer you a cadetship. We're only meant to do one a year, but they've allowed me to make an exception. Call me back, all right?"

"What?" Jean said. Rose's head was now in her hand, warm soapy water slipping down her forehead.

"Is it Frank? Be careful with him, Rose," Jean told her. "It's good to be direct, but you've got to be kind as well. I don't think he's the type to handle rejection well."

"No, it's not that," she said. She didn't have time to worry about Frank and his bullshit ego trip. Her head was looping with the message. There wasn't room for anything else. Her future was right there, being held out to her on a silver platter. She had been all set to tell them to pull the article. But now…now that she could have it all, that she could get out of here… Start again. Have the future she'd always wanted. It felt different. At the same time, the first article had created such a mess. Telling them not to run it was the right thing to do, she was sure.

"They left a voice mail," she said. "*Sage*. They offered me that cadetship."

"Really?" squealed Mia, turning now. Looking at her properly for the first time that night.

"And?" Jean prompted. "You'll take it of course?"

Rose looked between them.

"Yeah. I mean, I guess so."

Mia began to scream. Loudly, almost hysterically, right in Rose's face. Jean put three shot glasses on the bar and filled them with Bundy. Rose stared into Mia's gaping mouth and couldn't help smiling. She picked up one of the shot glasses.

"Cheers," Jean said and the three of them clinked their shot glasses together, and Rose downed her drink. It burned her throat in just the right way.

Jean looked at her proudly. "You deserve it."

Mia rolled her empty shot glass between her thumb and forefinger. She looked up at Rose again and said, "I'm sorry."

Rose was about to retort that she should be sorry, she'd been a really shitty friend, when Jean's face lit up. "Good. You girls need to work this out."

She put the bottle of Bundy between them. "Here's a going-away present, Rose."

Now was not the time for Bruce Springsteen. Instead, Mia decided on Divinyls and flicked the volume knob way up. She danced, the rum in her blood now. She kicked up her legs and Rose laughed at her, spinning in a circle.

"I'm leaving now!" Jean yelled, her bag on her shoulder.

"What?" they called.

"Don't make a mess!"

"We won't!"

They danced quick steps up on their tiptoes, around and around, arms in the air, singing all the words they knew about being tired and wired and desperate and low. The beer signs were glowing. They looked beautiful. Everything in this place was looking so glittery and beautiful. She grabbed Rose's hand and spun her and they laughed and giggled and went to sit on a chair but it slipped to one side and they rolled onto the freshly mopped floor.

They lay there. Staring at each other. Panting.

"What am I going to do without you?"

"Nothing. You're going to come with me."

Rose turned onto her back, staring up at the ceiling.

"I can't believe this isn't going to be our life anymore."

Mia stared at Rose's profile. It was better this way. Better that Rose left. Extending her hand, she reached toward Rose's bare arm. She stroked downward, her fingertips millimeters from Rose's skin. She could feel the warmth radiating off her.

Rose turned to her. Mia pulled her hand away.

"Is your head spinning?"

Mia wasn't ready for this night to end. "Not yet. Time for another shot."

She heaved herself to her feet.

33

That morning, Frank and Mia woke in much the same way. Both curled toward the side of the bed, worried they might be sick. Their bodies both stank of sweaty liquor and unbrushed teeth. The night before began to open up to both of them. Both winced. Frank, at how he'd acted at the tavern. Mia, at the memory that she had driven home. Together, they wished that they hadn't had that last drink. Together, they wished there was someone in their bed with them, someone who was there to hug them and tell them that it would be okay. Someone to make them feel less desperately alone.

Then they both had the same exact thought. It made them pull the sheet over their heads in their respective rooms, the lounge room in Mia's case, and wish to go back to sleep. Wish to disappear completely.

They both thought, *I've really lost her now.*

34

Rose woke up in Will's bed. She felt bleary and hungover. She pressed up closer to his warm body, their sweaty skin sticking together, and stroked her fingers over his sparse black chest hair absentmindedly.

"Morning, sleepyhead," he said.

Usually that kind of cutesiness would make her groan, but she could feel a goofy smile spread over her face.

"How drunk was I when I came in last night?" she asked, her memory wobbling.

"A little—you basically bashed my door holding an empty bottle of rum and asked if I wanted to share it with you."

"Oh, God," she said, though secretly she was glad that was the worst of it. She was afraid to think of the things she might have said: that it was her behind the notes or, perhaps worse, that she was worried she might be falling in love with him.

"Did I tell you I got a cadetship with the *Sage Review*?"

"Yep," he said and kissed her on the edge of her nose, "and I'm thrilled."

"I'm not leaving straightaway," she said. "I'll make sure we find her before I go."

He squeezed her closer. "Don't you worry about that. I'll figure it out."

She pressed her face into his chest. He was being nice but it wasn't what she wanted to hear. She wanted him to need her.

"I should get going," she said, rolling off him.

"No, just a bit longer." He pulled her back to where she had been. "Stay."

"Fine. Five minutes," she said and let herself relax, listening to his heartbeat. She was too hungover to rush around today. Soon, she'd be gone and Will would stay here until he'd found his kid, and who knew how long that would take.

Instead of slowing, she noticed his heart rate was actually quickening.

"Rose?" he said, just as she was about to ask him if he was okay.

"Yeah?"

"When you go…" He paused to swallow.

"I really don't want this to end." He breathed the words more than said them, making her hair flutter.

"Neither do I," she said. "Not at all."

He breathed in, then shuffled over to look at her. "Good."

"I've got to go now though."

"Stay."

"Nah, I've got heaps to do." She got up, put a hand over her chest as she looked for her top. She'd slept in just her underwear and had an awful memory of doing a drunken, and wholly-unattractive, striptease for Will.

"My article is coming out today," she said, as she picked up her T-shirt. Guilt washed over her; all those parents were going to feel sick when they read it.

Will pushed her back into the bed, and she pulled the sheet over herself.

"I think you are going to be a very successful newspaperwoman," he said, rubbing his hand over her hair. He pushed the sheet off, so her breasts were exposed. He ran his hand over them, his thumb stroking her nipple.

"Thank you." She tried to keep the gasp out of her voice, the guilt evaporating with his touch.

"I knew it the first time I met you, when you told me that bullshit story."

"It's not all bullshit."

He just looked at her, eyebrows raised.

"There really was a family that lived here called the Eamons."

"But they are alive?" he asked, pulling her underwear back off.

"I doubt it," she said, feeling exposed. "It was like eighty years ago."

He was fully dressed now and she was totally naked.

"I've got to go." It came out a whisper.

He ran a hand down her breasts again, and she arched her back toward him.

"I'm not stopping you," he said and put her knees up over his shoulders. He dipped three fingers between her legs. She wanted to scream.

"Off you go, then," he said. He moved them, in and out, inch by inch. He pressed his other palm down onto her stomach, feeling it spasm.

"Go on," he said and leaned down. He put his mouth down in between her legs, hot and wet and slippery. His finger moved in and out of her. His tongue licked her, sucked on her, and it was too much. Too much to bear. Finally, she did scream. She couldn't help it. Her whole body jerked as she came and came again. Every muscle clenched and released, and she never, ever wanted him to stop.

Finally, she pushed him away, exhausted. Her whole body

was slick with sweat and she felt like she was underwater. Every muscle heavy and slack.

Slowly, he pulled her underwear back on. He took her shorts off the floor and put each of her feet into them then slid them back up. The rasp of the denim against her legs was almost too much for her skin to take. She stretched, her arms reaching high above her head, then got up.

"Where are you going?" he asked, as she clipped on her bra.

"In case you haven't noticed, I stink. Laundry day is overdue."

She leaned down to grab her T-shirt and he pulled her into him and kissed her softly. She pushed him off.

"Gross."

She rushed down the street toward her old home, still grinning. She'd meant it when she said she'd try to help Will. She knew everyone in this town; together they'd find this woman and her kid.

Passing the lake, she smiled. Usually, she would avoid looking at it, hating the way it brought up memories of the relationship she used to have with her mum. But now the memories of what they used to have didn't feel so tainted. Things would never, ever be like they were again, but perhaps that was okay.

Rose let her arms stretch out. God, she must stink. There was a wind coming through; it was a hot wind, but still. It blew her hair around her face and, most important, her smell away from her nose.

Turning onto her street, she noticed something was different about the houses, but she couldn't put her finger on what. Now that she was really going to be a proper journalist, she'd have to be more observant. Excitement fizzed through her. She was a journalist. Everything was changing. It wasn't just a maybe. It was a real solid thing. After she'd done her laundry she'd go and find a copy of this morning's *Sage Review*, where her words would be printed in the pages.

Although, there was one issue. Something that almost made her laugh at the irony. She couldn't leave Colmstock until the case was solved, until the person who wrote the letters was apprehended. Damien had wanted her to follow the story until its conclusion. But, of course, there wouldn't be a conclusion. No one would be arrested, unless it was Rose herself. The anxiety, which had become all too familiar, stirred inside again, but she tried to dismiss it.

Maybe she'd write another note, saying that the "Doll Collector" had changed his mind about murdering children for some reason or another. Although, that wouldn't stop another doll from showing up.

As she turned down her path, it occurred to her what looked different about all the houses. Stopping in her tracks, she looked up and down the street. Usually, because of the heat, curtains were drawn and windows were open. People often even left their front doors open, with screen doors fastened, of course. But now all the houses were shut down like fortresses. Doors and windows closed, and curtains pulled tight.

Unlocking her front door, she went straight into the laundry. She emptied her backpack of clothes that stank of sweat and beer and sex into the washing machine and poured in some powder. Snapping the lid shut loudly, she heard the sound of little footsteps.

"Posey!" Laura almost pushed her over with the force of the hug. "I missed you," she said, her face in Rose's stomach.

"I missed you too." She stroked Laura's hair. It was true; she missed little Laura. Leaning down, she kissed the top of her head.

"You're moving back in?" Laura asked, and without waiting

for an answer, she started jumping up and down and screaming, "Yay! Yay!"

Rose squatted down to her level. "Not quite, but I'm going
to come to visit lots. Okay?"

Laura stopped bouncing. She glared down at her feet.

"Okay?" Rose touched Laura's chin so she'd look up.

"I don't like you anymore," Laura said and ran out of the
room.

Rose groaned and stood up. She pulled her clothes off and
tossed them into the cycle she'd already started. Grabbing a
towel, she wrapped it around herself and headed to the bathroom.

She turned the shower on hot and got underneath it. She
washed her hair, covered herself in soap, scrubbed everything
so it was new and clean. When she came out she wrapped
herself back in the towel, took out her hair dryer. She heard
the front door slam shut and rolled her eyes. When was Laura
going to grow up? She knew that the kid had probably waited
for the water of the shower to stop just to make sure Rose
would hear it. She turned the hair dryer on.

When the cycle finished, she threw her clothes in the dryer
and pulled on her old dressing gown. Doing up the sash, she
walked past Laura's room.

"Nice try," she said through the door, waiting to hear the
scuffle of feet as Laura came out from under the bed looking
disappointed. But there was no sound at all.

"I'm going now—come say goodbye," she said, coming into
the room and almost tripping on a toy puppy.

Rose got down and looked under the bed. There was a toy
bunny and some dirty socks, but no Laura.

35

"Laura's gone."

That was what Baz had told Mia on the phone, but she still couldn't believe it. Not really. She didn't believe it when she ran to her car, jumped in and started the ignition. She didn't believe it the whole drive over. But when she pulled up to the curb and saw the two police cars outside Rose's house, when she saw the crime-scene tape, she had to swallow her denial. This was really happening.

Mia ducked under the yellow plastic perimeter. There was no one out there to stop her. The front door was open, so she walked straight in. Inside, three uniformed police were standing in the doorway to Laura's room, talking.

In the lounge room Rose was sitting on the couch with her head down. Sophie and Scott sat on either side of her. Frank and Bazza were questioning them, perched on the coffee table, since there were no other chairs.

Frank was talking, his voice light for the kids. "So you haven't seen any funny-looking people hanging around?"

Sophie and Scott shook their heads.

"Does Laura have any secret friends?" Baz asked. Mia hung back, knowing this conversation shouldn't be interrupted.

"Yeah, she's got Bob," Sophie said.

Bazza and Frank looked at each other briefly. Then Frank shuffled a bit closer to Sophie. "Who's Bob, honey? You don't need to be scared."

Sophie shrugged.

"Laura doesn't want us to talk to him," Scott told him.

"But you checked him out, didn't you, son? You wouldn't want your little sister in trouble."

Scott shrugged. "Nah, Bob's lame."

"Is Bob a kid like you? Or is he more my age?" Baz asked.

"He's way older than you," Scott said, and every adult stiffened.

"He's three hundred!" Sophie added.

"Nah-uh! Seven hundred!"

"That's stupid! Turtles don't live that long."

"They do!"

"Stop." Rose spoke for the first time, but kept her head down. They stopped arguing and leaned back, annoyed, arms crossed.

"Is Laura going to die?" Sophie asked.

"No," Frank said quickly.

"But I thought when people got kidnapped they died?"

"Not always," Rose told her.

"How long until she dies?" Scott asked.

Finally, Rose looked up, straight at Frank.

"At this stage, it's impossible—"

"Baz?" she asked, eyes pleading. She needed the truth.

"Realistically, after twelve hours we expect a body."

Rose shot Frank a look before he could say anything to Bazza. "Go play outside," she said to the kids.

"Finally!" They got up and ran out.

"It's already been three hours," she said so quietly that Mia could barely hear it from where she was standing. "She's only five."

Mia crossed the room and sat down next to Rose, wrapping her arms around her. She felt so hard and still. Like a statue. Her body didn't react to the hug at all.

"We'll find her," Mia whispered in her ear, because they would. Nothing bad would happen to Laura; it couldn't.

She sat back, her arm still around Rose, and faced Bazza and Frank. How they must look to Rose right now. Still wearing their jackets, badges in their buckles, notepads in their hands. She'd served these guys countless drinks over the years, but she'd never really thought of them as cops. But now authority came off them in waves. And power. It was terrifying. It meant this was real. Frank was looking at Rose in a way, a way that told Mia he thought the worst. He thought something awful had happened to her sister.

"Get some rest, Rose. We'll be in touch if there is any news."

Rose glared at Frank. "No. You'll tell me now. How likely is it you'll find her?"

"At this stage, there is no reason to—"

"Stop it. Stop playing the policeman and tell me."

Frank looked down at the notepad in his hands. He couldn't do it. He couldn't even look her in the eye.

"We've had our team working around the clock on the notes for the last week. We have trace evidence, we have a psychological profile—"

"You said the notes could be a hoax."

"We are very confident that they will lead—"

"She's right!" Mia said. "What if some other sicko wrote them?"

"Then we'll lock them up too."

"And the notes are all you've got?" Rose asked urgently.

Frank continued looking at his hands. The door clanged

open and Rose's stepdad walked in. He was trembling, his face ashen.

"Frank? What's going on? Where's my daughter?"

Bazza and Frank got up and walked over to him. Now that Rob was here, he was the focus. Slowly, with no one else watching but Mia, Rose stood. She walked shakily around the men toward the door. Her feet slipping into the broken sneakers that were near the front door. She wasn't even looking.

"Where are you going?" Mia called after her.

"I'm going to find her."

Mia didn't follow.

Mia drove in silence. Usually, she would never drive alone without the radio blaring. Not tonight. As she drove past the fossickers she saw police flashlights. Tents were being kicked in, structures destroyed. A teenage couple was being screamed at by an officer. They must be looking for Laura there. Every time a crime occurred in town, this was the first place they came. Mia had never heard of any of the fossickers actually getting arrested, but if the police suspected them there must be grounds. After all, there had to be a reason why they ended up there in the first place.

Jean hadn't put Springsteen on at work either. That was a first. The two of them stood behind the bar; the only sounds were Jean padding numbers into the calculator, and the occasional tinkle as the cutlery Mia was shining dinged against each other. Apart from the two of them, the place was totally empty.

"Maybe we should close up—no one will be coming in tonight."

"They'd better not," Mia said. "I'll kill them if they come in here for a drink instead of out there looking."

Luckily for them, no one did come to the tavern. Mia had meant it. If a cop dared show his face in here she would send them packing. Maybe Jean knew that, because an hour later, they decided to call it a night. Mia felt long past exhausted, although she knew there was no way she'd be able to sleep.

Closing up didn't take long. There was no point mopping the floor, since only she and Jean had trodden on it. There were no glasses to wash, no point cleaning the taps since they hadn't poured any beer. All she really had to do was lock the back door. As she did, she walked past the guest's room. The light was on, fanning out from underneath the door. What the hell was Will even still doing here? Something was going on with him, she could tell. Rose had thought so too.

She knocked loudly on his door.

For one crazy moment she half expected to hear Laura's voice scream out, but of course it was only Will who replied, "Yes?"

"Do you need your room cleaned?"

"No."

"Are you sure? Must be starting to smell rank in there."

There was no answer. She hesitated, listening for anything that might not be right. But there was nothing, so she turned off the hallway light and headed back toward the front.

Jean was waiting for her, her bag on her shoulder. They flicked off the main lights without speaking, and Mia walked down toward her Auster as Jean fished for her keys.

Mia unlocked her car door.

"Let me know, okay?" Jean called, as she walked to her own car.

"I will."

She watched Jean walk across the road, away from Eamon's. Jean had always looked so powerful to Mia, like such a force to be reckoned with. Now she just looked like an old woman.

Mia wished she'd followed Rose. She needed to do something. Needed to help. Looking up, into the lit-up police station windows, she saw Baz and Frank sitting in the break room having a coffee. She slammed her car door shut.

36

How could she ever have thought that things were going to be okay? Things were not okay. They would never be okay again. And it was Rose's fault.

She'd made a mess. A big fucking mess. Things were bad and it was her fault. Writing the notes had made her believe there was no real threat, that it was all her invention. She'd never even considered she might be right. That what she had written in the notes might be true: the person who had left the dolls was marking his victims.

Some monster had her sister.

Her stomach clenched and she wanted to cry but that would be selfish. There wasn't time to cry. She had to find Laura.

But she had no fucking clue where to look. Where would someone take a little kid? She shivered. The air was heavy with heat and the blistering wind was still blowing, but her sweat felt ice-cold. It was like she'd made this happen. Like she'd willed it into being by what she had written.

For a while, Rose had jogged down the streets, straining her ears, hoping to hear something, see something. Now she just walked. Slamming one foot down on the road after another,

her feet rubbing painfully in her mum's old sneakers, but she wouldn't stop going until she found her. Usually, Rose would never walk around town by herself at night. But how could she be scared now? The worst thing possible had already happened.

The notes. They'd changed everything, created a nasty, festering mess that she couldn't even see her way out of. She hadn't ever thought pen and paper could do damage like this. She hadn't thought that something she had done could have such a massive ripple effect. It had always felt like it was just her against the world; if she wanted something to happen she had to make it happen. And making something happen, making anything change, felt completely impossible. But now she had changed everything, not just for her. The whole town felt changed, more paranoid and suspicious. It was her fault. Laura was gone and it was her fault.

But Laura couldn't be gone. People didn't just vanish.

Part of her wanted to turn around and run back to the police station. She didn't know what the right thing to do was anymore. She could find Frank or Baz and tell them the truth. That it was her who had written the notes, that they had absolutely nothing to do with Laura. But then they'd just waste more time focusing on her and the fucked-up thing she'd done rather than finding Laura. The only purpose would be to get rid of this feeling. This sickening, stomach-twisting guilt that she was sure would take over if she stopped moving. Back or forward, back or forward? Which way should she go? Was it selfish to turn herself in, help the police and appease her guilt? Or was it selfish not to come clean, to keep lying, to believe she had a better chance of finding her then the cops did? It went around and around impossibly. Back or forward. Back or forward.

The library rose in front of her.

She stopped walking.

You're just a big old slow coach.

Laura's voice had been so breathless and happy. The sun was out. They were going to the library. Everything was easy and normal and nice.

Rose's knees screamed in pain. Without even knowing it, she'd fallen to the road. She had begun to wail. Not cry. Wail. Agonized, painful sobbing cries coming out of her. Gravel dug into her hands and knees but she couldn't even fucking feel it. Laura. Her Laura. Tiny and perfect and just wanting to spend time with her big sister. She turned over so she was sitting, head between her bleeding knees, trying to breathe. Trying to stop the wails that came out on top of each other with such force that she couldn't even breathe, that she might just be sick. She had to get up. She had to keep looking. But she felt so small, so insignificant. She felt like a child and she just wanted someone to help her. Someone to tell her it was all going to be okay. So she rocked herself back and forth, and told herself to hush. Told herself that it was going to be fine.

Slowly the wails quieted, and it was just her ragged breath she could hear between her knees. That, and something else. A dull thud, like something heavy dropping a small distance. Then a yelp, so soft it was barely perceptible, but unmistakably human.

She got up. She had heard something. Definitely. It had come from the courthouse. The black, collapsed shell of a building.

The rubbish. The T-shirt. She'd seen it herself out of the library window. Someone was hiding there. Someone who was willing to be somewhere dangerous in order not to be seen. She didn't have time to prepare, time to steel herself and decide whether or not it was a good idea. She was already charging forward. Pushing the police barricade out of the way. Stepping softly on the burned debris. Whoever it was, she didn't want them to hear her coming.

37

Frank and Bazza huddled over their coffee mugs. It had been a long day. Frank knew he stank. He'd sweated, dried off and sweated again continuously since he got the hysterical phone call from Rose that morning. They'd bashed on so many doors, cruised so many streets, done everything he could possibly think of to find the kid. To begin with, he'd been so sure that they would. He'd pictured being Rose's savior. She could never be angry with him again after that. What was it that she had printed in this morning's paper? Something to do with the police being "ill-equipped to deal with this situation." That was aimed at him; he knew it. The sergeant seemed to know it too. But he had been sure he'd recover the kid, apprehend the freak who called himself such a ridiculous name and prove them all wrong.

But they hadn't found her. Not even a trace. And now they were out of places to look. He kept thinking of that line: "Pretty hair, pretty faces. When I'm done they won't be pretty anymore."

He had a bottle of bourbon in his desk drawer. He'd had a few sips already. Just to clear his head. But he wanted another.

Desperately, he wanted to obliterate himself so he wouldn't think it anymore—"Pretty hair, pretty faces." That poor fucking kid.

"Mia?" Bazza said, looking over Frank's shoulder.

Frank turned. Mia was storming toward them, looking pissed off.

"You're not meant to be in here," Frank said, but she didn't even look at him. Instead, she picked up his coffee mug and threw it into the sink. It shattered.

"What the fuck!"

"It's not coffee time, Frankie. You need to be out there looking for Rose's sister."

"We have been looking! We can't find her," Baz said.

"You can't have looked everywhere."

"Just about," Frank told her.

"What about him?" She pointed toward the tavern, framed by the dark window. "None of this happened until he got here. Plus, Rose saw him hanging around outside the school yard and he's got a teddy bear in his room."

"That's not evidence."

"Doesn't seem like evidence has mattered before."

Bazza shrugged. Both he and Mia turned to look at Frank.

He'd caught the looks Will had given Rose, staring at her unashamedly, superior. Telling him what to do with Steven homo-Cunningham, like he didn't know who Frank was in this town. Arrogant fuckhead was so self-righteous.

Mia raised her eyebrow. This was his chance. His chance to win Rose back. To prove to her who the real man was.

He didn't need to be asked twice.

Frank kicked in the door of room one with a crash.

"Hey!" yelled Mia. "Jean is going to kill you!"

Will jumped out of bed. He'd been reading, glasses crooked

on his face, tired eyes confused. Baz rammed him. Head in his chest, he pushed Will onto the bed. Will twisted out from under him. Quick for a guy who'd been taken by surprise.

"What the hell are you guys doing?" he yelled. He pulled back his arm and hit Bazza in the temple with his elbow. It made a clonking sound.

Frank lunged at him, tried to grab his arms, but Will pushed him off and Frank stumbled into Mia. She fell backward into the door of room two, pushing it open. Fucker had made him hurt a girl.

Bazza got up with a yell. He grabbed Will's arms from behind. Pinned them to his back. Will twisted around. Trying and failing to free himself.

Frank got closer to him, waited until he had caught his eye, then punched him solidly in the jaw.

"I've wanted to do that from the first second I saw your smug face," Frank said, and boy, was it worth it. He stretched his fingers, enjoying the throbbing of his knuckles.

"Did it feel good?" Baz said from behind Will, holding the guy up as he staggered from the blow.

"You bet."

"What's happening?" asked Will. Frank loved how shocked he looked. How his eyes were watering slightly. Was the arsehole going to cry?

"Hey, guys!" Mia said from behind him.

"I haven't done anything!" Will said, squirming, but Bazza's grip was strong.

"Hold him steady."

"Frank! Come here!" she yelled. He shouldn't have let her come.

"I'm busy." He pounded Will again; his head cracked back.

"There's blood."

He turned. Mia was standing in the other motel room,

looking into the bathroom. He went in. The bleach smell hit him first. The bathroom sink was full of pink water. He took a step closer. There was a bedsheet in there, a dark red splatter staining it. The bastard was trying to wash it out. He had already started erasing the crime scene.

"That's a lot of blood," Mia said, and what she really meant was that it was a lot of blood for a kid.

"You did that! It's Steve's," Will said from behind him. Frank watched Mia turn to him, eyes blazing. He'd never seen that expression on her face before. Not when someone didn't tip, not when a drunk guy pinched her on the arse.

"You're a monster!"

Frank looked away from the sink. He felt queasy. It meant they'd probably only find a body. He didn't want to see Laura's dead face, pick up her stiff little body from wherever this creep had stashed it. He still had a faint bruise on his shin from where she'd kicked him. He noticed something, a small blue corner, protruding from under the pillow on the bed. He took a pen out of his pocket and walked over. Carefully, he used the pen to pull out a blue spiral-bound notebook. It had lined paper and rounded edges. The same kind as the notes.

"You've been a busy man," he said to Will. All along, he'd been right about this freak.

"Where's the girl?" Bazza said, jerking Will from behind.

"I can't believe this—you've set me up!"

The freak wasn't even original. Mia got down on her knees and looked underneath the bed.

"Laura?" Mia opened the door to the bathroom. Empty.

"Are you here, honey?" She opened the closet. Empty too. Mia ran into Will's room. She repeated her search in the closet, bathroom and underneath the bed. Nothing. There was a suitcase on top of the drawers. Not big, but big enough. Frank tried not to cringe as Mia slowly unzipped it.

"That's private property!"

They all ignored him, breaths held.

But no, there was no kid in there either. She pulled out some dirty T-shirts and socks and underneath it all, the teddy bear. She held it up, looking at Will, her face twisting.

"I should have known," she said.

Frank put his gun to the dirty kiddie fiddler's head, pressed it hard so it would leave a mark. "Where is she?"

Will looked at him straight and steady. "I really don't know."

"I'm not going to ask you again."

They stared at each other. Will didn't even blink. The guy had no idea what was coming to him. If he were in his right mind, he'd be very afraid right now.

Frank spun the gun in his hand and brought the butt down on the top of Will's head, enjoying the cracking sound. He watched the pervert's eyes roll back as he slumped to the floor.

38

Rose pinched her nose. The burned stench was like a slap in the face. It made her eyes water. The courthouse was dark, much darker than she'd been expecting. The floor was covered in broken glass; the fluorescent lights above had exploded, and power cables dangled limply from the ceiling.

She had reached the waiting area. Rose remembered the way it used to look, before all this. It was the place where families had held hands anxiously. Where suited lawyers had talked in hushed whispers to pale-faced witnesses. Where people had tensed their bodies, desperately hoping for guilty or innocent. Rose had seen them all. She had hung around here a bit, following stories or looking for new ones. Now the place was barely recognizable. The cushioned seats were burned off, exposing the steel underlays. The carpet was just gray ashes and the bins were melted into warped modern sculptures.

On the floor were shiny splatters. The kerosene. Again, she thought of the paper-plate kids. She just couldn't imagine them coming in here at night with a canister of petrol. Matches and some scrunched-up newspaper, sure. But this?

The burned plastic smell was so strong; it made her throat

feel like it was going to close up. She kept going. Still treading lightly, looking around for a sign of life, her heart hammering.

The door to the courtroom was closed. The cowardly part of her heart was screaming to run. To come back with the cops. Not to go into that room alone, where some maniac was lurking, with no weapons. Or even a torch. But she couldn't stop. If Laura was in there, she couldn't leave. She wouldn't let Laura be in this terrifying place for one minute longer; she would be so scared.

Rose's hand shook violently as she reached up to the doorway. Her nerve endings flaring, screaming danger. She pushed the door open, her chin wobbling, weak with cold fear.

The roof was gone from the courtroom. It had fallen inward, on top of the chairs, the judges stand, the witness box. She could see the moon, bright in the sky. It lit up the destroyed room. There was no one inside.

Instantly, the fear turned to misery. Laura wasn't here.

Rose would have taken the fear. Fought the monster. She would have let her skin be slit, her bones be smashed, her hair be ripped out. Any pain would have been more bearable than this devastating disappointment. She turned out of the room, kept walking. Looking in the bathrooms, with their crackled tiles and doorless cubicles. The staff kitchen, which was as black and empty as every other room. The surface of the fridge was so blistered it looked like scales. The smell of the melted microwave made her want to be sick. But she kept going. She went out to the back, forcing open the door, which creaked so loudly she was sure that the ceiling would fall in on her. But it didn't.

She took her finger off her nose and pulled in lungfuls of air. It was still thick with the acrid burned smell, but it was more breathable than the fumes that had been confined inside. Rubbing the wetness off her cheeks with her dirty hands, she looked around. There it was, to her right. The crumpled-up white T-shirt she'd seen from the library window. Bending down, she tried to inspect it. It was dirty from ashes and stained with sweat. She got up and, not seeing the huge crack in the pavement, she tripped and fell onto her already-bleeding knees. The pain split up her thighs, hot and jagged. She flipped around onto her butt and looked at them; blood was mixing with ashes, dripping down her calves, looking like black oil in the moonlight. Her legs hurt like hell, but she forced herself up.

The only place left to look was the storage room, and the sooner she looked in there the sooner she could get the fuck out of here. But she didn't want to look there. That was where Ben had died. The walls of the shed were steel sheets, and inside it was filled with files. Basically, it was a large oven. She knew there wouldn't be a body or any kind of remains; apparently the kid had been so incinerated all they found were ashes. But still. He had died in there in such a horrible way, and she didn't want to trample all over it.

The silvery light of the moon glinted off the shards of glass that were left in the window. There was a shape in there. For a split second Rose's heart stopped. Really, truly stopped beating. There was a shadow in the window. A shadow that looked like a head and shoulders, staring out at her. But it couldn't be. It must have just been a shape inside the shed. A melted filing cabinet or a broken cupboard. With a sick feeling she realized she'd have to go and look. She took a step forward.

Then the shadow disappeared. Ducked down out of view.

There was someone in there. Someone who had been watching her stumble around in the dark. Someone who was hiding now, waiting for her approach. Fuck. She'd never been scared like this. Never.

But she wasn't going to run away. She was going in. Into the lair of the monster who had stolen her sister. Her head felt light; her legs were wobbly. But she stepped forward. Letting her feet crunch in the debris now, feeling sure she was going to vomit. Whoever it was had already seen her. Reaching down, she picked up a blackened beam of wood. It splintered her palm, but she held it tight.

"Let her out," she said, her voice so loud in the silence it made her body shake. No response.

One step. Two. Three and she was there. Looking into the black building.

"The police are on their way. I'm going to smash your fucking head in if you lay a hand on her." She stepped into the building.

Straining to see, she looked around at the burned-out filing cabinets. There. There it was in the corner. The shadow. All curled up like it didn't want to be seen. Not big enough to be a man.

"Laura?"

It let out a cry. But it wasn't Laura's voice.

"Come out," Rose said. And the shadow moved forward, obeying her. The moon lit up the figure's face. It was Ben. The ghost of Benny Riley.

Rose screamed, the beam dropping from her hand with a thunk. Ben screamed too. Loud and piercing.

"What the fuck!" Rose yelled and knelt down on the floor.

"Leave me alone," Ben said.

She reached out before he jerked away; she touched the skin of his forearm. Real, warm, soft flesh. Ben wasn't a ghost; he was real.

39

It had been Mia's idea to set Frank on Will. But knocking the guy out sure wouldn't achieve anything. If Laura was still alive, bleeding somewhere, then every second counted. They needed to find her.

Will was still out cold. They'd moved him into the bathtub. He was slumped there, head thrown backward in a strange angle, his forehead swelling. Looking at his empty face, she wondered how on earth he could have done it. How anyone could actually have gone through with something so evil.

Frank turned on the cold water. Not half a second passed and Will's body jerked and his eyes opened.

"Rise and shine," Frank said.

Will tried to sit up. But he couldn't. His hands were handcuffed to the rail on the wall.

"What the fuck is this?"

"We need you to tell us where Rose's sister is. Where is Laura?" Her voice didn't sound scared, which was how she felt; it came out strong and commanding.

"I told you—I don't know!"

His eyes were flicking all around the room. He was really starting to panic now. Good. The cold water inched deeper.

"I'd love to believe you. I really would," Frank said.

"I wouldn't," Baz muttered.

"But you see, we've got a bloody mattress. We've got the notebook." He held it up, a washcloth between his fingers and the cover. "It's even got your drafts inside. Wanted to get the wording just perfect, did you?"

Mia leaned forward to see the pages, but Frank had already begun wrapping the washcloth around it. Being careful not to touch it with his bare hands.

"Rose has been staying in that room. Ask her," he said, eyes still spinning around the room.

"Mia?" Frank didn't break eye contact with Will.

"Nope."

"Are you trying to say Rose abducted her own sister?" Frank said sarcastically.

"I don't know! Maybe they're drafts for her articles."

"That's a terrible story, I have to say."

"Please," Mia said. They didn't have time for the crazy excuses, for the dumb macho back-and-forth. "Tell us where Laura is. She's just a little kid."

Will looked at her, straight in the eyes. "I don't know."

If it hadn't been for the evidence, she might have believed him. That scared her. To be able to lie like that, to have hurt a child and look at her so innocently. Will must be some sort of psychopath.

"Ready?" she said to Baz.

Baz didn't hesitate. In a single, fluid motion, he took the hair dryer off its hook and threw it into the bath. Will writhed to get away from it, the water splashing all around him, his eyes wide in horror. But nothing happened. Her finger was on the power switch and she hadn't turned it on.

"Where is she?" Frank asked.

Will was panicking now, screaming, "I don't know!"

Mia's shoulders tensed. She didn't want to have to do this. But she would. She would do anything to save Rose's little sister.

She did it. She flicked the power on and off as quick as she could. Will's agonized scream made the hairs on her arms stick up. It was the worst sound she'd ever heard.

"Where is she?" Frank yelled.

40

It had taken Rose a long time to convince Ben to come with her. To be fair, she had yelled that she was going to smash his head in, so his hesitation was probably warranted. Eventually, after Rose had talked slowly and smoothly, he'd taken her outstretched hand.

"Will you take me to my mum?" he asked as they walked down the road. He'd already asked her this, but she answered him again anyway.

"Yep. That's where we're going right now."

He smiled up at her. "Can't wait."

"When was the last time you saw her?" Rose wanted to know what the fuck was going on. This kid was meant to be dead. She was taking him back to the police station, where, maybe, Laura would be waiting. It had been so stupid not to take her phone with her when she'd walked out. For all she knew, they'd found Laura hours ago. Deep in her heart, she had a dark feeling that they hadn't.

"In the car. When she dropped me off."

"Your mum took you somewhere?" Rose asked, tugging his hand so he'd cross the road with her. The night air felt exquisitely clean and light in comparison to the rank enclosure of the courthouse.

"She said it would be fun but it wasn't. We poured petrol everywhere and it stunk. I got a headache."

Rose remembered the fire lighting up the Rileys' horrified faces. That made no sense.

"She took me to her friend the nice nun. She said my dad was going to pick me up from there, but he didn't. So I left and a man gave me a lift in his truck but I couldn't remember my address. I knew she'd come get me there," he went on. "She always says that when things are scary I have to go wait for her in the shed and she'll pick me up once he's in bed."

Rose had no idea what that meant.

"Once who's in bed?"

"Him. I thought he was my dad, but Mummy said that my real dad actually loved me and wouldn't hurt me and he'd come pick me up."

She knelt down then, looked right into his dark brown eyes. Will's eyes.

"You just tell everything to the police, and they'll bring your mum, okay?" she said.

He nodded, and they climbed the three steps to the station. She pushed open the door and pulled Ben inside after her.

The air-conditioning of the station felt like it was burning her hot skin. She was feeling woozy, the panic, the fear, the pain in her knees all mixing together in her stomach. She squinted against the bright fluorescent lights.

Behind the desk the receptionist gaped, recognizing Ben instantly.

"Where's Frank? Get him," Rose said.

"He went to follow a lead on your sister. Hold tight, okay?" The woman swung around in her chair and opened the security door behind her; Rose could hear her footsteps slapping on the lino as the door swung shut.

In the light, Ben looked bad. He was much thinner than last time she'd seen him and his skin was smudged gray and black. She probably didn't look much better. The woman had said Frank had gone to follow a lead. Which meant they hadn't found Laura yet. The boy smiled up at her, and even though she wanted to cry, even though every part of her was feeling crippling, gushing grief, she smiled back at him.

After the cops had come out and rallied around Ben, she left. She had to get Will. Tell him everything; tell him she'd found his child, but lost her sister. Somehow she was sure he'd make this whole crazy mess make sense.

Rose scooped through her bag for her key to the tavern. Her hands were covered in ash, a thick line of it under each fingernail. Her left, the one that had picked up the beam, hurt when she put any pressure on it; she hadn't yet dug the splinters out of her palm.

The neon beer signs flickered in the windows, making it even harder to find the glinting silver in the dark.

Eventually she felt the coldness of it between her fingers. She unlocked the front door and quickly locked it again behind her. She noticed the yellow light in the back hallway was on, and it too flickered in front of her. Perhaps it was the exhaustion, or seeing Ben back from the dead, but for one awful second she was sure it was the Colonel.

She walked slowly toward the hallway, certain that at any second a white figure in an army uniform would jump out. But none did.

The door to Will's room was ajar. Looking inside, she saw that he wasn't in there. Then she heard a voice. Bazza's voice.

"I don't know if he can handle another one."

It was coming from her room.

"He has to tell us." Mia's voice.

What the fuck was going on? She walked into her room. There was no one there. Then she heard Frank's voice, loudly, through the closed door of the bathroom.

"What have you done with her, you sick pervert? Where is she?"

Rose pushed the bathroom door open, not prepared for what was inside.

Will lay in the bath. But he didn't look like Will anymore. His hair and eyebrows were singed. His face was swollen and bloody.

"Stop," he whispered. "Please."

"What the fuck are you doing?" Her voice came out strange and quiet. Mia turned to her. Her hair was all messed up, and her eyes. There was something wild in her eyes.

"He's got Laura!" she yelled. "Where's Laura?" she screamed at him. Her finger clicked the hair-dryer switch on and off. Will groaned and the lights flickered again.

"Stop it!" Rose yelled, rushing toward Will. But Frank grabbed her. Held her wrists tightly, screamed right into her face.

"He's got your sister!"

She twisted her arms around, almost breaking his arms to get him off her. She grabbed Will's face in her hands.

"Are you all right? Are you okay?"

He looked at her, but there was no recognition in his eyes. Rose got into the water, the coldness of it shocking on her sweaty skin. His wrists were bleeding where they were hand-cuffed to the bar. She pulled them trying to get them off. Trying to free him. The water around them was turning black from the ash on her body.

"Unlock him! He's done nothing!"

She could still save him. If she could just get him out of the water, give him CPR, maybe he would be okay. She grabbed his head again; there was still some movement in his swollen eyes.

"He wrote the notes. There's blood on the bed," she dimly heard Frank say.

"You idiots! You fucking idiots! Let him go."

No one moved.

"Mia!" She looked at her friend right in the eyes. "Call an ambulance. Please."

Mia seemed to come to attention. She pulled her phone out of her pocket.

Thank God. Maybe it wasn't too late. Rose kissed Will's lips, but they were slack underneath hers. She tried to lift him. She might have been screaming. Her throat contracting until it hurt.

"He wrote the notes, Rose," Baz said quietly. "We'll find her."

"I wrote them," she said. "Laura's gone."

Will's face. She couldn't bear it. The three of them were staring at her in the bright, white light. She couldn't even see them. She could only see Will. His eyes seemed to focus, but only for a moment.

"Honey," she said. "Will? Please don't leave me."

"They're on their way," Mia said.

"What do you mean?" Frank said, staring at Rose now.

Rose put her head on Will's chest, holding him, listening to his soft heartbeat, ready to do CPR if it stopped, until she heard sirens.

"What did you mean, Rose?" Frank asked again, but she ignored him.

"Frank, we better take those cuffs off," she heard Bazza say dimly.

"No," Frank said. "It was him."

Arms steady, Rose pulled herself out of the bathtub, water cascading from her wet clothes, the weight of it sploshing down into the bath, the rest of it splattering onto the tiles, the dirt from the soles of Frank's black leather shoes seeping between the tiles, becoming mud.

She walked up to Frank and pushed him hard; he slipped backward, holding on to the towel rack to support himself.

"You aren't listening. Take his cuffs off! I wrote the notes, you idiot! I did!"

The sirens were louder now.

Frank grabbed her wrist. "I'm going to fucking kill you," he whispered.

The sirens were right outside the tavern now. Slipping a little, she walked into her room, then continued out the back door. The lights were glinting and glittering.

"He's in there!" she called, pointing into the back door.

The paramedics ran past her, toward the tavern. One stopped and looked at her carefully.

"Come sit down," she said, reaching out to guide her toward the ambulance.

"No! It's him. Go help him. It's bad."

"Okay. But wait here, okay?"

"Go!" she said, and the woman rushed past her into the back door of the tavern.

Her sight was slick and shifting. Her nerves were overstretched. She didn't even know where she was going but her feet started moving. She started walking, the night air on her wet skin, the bitumen crunch under her mum's old sneakers. She couldn't even feel the blisters now.

The lights flickered behind her, the red and blue getting dimmer. She couldn't be there to see. If he died it was her fault.

Her feet were taking her across the road, not looking, toward the lake. Toward home. That made sense. To go home. To let her shoes tread the well-worn path. Follow the route they were used to. He couldn't die. He couldn't.

There was a bird squawking. Some sort of bird, angry at another and screaming. A dog barked once, and it was quiet again.

Quiet enough to hear the car that rumbled behind her, to hear it slowing down as it reached her.

41

There she was. Walking home like nothing happened.

Frank's wet shoe slipped a little against the brake as he slowed the car, making a pitchy squeak. The headlights cut through the dark, lighting up the lone figure, making her skin shine a pale gold.

That slut. All this time, she'd been playing Frank. Laughing at him. Making him look like an idiot. A fool.

She'd written the notes to make fun of him, to show him that she had the power. She'd been fucking that freak Will. He'd known it. Frank had seen the way she'd looked at him.

Slut.

He pressed hard on the brake. Rubber on steel. Turned off the car. Got out, slamming the door.

"Hey!"

She stopped. He could see the muscles in her shoulders. See them tense.

"You can't just walk away."

Rose turned, and she had the fucking audacity not to look scared. Her eyes were blank, her wet hair dripping down her black-smeared shoulders.

She should be scared. He owned this town, not her. She'd never respected that, never. She'd been laughing at him this whole fucking time.

"You know you're a fucking bitch, don't you?"

She nodded.

"You know you're a cunt?"

Rose didn't say anything, didn't nod. Just looked at him. Looked at him the same way she always did, like she was superior to him. Still, the slut thought she was better than him.

It was too much. He'd show her.

He lunged toward her; he was going to take her. Take the fucking bitch. And there it was. Finally. Fear. Frank grabbed at her breasts, feeling them for an instant, finally in his hand, before her greasy slut body wrenched away from him. And she ran. Her breath coming out in scared little whimpers. Bitch.

42

Rose ran toward the closest house. Their lights were on. They were awake. Three steps up to the front door and she was bashing on it. Pounding with her fist. But no one came.

"Help!" she screamed.

But no one came.

She flung herself away from the door, jumped over the bushes into the next yard, the twigs tearing at her already-bleeding legs. Scrambling to their front door, she hammered on it. The screen dug into her fist, and it rattled, loud. She whirled around, looking for him. Looking for Frank, whose eyes had turned vicious. His car was still there, but she couldn't see him. Her breast still pounded from where he had grabbed it; she could still smell his stinking breath all over her. Stale coffee and bourbon.

He could do anything he wanted to her and get away with it. She pounded on the door again. They were in there; she knew it.

"Fuck!" she yelled aloud.

"Ladies don't swear like that." She heard his voice so close, too close, she was running again. Away from the houses this time. Toward the lake. There was something there in the dark. A light, orange and flickering. A torch maybe. Someone who was out; someone who might help.

The long grass ripped against her ankles as she sprinted through it, running fast, her breath too loud in her own ears to hear anything else. Running past the lake, toward the orange light.

Something slammed against her. Frank. His weight on top of her. And she was on the shore of the lake. Cold mud on her back. He was trying to get ahold of her.

"Get off!" she screamed.

"Say you're sorry," he said, pushing on her shoulders, looking at her. There were tears in his eyes.

"You tortured him!"

He laughed, a strange woofing sound. "The bathtub was Mia's idea."

Rose stopped struggling; that couldn't be true.

"Say you're sorry."

She spit upward, into his face. "You're not going to get away with it!"

His elbow slammed onto her chest, pushing the wind out of her, hitting the bone with a crack. She looked up into Frank's face but there was nothing familiar about it anymore. Her spit slid down the side of his nose.

All his weight was on top of her. She couldn't breathe. He was too heavy; it felt like her ribs would snap.

"Don't you get it, bitch? I'll do whatever the fuck I want and you can't stop me. Try it—go on." He grabbed at the top button of her shorts, whispering now, "I'm going to ruin your fucking slut life. Try and stop me."

She jolted her body, trying to roll him off, but she couldn't. He laughed, the tears still there, as she tried again. She tried to pull in a breath, but her lungs wouldn't fill under his weight. Stars began to flicker in her vision.

"Go away, dickhead!" came a little voice. Rose tried to look around but she couldn't, her head stuck in the deep mud. She couldn't look anywhere but Frank's face. His eyes crazy, his nostrils flaring.

Something flung out into her field of vision. A small foot in a small shoe, right into his temple. He wobbled, stunned, hands coming off her to go to his head, losing his balance. She swung her body around and this time he crumpled off her.

Scrambling to her feet, she ran to get away from him. Breathing in hacking breaths of air. The night was alight now. The swing set was no longer covered in weeds and bushes, but with the licks of fire. The backs of children were already far ahead, bolting on little legs. Rose ran, hearing him screaming behind her. There was another car, idling behind Frank's. The old Auster she knew so well. Mia inside. Not looking for her, not trying to save her. Just idling, deciding what to do.

43

The drive was silent. Mia didn't ask what had happened, just listened to Rose catch her breath. She was still sopping wet. Beads of water still dripping down her shoulders from her hair. Her face was streaked with gray ash; her clothes were blackened still, despite the water. The back of her hair was matted with mud. It was getting all over her car's headrest. Tomorrow morning, Mia knew she'd have to scrub to get it off.

She wanted to tell Rose that she'd done it for her. That Will was to blame. Mia would have never done something like that for anyone else. Rose was in pain now; she could see that. Frank had hurt her; he'd wanted payback for all the trouble she'd caused. She would have stopped it if the paper-plate kids hadn't. She was sure she would have. But something had stopped her from getting out of the car, because she knew Frank was only doing these things because he loved Rose too and she'd let them all down. Rose had caused so much pain; maybe she deserved to feel a bit of pain too.

They pulled up outside Rose's house, but she didn't get out. "Did they say anything? Is he going to be okay?"

Mia shrugged. It hadn't looked good when she'd left.

"Don't know. They're going through his stuff now though. They'll find her."

"It wasn't him."

Mia didn't want to hear it. The notes didn't matter. She'd seen the blood in the sink. She knew Will was responsible.

Rose picked up her bag and got out of the car. She didn't say goodbye.

Mia watched as her friend walked up the path to her house, head forward, shoulders hunched. Then Rose stopped dead. She stood totally frozen on the footpath, her back to Mia. As still as a statue.

Mia unclicked her seat belt. She got out of the car, catching up to Rose.

"What is it?"

Rose turned. She put her finger to her lips. They stood together in silence. The night air brushing angrily through the leaves, the quiet hum of electricity running down the power lines. Then, very softly, the sound of laughter.

Unmistakably, a child's giggle.

Rose marched around to the side of the house. Mia followed. The bushes were thick, almost covering the junk that had been there for as long as Mia could remember.

"Come out," Rose said.

Silence.

Then the sound of movement in the black shape. The crunching of leaves. Laura, wrapped up in her sleeping bag like a caterpillar, shuffled out from inside the rotten old doghouse.

"You found me! Took you so long I fell asleep."

Rose bent down. She pulled Laura in, hugged her tight to her chest.

"You've been there that whole time?" Mia said; her voice didn't sound like her. It was high-pitched, strangled. She looked down into the doghouse. The silver moon lit up the corners of things. Biscuit wrappers, a juice box, a stuffed turtle.

"You were being such a meanie, Posey. Are you sorry now?"

Rose pulled away from Laura and slapped her across the face. The kid looked at her, shocked in muteness. Then she started to bawl.

The crying was heard from inside. The front door opened; Rob and her mother emerged. Rob got down on his knees.

"Laura!" he yelled, and Laura ran to him, diving into his arms. His head pressed to the top of hers, he started to cry.

"Thank God," he said. "Thank God."

Rose walked past them into the house.

As soon as Mia's car turned the corner, she saw it. The fire had spread. The swing set was like a huge bonfire, the grasses around alight. Even the polluted lake was on fire, murmurs of flame gliding on its surface. Snakes slithered out from the dry grass, escaping from the smoke.

The black night was filled with dancing embers floating like fireflies across the sky.

44

Rose must have checked the locks dozens of times during the night. Staring out into the black squares of the windows as her unsteady fingers squeezed at the latches, making absolutely sure they were secure.

She sat on the side of her bed. She could still hear the shower dripping. She'd managed to go to the bathroom once the sun had started rising, once there were no shadows for someone to hide. It was filthy now; the muck from her body had stuck to the white porcelain. Her clean skin was covered in cuts and scrapes. All down her legs, on her back and her elbows. Her knees hurt to bend. A bruise was black in the center of her chest. It was the same size as Frank's elbow.

There was a soft knock on her door.

"Rose?" It was her mother. Rose had hidden in her room last night, unable to face anyone. Even the idea of speaking was too much. She didn't answer.

The door opened and Rose's mother entered, still in her pajamas. Her eyes were focused on her daughter for the first time in a long while. She looked her up and down.

"Honey." She knelt down. "What happened last night?"

She could get a gun. That was it. Rose would get a shotgun. She'd go and find Frank and shoot him right between the eyes. Will couldn't really be gone. She should call the hospital, find out for sure. But she'd seen his eyes.

Her mother took her arm from her side and looked at the scrapes. Then she saw the bruise. She touched it only lightly, but still Rose flinched.

She could get a gun.

"What's happened to Rose?" Scott and Sophie were at the doorway of her room.

"Come on—leave her alone." She heard Rob's voice. "Go to your bedroom."

"But that is my bedroom!" Sophie said.

"Now."

Her mother knelt down in front of her and wrapped her arms around her. She squeezed her tight, and Rose heard crying. Her mother was crying.

"Why are you crying?" she said, her voice sounding strange.

"Why?" Her mother pulled away and looked at her. "Because someone hurt my baby."

She used to call Rose that all the time. Her baby. Rose's eyes went hot. Tears dribbled down her cheeks. Her nose began to run. It hurt. She was crying, but it hurt. She felt like she was choking.

"Mummy," she said, and her mother pulled her tighter. She rocked her, back and forth, until she got the tears out, until she could cry without gagging.

"Who was it?"

Her mother broke away from her, and they looked up. Rob stood over them. He looked angry, and she drew away from him.

"Who? Who did this?" he demanded.

"Frank."

"Right."

Rob turned and left the room. She looked at her mother. The two of them got up and followed him. He was getting in his car, starting the ignition.

"I'm going to get him, that fuck! I'm going to kill him," he was saying.

"Don't," Rose said. "Stop it."

He paused and she swallowed.

"Why would you do that? He's a cop. He can do anything."

Rob stilled for only a second. Then he started the ignition. "Fuck it. I don't care. No one messes with my family."

"But I'm not your family."

He looked at her. "You're not my favorite person in the world, Rose. I'll give you that. But you're definitely my family. When I married your mum, I took you on too. Didn't expect you'd want to live with us for so goddamn long, but still."

She looked at him, shocked. Her mother spoke instead, lightly touching his arm. "Leave it, honey," she said. "Rose is right. It's Frank. They'll crucify you if you touch him. It won't fix anything."

Rob thought on this, then banged the back of his head against the headrest. "Fuck!"

He turned off the ignition.

"If you want to help, can you take me to the hospital?" Rose asked. "I need to check if someone is okay."

"Jump in," he said.

She did, but when they'd only got as far as the lake, she asked him to stop. The swing sets were char, the grass was black ash, but there was still thick smoke panting out from behind the clearing.

"Embers from the fire got in the mine last night," Rob said. "It's still burning down there."

She swallowed, and he kept driving.

He didn't offer to come inside with her when they arrived at the hospital. Perhaps he knew she wouldn't have wanted him to, or perhaps seeing her bruises was too difficult for him when he knew there was nothing he could do about it. He said he'd wait for her, which was all she wanted.

When she got to Reception the nurse gave her a form.

"I'm not here for me," she said. "I want to see a patient. William Rai."

She couldn't look at the nurse. She knew what she was going to say. *Dead on arrival.*

"Are you sure, darl? Let me get a nurse to check you over."

"Is he here?" She'd almost yelled it, and the nurse raised an eyebrow at her. She typed his name into the computer. *Dead on arrival. Dead on arrival.*

"Floor eight," the nurse said.

Rose had to stop herself from running to the elevator. She pressed the up button again and again until the doors opened. Then she fidgeted and shook as the elevator rose in its shaft.

She flung herself out the doors to the desk on floor eight.

"What room is Will Rai in?" she asked.

"Eight seventeen," a nurse said, and she was already running. "But you can't go in!" they yelled after her.

She knew which room it was before she got there. Baz was sitting out the front of it on a chair. He stood when she approached.

"I can't let you in, Rose," he said. "He's under arrest."

Rose tried to push past him. "Is he okay though? Is he going to be all right?"

But she'd already heard it. The heart monitor. It was beeping in a steady rhythm. He was alive.

"I don't know—the doctor said he's optimistic," Baz said, holding her arms.

She twisted around and got a glimpse of Will through the

small window. He was lying on the bed, cords and tubes connected to his body. She couldn't see his face.

"Did Frank do that?" he asked her, seeing the top of the dark bruise on her chest that her T-shirt didn't cover.

She pushed him off her. If he wasn't going to let her through, she wouldn't bother speaking to him.

"Rose? Did he do something to you?" Baz called, as she slowly made her way back to the elevator. But she ignored him. Optimistic. That was good. Surely that meant Will was going to be okay. She pressed the elevator button and waited, trying to think of a way she could get past Baz.

The doors opened, and she got in next to a man in a hospital gown with bandages over his face. Doctors didn't say *optimistic* unless they really meant it. It was part of their jobs to be careful about people's feelings, she was sure.

"Rose?"

She looked up; the word had come from the man standing next to her. The voice sounded so familiar, with its slight English accent.

"God, you look almost worse than I do," he said. "I've just been up at Dental to see about some new teeth."

"Steve?"

Later, when her mother had left for work and Rob had gone out with Laura for a talk, Rose sat in front of her computer. She stared into a white square, the empty document on her computer screen. Writing usually made her feel powerful, but she'd never felt so helpless. Damien wanted an end to the story, and last night, it had ended.

Her fingers rested on the keyboard. There were grazes across her knuckles, the red bright against her skin. Underneath each of her fingernails, the dirt and muck were still trapped. A curved line of black against the cream. Her left wrist was swollen and red. Shaking, she called Damien. She forced her voice to be steady as she told him about what Frank, Mia and Baz had done to Will.

He let out a long sigh, then asked, "Do you have any evidence?"

"No. Apart from him being in the hospital. Isn't that evidence?"

"Did anyone else see all this? Anyone that wasn't involved?"

"Only me."

"The thing is, Rose," Damien said slowly, "we've already covered the police-brutality angle. It worked with the video—people like a bit of blood. But throwing an accusation like torture at them with nothing to back it up isn't a good idea. It won't sell enough papers to make up for a potential lawsuit."

But it's the truth! she wanted to yell, but she stopped herself.

The truth didn't matter; she knew that now. The facts had been decided, the truth meant nothing and her voice was powerless. What had happened with Steve should have taught her that. People didn't care about human life like she'd thought they did. People cared about purity. They cared when something unexpected happened, something that confirmed the deep-seated fears they already held. They wanted black and white, someone was good or someone was bad, and nothing in between. Or at least that was what the papers thought that they wanted; it was all they were willing to give. If something didn't sound good in a headline, it wasn't news. And if something wasn't news, it didn't count.

"Rose?" he asked down the line. "So have they arrested this guy? That could be an easy way of wrapping it all up. Then you can get over here and start your cadetship, leave all this crap behind you."

"I'll send you something soon," she told him and said goodbye.

Her throat contracted, squeezing so she almost couldn't breathe as she began to type.

LOCAL POLICE SOLVE MYSTERIOUS
CASE OF PORCELAIN DOLLS
by Rose Blakey

The local police of Colmstock are being hailed as heroes, as the man who terrorized the tight-knit community who titled himself The Doll Collector has been apprehended. William Rai, a thirty-two-year-old graphic designer, was discovered to be the source of the terror. He violently resisted arrest, leading to the officers being forced to take drastic action.

The people of Colmstock are relieved to know they can return to their safe, peaceful lives.

She looked at the words on the screen. They would get her out of here, once and for all. They'd get her to safety. Slowly, she put her hand on the mouse and clicked Delete.

Damien wanted a story, but it didn't have to be this one.

45

"I know this is hard to talk about, Mrs. Riley—"

"Liz."

"I know you've had a real shock, Liz, but I need to know what happened."

Elizabeth Riley wasn't listening to Frank as he spoke. Instead, she was watching her children play together. A sight she had thought she'd never see again. Ben was lying on the carpet and her daughter, Carly, was tickling his feet. They were both letting out loud whoops of laughter. It was the best sound in the world.

"I need to know where you took your son, and why."

She looked back at Frank. He was talking to her harshly, but quietly, looking around the room filled with women and children. He obviously didn't feel very comfortable being the only man in a women's refuge.

"I didn't take him anywhere."

Now she had her children somewhere safe, she definitely wasn't going to be confessing to anything.

"That's not what Ben said," Frank continued, in that same low voice. "He told us quite a story about a place full of nuns.

I'm thinking that you took him to a Catholic home, some-where out of town."

"Why would I do that?" she asked. Since she'd left her hus-band, her confidence was beginning to trickle back. This was her second chance. When she called the refuge and they'd said yes, they actually did have a room for her this time, it had been a sign. If her husband had found out what she'd done, he really would have killed her.

"I know about your husband's temper, ma'am."

"That's a very polite way of putting it."

"I know that he was rough with you and the kids, espe-cially Benny."

"If you knew all that, why didn't you do anything about it?"

Frank shifted again, uncomfortably, looking around at the sea of women.

"I—"

"Please, I don't want to hear any more about recourses."

Liz stopped herself. She was about to get upset; she was about to talk about the way Ben had felt the full force of her husband's "temper," about how she was sure that it was he who had caused Ben's brain damage. She would tell him how she'd started moving on, rebuilding her life, met a nice guy. About the morning her ex-boyfriend had turned up on her doorstep, saying he'd changed, and somehow she'd believed him. She slipped under his spell again. She would tell Frank how she hadn't known she was pregnant. How she tried to hide the vomiting, cover the growing weight around her stomach. How when he found out he beat her so badly she almost miscarried.

How she knew if she didn't pretend Ben was dead, he really would be soon enough.

But telling him those things wouldn't help the situation.

"Listen, I'm on your side here," Frank said. "I just want to understand what's happened."

Ben let out another whoop of laughter, and the other mothers looked over and smiled. The sun was streaming through the living room window, where the women sat around, drinking tea, talking quietly. It was the most serene place she'd ever been. Frank shouldn't be here.

"How about I tell you what I think?" he said.

"If you like."

"Okay." His eyes were fixed on hers now, trying to intimidate her. "I think you hid Ben away somewhere, for protection. I think you staged the fire, tried to pass it off as the arsonist's doing to cover your tracks, and it got out of control. You didn't mean the courthouse to catch, and you definitely didn't mean for your own business to catch. Am I on the right trail?"

Liz looked back at him carefully. The guy smelled like her husband. That sweet smell of yesterday's drink trying to escape through his pores. The smell of mint chewing gum to cover up the swig he'd had in the car outside. He had the glassiness of his eyes, the same redness on his nose. And there was that same shadow on his face when he looked around at the women.

"Not at all."

Which was true. He was not on the right track. Liz had definitely intended the courthouse to light up; that was why she'd doused it in gasoline. If it had just been the shed, it might have been obvious. And she'd definitely meant for their milk bar to go up in flames; she only wished the roof had caved in. They would have got more insurance that way.

When her husband was apologizing, when he was promising he'd never lay a hand on her or Ben ever again, he'd say it was the job that was making him so angry. He said if it weren't for the job, for the long hours, for the income that barely covered their mortgage, then he'd stop. But he hadn't kept his word.

Her former boyfriend was meant to have come and picked up Ben from the convent where she'd left him, but he hadn't. She'd written him a letter one morning when things were really bad, when she could barely get out of bed she was so sore. He checked her phone records; he read all her emails. A letter was the only way. Perhaps Will never received the second letter she'd sent, perhaps he'd never received either of them, or maybe he wasn't as good a guy as she'd remembered.

It didn't matter anymore. They had a room for her and the children at the refuge now, and her husband had no idea how to find her. All her prayers had been answered.

"You told us that the children had been lighting the fires. Didn't they light another one last week near the lake? I heard you were there. You witnessed it."

He let out a patronizing sigh, and the grog smell blew into her face.

"Mouthwash," she said, unable to stop herself.

"Excuse me?"

"That gum you're chewing isn't covering the booze on your breath. Mouthwash is the only thing that does the job. Trust me. When I smelled mouthwash, I knew it was time to duck."

She held his gaze, not letting the resentment that was all over him scare her. She was sick of being scared.

"Thanks for your time, Mrs. Riley," Frank said, getting up.

"Liz," she said.

She didn't show him the door; he could make his own way out. Instead, she clambered down onto the carpet with her children and joined in on their tickle fight. Little fingers rubbing her feet, her underarms, smiling at her hopefully, waiting for a reaction. So she let herself. She let herself laugh. Really truly, honestly laugh. No one was going to hush her now.

★ ★ ★

Frank took a deep swallow from his bottle as soon as he got in the car. That bitch thought she knew him, but she had no idea. She was just like all the rest of them at the refuge, playing the victim as though they had no choice in who they married, no choice in it when they stuck around.

She'd torched half of Union Street, tried to make it out that it was the kids and there was absolutely nothing he could do about it. Then she had the balls to tell him off for drinking? No wonder Mr. Riley couldn't keep his fists to himself.

Screwing the lid back on tight, he threw the bottle of bourbon into his glove compartment, then turned his keys. He'd left his car out in the sun and the leather of the steering wheel was searing hot; he could barely even touch it. Winding down the window, he put the car into Reverse. He gripped the wheel with his knees and swerved backward, then changed to Drive and floored it out of the parking lot.

Since Rose had got that bullshit article published in *Sage*, that second note that he now knew the bitch had written herself, there'd been an influx of visitors in town. The road that turned off from the highway to Colmstock was usually his; he could do any speed he wanted without having to worry about idiots slowing him down. Now there was always someone driving like an old woman in front of him. Hack journalists wanting their piece of the pie, religious groups looking for a cause, children's groups trying to find a new level of outrage, they were all here. More than anything he wanted to expose Rose for the hack bitch she'd turned out to be. All of this, everything, was her fault.

It would feel so great to arrest her. To pull her wrists behind her back and cuff her, pull them tight and hear her squeal. But Frank wasn't stupid enough to do that; if he told the chief the truth about Rose the case against William would be almost nonexistent.

A cane toad crouched in the road a few meters away. It faced Frank, the road glinting in the sun all around it, its neck blowing out like bubble gum. Frank accelerated, heard the pop under his tires as it exploded underneath the car.

There was a girl riding a bike on the side of the road way ahead. That wasn't something you saw every day around here. As though summoned from his daydream, he saw that it was her. Rose. Her hair was blowing back behind her; a backpack was sitting heavy on her back. Pushing the bike to go faster, she was standing on the pedals, her arse up in the air. He had no idea what she was doing out here; nothing much was in bike-riding distance apart from the old Auster's factory.

Frank swerved toward her, squeezed the brake and pressed the horn down hard, and laughed as her shoulder clenched, as she veered off the road awkwardly, almost falling off the bike completely. Her foot hit the ground hard to stop herself.

Rose turned and caught his eye as he slowed. Just because he couldn't arrest her didn't mean he was done with her. He was just biding his time. He'd make sure she got what she deserved, one way or another. Looking around, he saw there were no other cars on the road. No witnesses. He turned sharply.

She didn't race away, just stood, feet on the ground, her slut legs either side of the bike seat. Bet she enjoyed riding that thing. Her arms were dirty too, as if she'd been clambering around a junk site.

As he reached for his door handle, he saw her turn, her eyes squint. A bright light appeared from the other end of the road. It was the sun bouncing off the windscreen of a car coming toward him. Frank pulled back onto the road. He'd get her. Now wasn't the time, but it would come.

Frank parked outside the station. He had to fill in the chief about his pointless interview with Mrs. Riley. Once that was over, he would knock off. It was early, but he'd done more than enough over the last months. He'd say he was going to do recon or something.

Taking just one swig from the bottle, he got out of his car, tossing a piece of mint chewing gum into his mouth. He wondered if he'd remembered to put deodorant on this morning; he could smell his own musty perspiration strangely and his underarms felt more damp than usual. Mornings were a bit of a haze these days. It didn't matter anyway; he'd be home again soon enough.

He waved hello to the front desk as he buzzed his way inside. As he walked past the interview room something made him look over. Maybe it was intuition, or that instinctual pull that cops in films were always harping on about. At first he didn't recognize the man. It was more the receding hairline and the impossibly shiny scalp that he identified, rather than the face. The nose was covered in a large strip of white gauze; each bloodshot eye was shadowed with a bluish-yellow crescent; the mouth had black stitches on each side, as though the whole thing was a gash to be sewn up. But none of that was the worst of it. The worst was when Steve saw him, when they locked eyes, and before he had a chance to look away, Steve's face broke into a jagged broken-toothed smile.

Frank almost ran into the chief's office.

"What the hell is Cunningham doing here?" he asked.

"He has some information for us," the chief said, not looking up from the piece of paper in front of him. "Apparently the council has had some people come forward confidentially."

Frank nodded. "Sure, but does he have to come in here? The guy looks like something out of a horror film."

The chief looked up at him then. "How'd you go with Mrs. Riley?"

Frank filled him in and kept his eyes on his feet as he walked out. Last thing he needed to see was that face again. Sure as shit he'd have a nightmare about it tonight as it was.

He got back in his car and got the hell out of there. Every intersection he stopped at, he considered getting the bottle out of his glove box for a sip. He resisted, even though his hands felt shaky.

He knew he should be stopping by the mine, seeing if there were any updates or progress. It was still alight. There was enough oil shale down there that apparently the fire could keep on burning, indefinitely, under the surface of the town. The area was cordoned off and firefighters and engineers from all over the region were milling around it, trying to control the blaze. He couldn't bear to go and see it again right now, to watch as Colmstock's last chance burned away beneath them.

After pulling into his driveway, he left the bottle in the car for tomorrow—he had another in his room—and slammed his car door. Hopefully his mum would have started cooking already. It wasn't even five o'clock and he was starving.

"Is that you, Francis?"

"Yeah," he said, closing the door behind him. It was good to be home.

"Come in here—we have a visitor."

Frank rounded the corner, expecting to see one of the old Nonnas his mother was friends with sitting on the sofa opposite her. It wasn't. Sitting in his house, on his sofa, directly across from his mother, was Rose.

"Hey, Frank," she said and smiled.

He stood rooted to the spot. How much of that bourbon had he drunk today?

"Your friend Rosie's come to visit me—isn't that sweet?" his mother was saying.

"Yeah," he said again.

"After hearing so much about her for all these years, it was such a nice surprise."

Frank gaped.

"Oh, don't get embarrassed, *dolcezza*," his mother told him.

"It was lovely to meet you too," Rose said, picking up her backpack and placing it lightly on her shoulder. "That panettone was delicious."

"Leaving already?" his mother asked. "But Frank's only just gotten home."

"I've gotta go," she said, giving his mother a small wave then heading out of the room.

Frank followed her to the door.

"See you later," she said, smiling back at him as she turned the knob.

"What the fuck are you doing?" he spit.

"Just being polite," she said, smiling again. Despite everything, he smiled back at her as she turned and closed the door behind herself. As she walked down the street, he saw she still had small half-healed cuts down her arms.

"What a lovely girl," his mother called out from the living room.

"Mmm," he said, as he went into the kitchen to find a glass.

"Looks like she's been through the wars," his mother was saying, as she slowly cleared up the plates from the lounge room. "When she leaned over I saw a hell of a bruise on her chest, and did you see those scabs on her knees? Poor thing. She said she fell off her bike this afternoon too—she was covered in muck when she first got here and was all coy about asking to use the bathroom. Honestly, she's very polite. The kind of girl you just want to look after. I'd like her as a daughter-in-law, I think."

His mother went on and on. Frank ignored her and went into his room with the glass.

The next morning, Frank woke to a cacophony of car doors slamming shut. His street was a quiet one, so this was out of the ordinary, but he was too tired to look out the window. His stomach was swirling and his head was too fuzzy to try to think about anything more than the dream he had just had. He had almost remembered it when there was a knock on the front door. He rolled over. He'd let his mother get it. There was another impatient knock and his mother's slippered feet shuffled down the hallway, and he heard the front door open.

"Mio Dio!"

He sat up then. Rubbed his face and pulled on a T-shirt. He opened his bedroom door to see his captain coming down the hallway toward him.

"What the hell?" he said, wishing he'd covered up his jocks.

"Frank." His captain nodded. "Let's just make this simple, okay? No one wants any fuss."

Frank looked past him. Baz was talking softly to his mum in his entranceway; Jonesy was lurched next to the door, and two men he didn't recognize, men in suits, stood with their arms folded.

"I don't understand."

"Please let me pass," his captain said. Frank hadn't been intentionally blocking him. He stood aside straightaway.

His captain went into his bedroom, followed closely by the two men in suits. Frank stood in his bedroom doorway, feeling like an absolute idiot in his underwear. He wished that he had moved the spirit bottle out of his room last night, but no one else seemed to be looking at it. Instead, one of the men in suits was pulling on some plastic gloves and getting down on his knees next to Frank's bed.

"Is this a joke?" he said, suddenly realizing that it must all be some prank, but he had no idea why. He wasn't getting married. It wasn't his birthday.

The man with the gloves on ignored him and pulled something out from under his bed. It was so out of place that it took Frank a moment to register what it was. A plastic-wrapped square of white crystals. Then the man pulled out another, and another, and his captain turned to him.

"Put on some pants, Frank. Let's just walk out of here. I've known you a long time. Don't make me use the cuffs."

SENIOR SERGEANT TIED TO MAJOR DRUG TRAFFICKING
by Rose Blakey

Breaking: In a corruption scandal, Senior Sergeant Frank Ghirardello has been officially charged with importing methamphetamines interstate. A raid was carried out at his Colmstock home early this morning with officers of the Crime and Misconduct Commission present. A large amount of uncut methamphetamines was seized from the premises.

The drug "ice" has devastated this small community, with state police stumped as to how it was infiltrating the town.

As well as the highly-publicized porcelain dolls case, the town has been overwhelmed by recent arson attacks. The most recent of which penetrated an open oil shale mine and continues to burn under the town's surface. Firefighters are working around the clock in an attempt to control the blaze; however, no arrests have been made.

In light of these events, a spokesperson for the Crime and Misconduct Commission has stated that a public inquiry of ongoing police misconduct is not being ruled out.

46

Rose stood outside Eamon's holding her suitcase. She'd intended to go in, say goodbye, but the idea of stepping up toward the door, something that she had done thousands of times before, was impossible. Through the grimy window she could see Mia pouring a beer; she could see Jean pulling out the rubbish bag and tying the plastic into a knot. It seemed they weren't going to hire someone to replace her. Although Jean would have to get someone soon. Rose had heard that Bazza had proposed. Mia had got what she wanted. Rose didn't hate her, but she also wasn't happy for her. She felt nothing.

Soon there'd be new girls working at the tavern with Jean, probably still teenagers, and it would start all over again. Standing on the footpath, Rose turned and kept walking down the street. She couldn't go in there, not now, and hopefully not ever again.

The road was hot to the touch now, as the fire continued to burn beneath them. Colmstock was veiled with murky smoke that irritated the throat and eyes. Every person she walked past had bloodshot eyes.

Yesterday, she'd gone to the hospital. Baz wasn't waiting

outside Will's door anymore, but after the commotion she made last time, the fleshy nurse behind the service desk had recognized her as soon as the elevator doors opened.

"Wait here," she had said as she had wobbled out from behind the desk. "If you go barreling down that hallway again I'll have security here to escort you out, understand?"

"How is he?"

The nurse bit her lip, and Rose's vision had started to blur.

"Are you family?"

"No, but I'm his girlfriend. Please," she had begged, "tell me."

"There's been damage to his heart—it might be long-term."

"Long-term," Rose repeated. The nurse nodded.

"So." She swallowed. "He's not going to die?"

"You didn't know? He's out of the woods, thank goodness. He regained consciousness the night after he came in."

She could hear the woman's words, but she couldn't believe it. His face that night, his limp body, was still in her mind.

"There're no cops here," she said, quietly.

"No. The charges were all dropped."

Rose swallowed. "Can I see him?"

"If you promise you'll wait here," the woman had said, and Rose had nodded eagerly, "then I'll go check he's okay for visitors."

"Okay."

The nurse motioned her to a seat, but Rose hadn't taken it. Instead, she had stayed standing, staring at her shoes on the linoleum floor. The day she'd met Will they had been brand-new; now they were frayed and dirty.

The speakers had crackled, ordering someone to the service desk. The waiting room had smelled of the disinfectant hand sanitizer. There had been a sign above a bottle, instructing visitors to use it before seeing patients. Rose pressed down on the pump, rubbing her hands together, the alcohol smell overwhelming, wincing as it got into the cuts on her hands.

She had been grinning, a huge nervous beam. He would look bad; she knew that. It would be a hard thing to see. But still, she had been elated because, she had known completely, she was in love with this man. The man she loved was going to be okay, and she would help him get better and it would all be okay. She would give up everything for him. Everything.

The nurse had come out of Will's room then, clicking the door carefully shut behind her. The woman had looked away from Rose's smile, and that had made her falter.

"Is he asleep?" she'd asked.

"No," the nurse had said, and Rose had worried that there was something wrong, that maybe he wasn't going to be okay after all.

"I'm afraid I can't let you see him." The nurse hadn't looked her in the eye.

"It's okay—I don't mind waiting," she'd gabbled, "or I can come back in the morning?"

"He doesn't want to see you," the nurse had said and shrugged awkwardly. "Sorry."

Rose had just stood, her hands still stinging from the disinfectant. The woman had looked as though she was about to put a sympathetic hand on Rose's shoulder, but reconsidered, and she had gone back behind the desk.

Rose waited at the bus station, her suitcase between her knees. Looking down the highway, she saw the heat made the road glisten and shimmer as though it were wet. She'd dreamed about having a ticket for this bus trip many times, imagining how elated she would feel, how proud of herself. But she didn't feel any of these things, only the sun heating her back, her sweat making the material of her singlet stick to her skin, the crawling sensation of something on her arm.

She lifted her hand to brush it off, but stopped. It was a lady-bug, slowly crawling up her arm. Putting her forefinger into its path, she waited for it to crawl on and then took a step over to a patch of burned grass. She watched the tiny insect creep off, just as the bus pulled in.

Giving her suitcase to the driver to stow underneath, she handed him her ticket. He nodded to her and she boarded, picking a seat toward the back. Settling in for the long journey, Rose stared at the back of the empty seat in front of her. When she'd imagined boarding this bus she had thought about how good it would feel to look at each part of the town she'd seen a million times, and know it was the last time. A few other passengers boarded, but Rose didn't look up. The bus rumbled as the ignition was started. Then it pulled out from the station and was on its way.

She'd left Will a note. It said that she was sorry, and told him about Ben. It said to call her if he could ever find it in his heart to forgive her. But she didn't expect to hear from him.

Out of the window, the burned courthouse flicked past, the library, the police station and Eamon's Tavern. They went up the main road and passed the kids walking home from school. Laura was there, in her uniform, rushing to keep up with her brother and sister. But Rose never saw them; she never looked out. She just closed her eyes, letting the bus carry her to her better life.

47

Sophie, Scott and Laura didn't notice the bus either.

"Wait! Wait!" Laura was calling.

They never, ever waited up for her. One day, Laura knew she was going to be bigger and taller than both of them and she wouldn't wait for them either. Give them a taste of their own medicine. But for now, her legs were too small and she hated being left behind more than anything.

She tried her best to go even faster. The houses whirled past as she ran, her backpack going bam-bam-bam on her back. When she got home she was going to do something. Maybe put clothes-pegs under their bedcovers, or bite herself and tell her mum that they did it. She thought about it and smiled and really she wasn't paying attention and that was why she fell.

Her foot hit an uneven edge on the pavement. And everything went upside down and then she was on the ground. She sat up and looked around, deciding whether to cry. But no one had even seen it. Scott and Sophie were getting farther ahead and now she would never catch up.

"Sophie!" she yelled but they didn't turn around.

She brushed the dirt off her hands. They were scraped a

little bit, but only pink with little scratchy white lines. It was her knee that hurt the most. Inspecting it, she saw red blood. One big droplet of it, coming out of a shiny circle with no skin at all.

"Oh, you poor thing!" An old lady with a dark red walking stick was shuffling out of the house Laura was in front of. It was the house that had the big, wild jungle garden filled with millions of rolled-up newspapers. Laura didn't know the lady, but she'd seen her in church a few times. Once she'd even seen Rose and the lady holding arms and crossing the street, like Rose did with her sometimes before she got angry with her and left.

"I saw your stumble through my window. Are you okay, sweetie?"

Laura nodded sadly. Her knee actually did hurt a big amount.

"Come on—up you get. I'll find you a Band-Aid."

She put out her wrinkly hand. Laura clasped on to it with her little fingers and the old lady pulled her to her feet.

They walked together up the drive and Laura had to watch her feet so she wouldn't fall over again on the newspapers. This lady smelled funny. Like the eucalyptus drops she had to suck when she had a cold. The lady led her through the door. For a moment Laura just saw the two armchairs with a little coffee table in between. But then she saw the rest of the room. It was the best thing she had ever seen ever!

There was a shelf all filled with dolls. At least twenty. Dolls, just like the one Rose had taken away from her. They had blond hair, brown hair, black hair; one even had pink hair!

"Wow!"

"Did you like the doll I left you? That was Abagail—she used to be one of my favorites," the lady said.

"My sister made the police take her," Laura said, thinking how silly Rose had been to think the old lady was a bad guy.

"You'll have to speak up, dear. My hearing isn't what it was."

"My sister stole her!"

"Oh, really? What a naughty girl."

Laura laughed. She'd never heard Rose being called a naughty girl before, but she was. She was a naughty meanie girl.

"Well, anytime you want to play with one of my dolls you can come right on over. They're meant for children and I don't have any of my own."

Pure, complete joy took over Laura and she couldn't even feel the sore on her knee anymore. She went over and picked up as many dolls as she could carry. They all had soft dresses that felt all smooth and nice, and some had curls that went *boing* when you pulled on them like a spring, and their faces were hard, but so lovely with little pink cheeks.

"Shoo! Let the little girl sit down, Jack." The lady pushed a big ginger cat off the armchair and it stalked out of the room. "I'll find you a plaster."

Laura wondered if she really meant it. If she could come here after school and play with her dolls and maybe even the cat too. It would be the most great thing ever. Way more fun than trying to play with Scott and Sophie and their stupid, dumb games.

Laura climbed up onto the armchair. It all smelled eucalyptus-y in here, but she decided that she liked it. She seated the dolls all around her. One on each armrest, three on her lap. She hadn't decided which one was her favorite yet.

Momentarily, a framed photograph on the coffee table distracted her. It was black-and-white like it used to be in the olden days. A mum and dad—the dad looked like a soldier

and had a funny mustache—and a little boy and a little girl
with a doll.

The lady came back in with two plates of cookies. Choc
chip, Laura was pretty sure. Hopefully not raisin or something yuck like that.

"Who's that?" She pointed at the little girl with the doll
and remembered to yell loud because the lady said she had to
speak up and that meant yell.

"That's me and my family. Before the bad things happened."

Laura didn't really understand how the old lady could also
be a little black-and-white girl who lived in the olden days.

"Innocence means everything to me. Everything. Mine
was taken away when I was far too young. The things I saw
in that great big house should never have been witnessed by a
child. I wish I'd knocked the place down rather than selling."

The lady looked sad as she set the plates down on the table.
And began opening drawers.

"Can I really play with all these dolls?" But Laura forgot
to yell this time.

"I just wish they'd change the name, don't you think? Using
my father's name on a place of drink would have him turning over in his grave, not that he deserves much sympathy."

There were Band-Aids in the drawer in front of her, but
she closed it anyway and looked at Laura, smiling.

"Don't you just look cute as pie. You will come over and
play with them, won't you? It makes me sad to see them all
here gathering dust. That's why I started giving them to girls
that looked a little poorly at church after poor Benny was gone.
It's not something the kids should have to face."

Not really listening, Laura picked up one of the dolls and
looked at its face. It was so pretty. Maybe it would be her favorite.

"This one's Hyacinth," the lady was saying. "I was going

to give her to little Joni, looks a bit like her, I think. But now Benny's back and all the kids are playing again it isn't really necessary, I suppose. Tell you what—I'll just keep them all here for now until you get tired of them. How does that sound?"

Laura grinned. The old lady grinned back. Laura would come here every single day after school to play with them. She liked the old lady. She was going to be Laura's brand-new friend, just for her and no one else.

"Now, let me see if I can dig up a plaster for that poor knee of yours and then we'll call your mum and tell her you're here." The lady shuffled off to the bathroom.

Sneakily, Laura took one of the cookies from the other plate instead of her own. She wouldn't notice. Laura stuffed it into her mouth. It was choc chip, no yucky raisins or sultanas. She chewed happily, swinging her legs.

★ ★ ★ ★ ★

Acknowledgments

Little Secrets was written over many years from places all around the world. Rose has been my companion at airports in Brunei, over iced Americanos in LA, from in-laws' houses in snowy Nottingham, at public libraries in Broome and, of course, from my dining room table in Thornbury, Victoria. She wouldn't exist at all if it weren't for the amazing people I'm lucky to have in my life.

A ginormous thank-you to my literary agent, MacKenzie Fraser-Bub, who has been with me on this book since I called her early one morning and rambled incoherently about dolls. Huge appreciation goes to my stupendous editor and new mother Kerri Buckley, who made good on her claim that "they'd need to pry this from my epidural-spiked hands to take it away from me."

To Jon Cassir, my fabulous film and TV agent, who read so many early drafts of this, and to the incredible Nicole Brebner and the whole team at MIRA publishing and Lilia Kanna and everyone at Harlequin Australia.

I am fortunate to be surrounded by wonderful writers who helped me through some tough drafts of this book: David

Travers, Martina Hoffmann, Rebecca Carter-Stokes, Claire Stone and Jemma Van Loenen.

Big Love to my own personal cheer squad—Phoebe Baker, Heather Lighton, Tess Altman, Adam Long, Isobel Hutton, Jemimah Widdicombe, Lou James, Eloise Falk and Lara Gissing, plus so many more! Thank you to Christian O'Brien for letting me borrow his true story about the kangaroo and the eyeball, and to Helen-Marie from Bonding Over Bindings, who in a single Tweet gave me the final piece of the puzzle for this story.

Finally, to my family—Tess and David Lamb; my dad, Ruurd; my mother, Liz; and my sister, Amy.

And for Ryan, always.